BEYOND the DOORS

BEYOND
the
DOORS

David Neilsen

Crown Books
for Young Readers
New York

TO PHOEBE AND GRIFFIN

Text copyright © 2017 by David Neilsen
Jacket art and interior illustrations copyright © 2017 by Isa Bancewicz

All rights reserved. Published in the United States
by Crown Books for Young Readers, an imprint of Random House Children's Books,
a division of Penguin Random House LLC, New York. Crown and the colophon are
registered trademarks of Penguin Random House LLC.

Visit us on the Web! randomhousekids.com

Educators and librarians, for a variety of teaching tools,
visit us at RHTeachersLibrarians.com

Library of Congress Cataloging-in-Publication Data is available upon request.

ISBN 978-1-101-93582-8 (trade) — ISBN 978-1-101-93584-2 (ebook)

Printed in the United States of America
10 9 8 7 6 5 4 3 2 1
First Edition

Random House Children's Books supports
the First Amendment and celebrates the right to read.

◆ CONTENTS ◆

ACT THREE: Opening the Door

BEYOND the DOORS

♦ PROLOGUE ♦

EDWARD ROTHBAUM WAS IN A GRUMPY MOOD.

He was currently late for a very important meeting with three very important people (and one not-so-important person) who had traveled all the way from Argentina to see him. He had been looking forward to this meeting for months and had practiced what he was going to say in front of his closet mirror three times. The key to this meeting was the poster boards he'd spent the past four weekends creating. They were very impressive poster boards, and they made a very convincing case. Armed with these poster boards, Edward was confident that the meeting with the three very important people (and one not-so-important person) would be an unqualified success.

Unfortunately, upon the arrival of the Argentineans,

Edward had discovered that he had left the poster boards at home.

Which was not good.

He had apologized backward and forward to the three very important people who had traveled all the way from Argentina for this meeting. He had even apologized to the not-so-important person. Then he'd set up all four of them on laptops to play Minecraft, ordered everybody pizza, and rushed home to collect his work.

All this had conspired to put him in a very grumpy mood, and as he pulled into his driveway and got out of his car, he slammed the car door shut with just a little extra oomph in a halfhearted attempt to feel better. Three steps later, Edward's guilt over being unnecessarily cruel to the car door reared its ugly head, and an unpleasant feeling of shame was added to his grumpy mood. The guilt wormed its way into the small, honorable, pacifist side of Edward's brain and chastised him over his selfish assault on the innocent car door. It pointed out—quite rightly—that the door could not reasonably be blamed for Edward's plight, and therefore had not deserved to be slammed with such vigor. The much larger and much grumpier side of his brain told the guilt to stuff it because he was having one of *those* mornings and taking it out on the car door had made him feel just a little bit better.

The guilt tucked its tail between its legs and fled.

Edward reached his front porch and fumbled in his pocket for the keys, all the while shaking his head and muttering angrily about his forgetfulness. "Dingbat! Dolt! Doofus!"

Edward berated himself alliteratively as he turned the key to unlock the door. "If this meeting doesn't go well . . ."

He shuddered to think what might happen.

He stepped inside and slammed the door closed with even more force than he'd slammed the car door a moment earlier—mainly because it was a bigger door and so could withstand a bigger slam. The lowly spark of guilt in his gut attempted to raise its head and reprimand him for all of this sudden violence toward members of the door family, but the rest of his brain growled at the guilt, causing it to slink away in fear again.

Edward took two very serious steps in the direction of his study and was poised for a third when all at once he froze, foot raised. His extra-keen "Dad" alarm was ringing. Something was wrong. He mentally went over his parental emergency checklist.

- Was one of his four children currently lying helpless on the floor in front of him? No.
- Did the furniture appear to have been oddly sorted, labeled, and boxed up in one of the tidying binges of his eldest daughter, Janice? No.
- Did he smell anything oddly unappetizing coming from the kitchen, implying that his son, Zack, was yet again experimenting with food? No.
- Were there signs of massive destruction and/or unnatural horrors leaking out from the room of his middle daughter, Sydney? No.

- Was a large number of small, helpless, and inevitably cute animals scurrying across the floor courtesy of his youngest daughter, Alexa? No.

Stumped, Edward absently loosened his collar and shuffled his jacket off his shoulders before the answer came to him. It was hot. Too hot. One of his children must have toyed with the family's YourHappyHome smart thermostat again.

"Man," he moaned. "That took me an hour to set up."

His children were always doing little things like that. Adjusting the thermostat. Leaving dishes in the bathtub. Filling up the DVR with episodes of *Say Yes to the Dress*.

Just trying to get my attention, he told himself, parroting what the therapist had drilled into his head last month.

If he was being honest, he didn't mind the little pranks his children were constantly playing on him. It showed they still cared, for which he was grateful. After their mother left six years earlier, Edward hadn't been sure he'd be able to raise four kids alone. Even though he wasn't technically a single parent (she'd promised to come back eventually), he might as well have been one. He thought he'd done an okay job so far. At least they seemed to be turning out more or less normal.

More or less.

But they won't turn out as well if my meeting tanks and I lose my job and we lose our house, his inner alarmist warned. The rest of him agreed, and he focused on getting his mind back on the task at hand—finding the missing poster boards

4

and returning to work before the three very important people (and one not-so-important person) finished the pizza, got bored with Minecraft, and booked a return flight to South America. He entered the hallway and strode determinedly toward his study and the waiting poster boards. Three steps in, however, he stopped, his foot once again hovering inches above the floor.

"Huh," he managed to utter.

In front of him was his familiar hallway, off of which were five familiar bedrooms, one familiar bathroom, and his familiar study. This time he didn't need his "Dad" superpowers to notice something was wrong. His eyes informed him just fine on their own.

The doors were missing.

Every door in the hallway was gone. He walked up to the doorway leading to his study and inspected the unexpectedly empty doorframe, running his hand up and down the edge. There were no signs of struggle or damage. The doors had not been violently ripped from their hinges. A freak, indoor tornado hadn't suddenly twirled its way down the hallway and carried them off. Somebody had simply unscrewed the hinges and removed the doors. As further proof, there was a small pile of screws lazing about at his feet. Screws that had until quite recently been employed to attach his study door to the hinges on the doorframe but that now were shamelessly lying down on the job.

"Huh," he mumbled again.

Who would do something like this? And why? A quick

scan of his study showed no signs of anything else having been touched or taken. A second scan spotted the poster boards he'd come home to retrieve. The house had not been robbed. Nothing was missing.

Except the doors.

Who steals doors? he wondered. *Is that a thing?*

As much as he wanted to, he couldn't blame any of his children for this. It was too odd to be a prank. Too . . . specific. Wiping beads of sweat from his forehead, he walked back out into the hallway and inspected the other doorless doorways. Every door had been cleanly unscrewed and removed, leaving a tidy little pile of screws on the floor.

It was very weird.

Something else began nagging him, something urgent. It set off flashes of warning within his mind. However, for better or worse, raising four kids by himself had given Edward the ability to ignore most anything, and the oddity of the missing doors demanded his every last kernel of thought. Where they had been taken, he didn't know. Who had taken them, he didn't know. Why they'd been taken, he couldn't imagine. He was even still having a little trouble believing they'd been taken at all, despite the evidence currently not staring him in the face.

With effort, he tore his attention away from the mystery of the doors, ignored the increasingly important something trying to get his attention, and concentrated instead on his pressing mission. He told himself to focus as he wiped the back of his hand against his surprisingly sweaty cheek. He needed to grab the poster boards and return to work before one of his Argentinean guests was killed by a Minecraft Creeper.

He was about to turn and head back to his study when his increasingly freaking-out subconscious finally reached through his obliviousness and slapped him in the face. Smoke. He smelled smoke. And he was hot. Very hot. Far hotter than he'd get from a poorly adjusted thermostat. His face was now absolutely dripping with sweat, and, for the first time, his ears acknowledged hearing a looming crackle and sputter—a disturbing sound, which he suddenly realized he'd been hearing ever since he'd entered the house.

He turned around to find the hallway engulfed in flames.

◆ ACT ONE ◆

Inserting the Key

◆ CHAPTER ONE ◆

Zack Is Mistaken

THE DOOR TO MRS. GIZZNULF'S SIXTH-GRADE CLASS CREAKED open with all the subtlety of a polka-dancing zombie. In response to this unexpected distraction, four students gasped, seven looked over with eager excitement, three jolted awake, and eight remained asleep. Only one student attempted to block out the eerily squeaky interruption and actually pay attention to what Mrs. Gizznulf was saying, certain it would be on an upcoming test. Seated ramrod straight in the third row two seats from the window, Zachary Rothbaum jotted down the teacher's every word with enthusiasm rarely seen in an eleven-year-old. Because he was focused with laserlike intensity on his task, it took Zack a few seconds to realize anyone had entered the classroom, which was unfortunate considering he was the reason the door had been forced open twelve minutes before the lunch bell in the first place.

"I apologize for the intrusion, Mrs. Gizznulf," Nurse Hibble announced meekly, poking her head through the partly open doorway just as much as was absolutely necessary. "I'm afraid I must borrow Zachary Rothbaum."

Mrs. Gizznulf growled, something she tended to do when either bothered or hungry. Nurse Hibble flinched and quickly withdrew her head from the classroom. "His presence is required in the main office," she called out from the safety of the hallway.

Every head in the classroom turned toward Zack at the same time, twisting in perfect unison with the precision of a Broadway chorus line. He tried not to squirm under the undivided attention of his entire class, but having forty-five eyes staring at him at once (two each for twenty-one students and Mrs. Gizznulf, plus Tom Gillogily's non-glass eye) caused his sweat glands to dribble irritating beads down his forehead.

Now what's she done? he thought. He held no fantasies that Nurse Hibble was here because of anything Zack had done or said or stepped in or eaten. Whatever the issue, it wouldn't be about Zack.

It would be about Sydney. As usual.

"Ahhhhh, Zaaaaack. You'rrrrrre wannnnted innnn the ooooofficccccce," purred Mrs. Gizznulf in a particularly thick version of her unidentifiable South American accent. A number of Zack's classmates whimpered and sank lower into their seats, as the strength of her accent was known to be directly proportional to the size of the English teacher's irritation.

Aware the safest way to avoid her wrath was to leave the room as soon as possible, Zack closed his notebook and quickly shoved everything on his desk into his backpack. "Yes, ma'am," he said, standing and heaving the bag over his shoulder.

He marched down the aisle of the suddenly silent classroom and managed to leave the room without hearing the sniggers and giggles one might expect to hear during a student's march of shame. This was partially due to Zack, who was moderately popular and could hold his weight on the playground, and partially due to Mrs. Gizznulf, who had demonstrated on more than one occasion her fanatical devotion to corporal punishment.

Mrs. Gizznulf ran a tight ship.

"What's she done this time?" he asked Nurse Hibble as they trudged down the hall. "Is the other kid okay?" While each infraction was unique, most generally involved Sydney leaving some sobbing fourth-grade girl holding a tissue to a bloody nose. With their father working and unable to get away on short notice, and Janice now in middle school, Zack was generally called upon when his excitable sister got in trouble. About every month or so, he was summoned to the office to deal with her after her latest scuffle.

As they passed the faculty lounge, Zack realized Nurse Hibble had yet to respond to his question. Worried this meant his sister had done more damage than usual, he tried again. "The other girl's okay, right?"

Again, silence, this time mixed with a quickening of Nurse Hibble's steps, so that Zack found himself almost jogging to keep up. Something was definitely wrong.

"Nurse Hibble?" he asked, hoping the third time was the charm.

It wasn't.

She stopped in front of the door to the main office, placed a hand on the knob, then paused and looked back at Zack. "I'm so sorry," she said. Then, as Zack's face twisted into worried confusion, she pulled the door open and ushered him inside.

Stepping in, he found Sydney sitting against the far wall, dazed and miserable. She was obviously upset, so whatever had happened must have been serious. Still, there didn't seem to be any blood on her clothes, which was a good sign.

"Sydney," he sighed. "Dad is gonna be pissed if you got in another fight."

In response, she unexpectedly buried her face in her hands and sobbed in a way he'd never seen. Internal alarm bells immediately clanged in his skull.

"Sydney, hey, I didn't mean that. It'll be okay. We'll come up with a good story—I promise. Sydney?"

A throat cleared behind him. He whipped his head around to hear the grim details from Nurse Hibble but stopped midwhip when he caught sight of Janice standing against the wall, tears running down her face. In her arms

was their youngest sister, Alexa, pulled from her first-grade class.

Without knowing why, Zack's stomach tightened and his tear ducts readied a deluge.

"Janice?" he asked. "What are you doing here?"

Again, the throat cleared. "Thank you, Nurse Hibble. You may go."

Principal McCarthy stood in his office doorway, wearing his most serious face. Behind him stood a tall, thin, chinless Latina woman with tears carving gullies down her cheeks.

"What's going on?" Zack asked the room. The weeping woman let out a pitiful moan as Principal McCarthy stepped forward to drape an arm over Zack's shoulder.

"Mr. Rothbaum," he said in his best "you're not going to want to hear this" voice, "I'm afraid there's been a terrible accident."

◆ CHAPTER TWO ◆

Janice's Suspicions

JANICE STARED AT HER FATHER, LYING MOTIONLESS BEFORE HER on the hospital bed, a series of tubes and wires connecting him to various machines and letting everyone know he was still alive. She tried to hold in the tears but was not overly successful. He seemed very peaceful and calm, and not at all like someone who had quite recently been caught in a terrible house fire, suffered severe smoke inhalation, and fallen into a coma.

A pathetic heaving of choked breath was uttered behind her. The overwhelming emotion in that breath threatened to send Janice over the edge, so she quickly focused on her father's bedding, searching for imperfections she could fix in the way the blanket had been gently tucked into the sides. Spotting a slightly mussed fold in the corner of the blanket by her father's left foot, she reached out to pull it taut.

"Give it a break, Janice, will ya?" mumbled her sister Sydney.

Janice stopped midreach. "It's messy," she said.

"It's fine," Sydney replied with just a hint of sisterly fury.

"The doctors say he could wake up anytime, anytime," said the smelly, pudgy lawyer guy whose name Janice had not bothered to remember. "All we can do is wait."

Another half gasp/half sob from behind caused Janice to wheel around and face the weeping individual. "Why are you weeping?" she asked.

Miss Guacaladilla, the chinless social worker who had been with them every moment since she'd ruined all their lives by coming to school bearing news of the fire, wiped her left eye clear of tears with the back of her hand, further streaking mascara across her already-mascara-covered cheek. "He's in a coma! He's lying right there! In a coma!"

"We know!" snapped Sydney. "You don't have to rub it in!" Zack moved quickly to her side, placing a calming hand on her shoulder.

"At least he's alive," said Janice. Her siblings all silently agreed. By some miracle—no one knew how—their father had managed to pull himself out of their burning home before succumbing to his injuries. Had he not, the children would be standing at his grave instead of his bedside.

"It's just so tragic," wept Miss Guacaladilla.

Miss Guacaladilla seemed to find everything in life

absolutely miserable, and her constant sobbing was not helping Janice or her siblings deal with the situation in a healthy, orderly manner. Janice felt a rising urge to intensely dislike the woman.

That's not fair, thought Janice, reprimanding herself. *She's just the messenger.*

Still, without having anyone else to blame, dumping everything on Miss Guacaladilla (she had asked the children to call her Lubella; the children had refused) made Janice feel better.

"Can he hear us?" asked little Alexa.

"Probably," stated Nurse Hallabug, who had been lurking quietly in the back. She had said she wanted to give the family some privacy, but Janice suspected she really just enjoyed watching people suffer. "We are almost pretty sure that there is a decent chance that it is possible that your father can hear you from time to time. If you don't mumble. We think." She smiled at them—one of those "I'm smiling to show how sad I am for you" smiles—and nodded.

Alexa looked up at Janice, who nodded back down to her. "Go ahead," said Janice.

The littlest Rothbaum inched closer to the hospital bed, standing up on her tippy-toes to get a better look. "Please wake up, Daddy," she said.

Miss Guacaladilla broke into new sobs.

Zack stepped next to Alexa and lifted her into his arms. Janice joined them and took her sister's hand, then was slightly surprised to feel Sydney take her other hand. The four children stood united next to their father, awkwardly waiting for one of the conscious and healthy adults in the room to do or say something.

A throat cleared. A nose sniffed. Someone loudly scratched an itch.

"Mr. Rothbaum should probably be allowed his rest," said Nurse Hallabug. "There's every reason to believe that it might be good if maybe he was left alone. Perhaps."

"Yes, well. I must be off, be off," said the smelly, pudgy lawyer guy with a commendable sigh. "Things to do, papers to file, and whatnot, whatnot."

Miss Guacaladilla gave a loud, teary sniff as she approached the four siblings. "I do hope you poor, sad dears are ready to depart," she said, wiping her face with the back of her hand yet again. "We must administer to your future."

"Our future?" asked Janice. "What do you mean?"

"Oh, you sweet, innocent, miserable children," announced Miss Guacaladilla in a warbling voice. "With your father in a coma, there is no one to look after you. Also, there's the upsetting matter of your house burning down. I'm so sorry to tell you, but you have nowhere to go. No one to help you."

The children looked at one another. It was obvious none of them had considered this at all. "What are we supposed to do?" asked Zack, speaking for the group.

"Oh! Yours is such an unfortunate fate!" bawled Miss Guacaladilla, her tears leaping from her face and sprinkling everyone with a fine mist. "I'm afraid you must come with me. It's time to put you . . . in the system!"

◆ CHAPTER THREE ◆

Sydney Throws a Fit

SYDNEY GLARED AT THE PAINTINGS ON THE WALLS OF MISS Guacaladilla's office. They were all wrong. Rather than paintings of people or trees or a bowl of fruit, they were just colors. Lots of dark, morose, gloomy colors. They made the paintings seem sinister and depressing, and made the room feel distinctly miserable.

This was not a happy office.

For one thing, Miss Guacaladilla never stopped crying. She'd cried when picking them up from school, she'd cried at the hospital, she'd cried when checking them into a motel for the night, she'd cried herself to sleep watching over them in the motel room, she'd cried the next morning when buying them a change of clothes since they'd lost everything in the fire, and she was crying now just sitting in her chair.

There was nothing happy about her.

"Such a tragedy, my poor, sad, miserable little dears," Miss Guacaladilla was saying. "It is almost too much to bear. To lose your home to the ravages of fire as your father lapses into a coma from which he may never recover. What a horrible way to start your young lives."

Way to cheer us up, thought Sydney, fidgeting in her chair and swinging her legs back and forth against the back of the social worker's desk. Zack absently reached over to still her knee, but she slapped his hand away.

"Are we going to stay with you, then?" asked Zack.

"What?" shrieked Sydney. "Miss Boo-Hoo? No way!" She gave the desk another solid kick in defiance and popped out of the chair to pace back and forth along the far wall of the office. Unfortunately, because of the minuscule size of the room, she ended up more or less just turning in circles.

"I'm afraid not, Zachary," answered Miss Guacaladilla through a flood of tears. "As much as I adore you all, and as much as I enjoyed our evening together, I am not legally allowed to foster children." She sighed, as if this were the one great disappointment of her life. "However, I swear on the life of my poodle, Bilbo, that I will not rest until I have secured a loving, legal foster parent for each and every one of you."

"Foster parent?" spat Sydney. "We don't need a foster parent. We have a real parent."

"A real parent who is—oh, how it pains me to say

this—currently unable to care for you due to his being in a coma. Has the universe no mercy?"

Sydney smoldered with untapped fury as she watched the obnoxious woman once again descend into a bawling wreck. She didn't want a foster parent. She wanted Dad.

"Won't it be difficult to find someone to take all four of us in?" asked Janice.

Miss Guacaladilla sucked in her breath as if she'd just seen an alien spaceship land outside her window. A very sad alien spaceship. "Oh, my poor, miserable, sad, forlorn, despondent, forsaken children!" she wailed. "No one will take you all. I'm afraid you will all be sent to different homes to live solitary lives, quite possibly in different cities or even different countries. It pains me to no end to admit that you may never see one another again! Why is life so cruel?" Miss Guacaladilla dropped her head to her desk and blubbered spasmodically.

Though her siblings froze in astonishment at this news, Sydney, who had never been frozen in her life, grabbed a thick, dusty book off the shelf and hurled it at the social worker. "No!" she roared. "That's wrong! That's all wrong!"

Zack managed to deflect the book before it did any actual harm, but Miss Guacaladilla raised her head nonetheless. "I'm so, so sorry, Sydney," she said. "I wish there were something I could do."

"Dad shouldn't be in a coma!" yelled Sydney, giving voice to the thoughts that had been filling her mind ever since this blubbering faucet had come into their lives. "He shouldn't even have been home! He should have been at work! It's all wrong! Wrong, wrong, wrong!"

"Sydney," began Zack. "You heard what the police said. He forgot his presentation. He went back to get it. I know it doesn't make any sense, but—"

"But it's wrong! And splitting us up? No! No, no, no!"

Sydney went into full-on RAGE mode, pulling books from shelves and kicking walls, chairs, and an innocent-if-disturbing toad-shaped doorstop. She hoped in some way to articulate exactly how wrong the entire situation was through this childish display, but resigned herself to the knowledge that her particular mode of self-expression would be misinterpreted as a tantrum. True to form, Janice rose from her chair and yelled at Sydney for throwing a fit while Zack ran over and wrapped his arms around her, trying to physically smother the RAGE out of her.

Alexa appeared about to cry but held off. Sydney figured her sister didn't want to compete with the social worker, who was crying a flood of her own.

"Sydney!" yelled Janice. "Calm down!"

Her words had little effect on Sydney, but then words rarely did. More physical than the other Rothbaum children, Sydney tended to respond to harsh language by destroying something. Since there was little in the office worth destroying, she chose to lash out instead. Luckily, Zack's more direct approach of wrapping her up in his arms as if he were a human straitjacket did the trick. After a few more moments of her screaming and kicking and biting (she'd have to apologize to Zack for that later), the RAGE subsided and Sydney slumped into a ball on the floor. Zack knelt at her side and stroked her hair as Miss Guacaladilla rose in a sad attempt to regain control of the room.

"You're absolutely right, Sydney!" she said. "You're a family, and you shouldn't be separated! But you're also minors, and the law says you must live with an adult. Since you have no living relatives—"

"Mom's alive," squeaked Alexa.

Everyone was silent, even Sydney. Miss Guacaladilla's lips trembled, foretelling another coming burst of sobbing. However, she inhaled deeply multiple times and just did manage to maintain control of her tear ducts.

"Oh, you sweet, innocent, darling little girl," she whimpered. "Your mother is nowhere to be found. We have looked everywhere since the accident, searched online in some truly unpleasant places, but have been unable to find even the barest hint of her. I'm so, so, so sorry."

Had she not just erupted in full force and utterly drained her battery, Sydney would probably have bolted into another RAGE at Miss Guacaladilla's words. Even though it was old news, the fact that their mother had simply walked out of their lives six years previously was a gaping wound in all their hearts.

Defeated, the four children sulked in their chairs and on the floor, waiting for Miss Guacaladilla to deliver the final judgment. The social worker took a moment to grab a tissue and blow her nose with a fierce honk before continuing. "As I was unfortunately saying," she wheezed, "without a living relative available, there is simply no possible way for me to place all of you with a single family. Now then, why don't you come around here where you can see the computer screen, and I'll scroll through possibilities in the database. Some of these families are actually quite nice, and not at all creepy. I even think there's one in Uzbekistan with a pool!"

Sydney prepared to tell Miss Guacaladilla exactly what she could do with her Uzbekistanian family and their pool when the door burst open, and in rushed the sweaty little man from the hospital.

"Stop!" he called out. "I found her, found her!"

Five jaws dropped—four because they thought the man had somehow found their mother, and one because a smelly, pudgy man had just burst into her office. Mr. Fletcher Groskowsky, Esquire, clomped up to the desk and plopped his plump posterior into the nearest chair, ignoring the chair's groan of protest. He then proceeded to wave a folded piece of paper in front of his face as if he were a dainty Victorian debutante wilting on a hot summer's day.

"You had to be on the third floor, didn't you, didn't you?" he asked, panting.

"Second floor," corrected Miss Guacaladilla. "And there's an elevator."

"No, no. This was far too important to risk an elevator." Mr. Groskowsky leaned forward. The four children and one social worker leaned forward. Miss Guacaladilla then leaned back because of how bad Mr. Groskowsky smelled. The children braved the stench in hopes of receiving joyful news.

"Did you . . . did you find our mother?" asked Janice.

"What?" snorted Mr. Groskowsky. "No! Of course not! Of course not! Don't be ridiculous! I found Gladys Tulving!"

The children were speechless. The social worker was speechless and teary. Finally, Sydney couldn't stand it any longer, so she punched Mr. Groskowsky in the arm.

Nobody seemed to mind. Not even Mr. Groskowsky.

"Who is Gladys Tulving?" asked Zack finally.

"Who is Gladys Tulving?" snorted Mr. Groskowsky again. "Are you serious? You can't be serious!"

Sydney considered punching him again but was stunned into pacifism by his next words.

"She's your auntie!"

◆ CHAPTER FOUR ◆

Alexa Is Overly Optimistic

ALEXA LEANED HER ITCHY NOSE AGAINST THE CAR WINDOW AND quietly rubbed it against the glass while gazing out at the rolling hills of wispy brown grass in the late-afternoon sun. She tried not to look too excited.

Zack and Sydney were crowded next to her in the back of Miss Guacaladilla's car—Zack looking all serious and Sydney looking all grumpy. Janice sat in the front, so Alexa couldn't see her face, but she assumed her big sister was looking all worried—as usual. Alexa knew her siblings were sad over the house burning down and Dad in a coma and everything. She was also sad, of course, but she didn't like being sad, so she'd chosen instead to concentrate on the sliver of happiness presented to the Rothbaum children.

They were going to meet Aunt Gladys.

She'd been told her aunt lived out in the country, and that made Alexa wonder what sort of cute, fluffy animals she would find out there. Her most recent pet—a rat she'd found behind the school dumpster and named Ratty—had very likely perished in the fire. Which was very sad. Except he was a rat, so it was not quite as sad as it would have been had he been something cuter, say a bunny or a chinchilla.

To be fair, however, it was not meeting her aunt that had Alexa excited, nor was it the possibility of finding something new to smother with love, such as a bear or a raccoon. No, what excited her was what the sweaty, smelly man had said after he told them all they had an Aunt Gladys.

◆ ◆ ◆

"They can't possibly have an aunt," Miss Guacaladilla had said after picking her jaw up off the floor. "Their father was an only child."

"Father?" Mr. Groskowsky had spat, flecks of disgusting goop flying out of his mouth. One of them landed rather near Alexa's elbow, and she gave a quick shudder and pulled her arms to her chest. "Don't be silly! Don't be silly!"

"Then I'm so very sadly afraid that I don't—"

"Their mother! Charlotte Tulving!"

All eight of the siblings' eyes bulged in shock.

"Mommy?" Alexa managed to ask, confused because she was pretty sure her mother's last name had been Rothbaum.

"That's what I said, what I said!" Mr. Groskowsky slammed his folded piece of paper down on Miss Guacaladilla's desk. "Gladys Tulving is your mother's younger sister! That's who your parents wanted you to live with should anything unfortunate happen to them."

"Which it did!" wailed Miss Guacaladilla.

"Yes," agreed Mr. Groskowsky, looking slightly uncomfortable. "Yes. Quite unfortunate."

"I don't remember this aunt being named in the will," Miss Guacaladilla mused between loud sniffs.

"No. No. It was . . . Let me think. It was after we'd finished the will. Later that day. The mother came in and wrote the aunt's name down for me."

"But you didn't revise the will," Janice said, acting all suspicious, as usual.

"No. It seems I didn't, I didn't," the lawyer admitted. Then he tapped his forehead a few times, like he was trying to jog loose a particularly pesky memory. "Strange. That's not like me." His eyes had glazed over as he tried to remember. Finally, he shrugged his shoulders. "Forgive me if I seem somewhat scattered. My office was broken into this morning. Nothing important was taken. Well, my door. Which is odd. Perhaps that's a thing? No matter. I distinctly remember your mother's note and the name she wrote down. Gladys Tulving."

◆ ◆ ◆

Now they were in a car heading for Aunt Gladys's house. Alexa could hardly contain her excitement because she had put one and one together and realized that since Aunt Gladys was Mommy's sister, she would know where Mommy was. In fact, Mommy was probably waiting for them at Aunt Gladys's house right now!

Alexa was about to finally meet Mommy!

As far back as she could remember (granted, not long, as she was only seven), Alexa had dreamed about her mother. She had seen pictures, of course, and Janice and Zack had told her what little they remembered (Sydney didn't remember anything, since she'd only been three when their mother had left), but other than that, Mommy had always been a blank book. Daddy never mentioned her, and there wasn't anybody else around who'd known her.

But while she didn't know much about her mother in real life, she knew all about her in her dreams. At night, asleep, Alexa and Mommy would spend hours playing games, having adventures, and just being together. Sometimes they'd go on a big trip into the African jungle; other times they'd ride beautiful horses across the open plains. Or they'd go swimming in a magical lagoon. It was always just the two of them, and it was always wonderful. And it pretty much always included ice cream. In her dreams, Mommy was loving, kind, smart, beautiful, and always at Alexa's side, no matter what happened.

Exactly where a mother was supposed to be.

Alexa sat up a little straighter as Miss Guacaladilla turned the car off the main road and drove up a long, bumpy gravel driveway winding its way around yet another empty, grassy hill. She flattened her face against the window, eagerly anticipating that first glimpse of their new home and—she was certain—of their mother.

"It is so sad that your aunt lives so far away from anything or anyone," Miss Guacaladilla was bemoaning. "You will all be tragically distant from modern civilization. You poor, poor dears. Why, you may even have to do without basic luxuries such as indoor plumbing, air-conditioning, or Wi-Fi access! Why must life be so cruel?"

The children did not answer, as they had learned to tune out Miss Guacaladilla's overly dramatic wailing.

The car inched forward, tires bumping over every single pebble in the driveway as if loath to miss a single one. Then, all at once, Aunt Gladys's home came into view.

Alexa gasped.

It was huge! And round! And . . .

"Not what I expected," admitted Zack.

"It probably looks bigger than it is," said Janice.

"It's ugly," announced Sydney.

Alexa ignored them and scanned the fabulous house for signs of her mother. When that failed, she looked for signs of Aunt Gladys. When that failed, she searched for signs of cute, cuddly baby animals. When that failed, she searched for any signs of life at all.

That also failed.

"Are you sure this is the right place?" asked Zack as Miss Guacaladilla braked to a stop.

"I'm so, so sorry, but this is the address Mr. Groskowsky gave me," she answered with a sniff.

"Who?" mumbled Sydney.

"The sweaty guy," offered Janice.

Everyone tumbled out of the car and stood in the shadow of the massive-if-odd building rising up before them and blocking the sunlight. Though at first glance it appeared to be relatively round, a closer inspection showed a bunch of awkwardly placed, angular extensions jutting out from the walls here and there. A few seemingly pointless towers stuck up from the roof as well, ranging in size from only a couple of feet tall to one that rose a full two stories above the rest of the house. These asymmetrical details, combined with the distorted late-afternoon shadows, made the entire house look as if it were glaring at the children with pure malice. An old, dilapidated shed stood guard a few yards away amid the barren remains of a garden that hadn't seen a green thumb in at least a decade.

Alexa shivered.

"How the heck do you get in?" asked Sydney.

"Maybe you don't," answered Janice.

Alexa couldn't blame her sisters for wondering. Though this was obviously the front of the house, there didn't seem to be a door. Also, a wide moat surrounded the house, and Alexa saw no way across. All in all, it was not a very inviting place.

"Oh no! There's no way in! How horrible!" Miss Guaca-ladilla quickly teared up at the inhumanity of it all.

"There's got to be a bell or knocker or something," suggested Zack.

"I wouldn't want to get your hopes up," she replied. "But I will look, if only to confirm your hopeless plight." The ever-sobbing social worker dabbed her eyes dry with her pinkie and carefully walked to the edge of the moat, looking first left, then right.

The children stayed by the car.

"Do you see anything?" called Zack.

"No," she admitted. "No, I'm afraid I simply do not. It is but a dreary tomb of desolation. And to think, you poor, poor dears are doomed to reside within it . . . forever!" She broke into an uncontrollable sob. The children ignored her.

"I don't like this," muttered Janice softly to her siblings. "Aunt Gladys knew we were coming, right?"

"I'm so, so, so sorry, dears, but no. I was unable to contact her before we left," said Miss Guacaladilla from the moat's edge, surprising them all with her amazing sense of hearing. "Your aunt does not have a phone. Or an e-mail address. She doesn't even tweet!" A single tear skirted down her nose at the thought of a life without tweeting.

"Are you even sure she's home?" asked Zack.

"Or alive?" asked Janice.

What the endlessly weeping Miss Guacaladilla was about to say the children would never know (though they assumed it would have been incredibly depressing), as all at once Janice and Zack's questions were answered without the social worker's help.

"I don't want any!" came a voice from above. All five car-weary travelers looked up to spy a small female head poking out of a window on the third or fourth floor (it was hard to tell which).

"Oh! Dear me! Are you Gladys Tulving?" asked Miss Guacaladilla.

"Who, me? Am I? I am. Am I? Yes. Possibly." The woman seemed to be deciding on the spot. Then she added, for good measure, "I don't want any!"

"My name is Lubella Guacaladilla," claimed Miss Guacaladilla, ignoring Aunt Gladys's odd behavior and launching into her official, yet still quite sad, tone of voice. "I am with Child Services."

"No children! Not here. Thank you. Not in years. I was a child. Not anymore."

Alexa caught Zack raising his left eyebrow at Janice, who responded by rolling her own eyes at the sky.

"No, I'm sorry, but I'm not here . . . I mean, yes. I know you are not a child." Flustered, Miss Guacaladilla gestured behind her. "These are the children."

"What are they selling? I don't want any. Is it cookies? I like pie."

Alexa giggled. Aunt Gladys was funny.

"May I come in and speak with you, please?" asked Miss Guacaladilla. "You see these poor, miserable children? They are yours. Or rather, no. They're not your children—I'm so sorry. They are your nieces and nephew."

Aunt Gladys paused in her window, obviously confused. "No cookies?" she asked, sounding slightly disappointed despite her gruff rebuke. "Nieces? Nephew?"

"From your sister," confirmed Miss Guacaladilla, pressing her advantage.

Aunt Gladys promptly dropped down beneath the window with a squeak.

"Ms. Tulving?" asked Miss Guacaladilla, a bit concerned. "Ms. Tulving? Are you all right? Oh dear, what have I done? What horrible thing have I done?"

A single, shaking hand rose up from below the window and grasped the sill. Then a second. Together, the two hands pulled Aunt Gladys up until she was able to just barely peek over the window ledge and gaze down at her four family members. "Charlotte?" she asked, sounding for all the world like nothing more than a frightened little girl.

Alexa swelled with hope, thinking Aunt Gladys had just called for her sister—Alexa's mother—to come to the window. But the hope was quickly dashed as Aunt Gladys shook her head clear and stood. She folded her arms defiantly and glared down at the children.

"Charlotte's children are not welcome," she said.

The siblings looked at one another, confused and slightly crestfallen. As one they turned to Miss Guacaladilla pleadingly. The social worker waved at them reassuringly and turned back to Aunt Gladys.

"Ms. Tulving, these poor, miserable, downtrodden little children have lost their home. Their father is in a coma. Their mother is nowhere to be found. You are their only living relative who is both not in a coma and not someone who mysteriously disappeared six years ago. Surely you can open your heart and home to your family under such tragic circumstances?"

"No," answered Aunt Gladys, slamming the window shut.

◆ CHAPTER FIVE ◆

Zack Notices Something Odd

ZACK FELT AS IF SOMEBODY HAD SLUGGED HIM IN THE GUT.

Nobody moved, nobody spoke. They all simply stared up at the shuttered window in shock, willing it to reopen.

It didn't.

"Can she just reject us like that?" asked Janice.

Miss Guacaladilla was stunned beyond the capacity to speak.

"No way!" said Sydney. "She has to let us in! We're family!"

Miss Guacaladilla continued to not say anything.

And then the crying began.

Of course it was just Miss Guacaladilla, so Zack didn't really mind, but it jolted him into action. "It'll be okay," he promised.

"It is NOT okay!" barked Sydney. Zack saw her cheeks reddening—a sure sign of imminent eruption—and he quickly moved to still the volcano gurgling inside his sister.

"We'll make it okay!" he insisted. "I promise, we won't let them—"

But whatever he wouldn't let "them" do was forgotten when the eldest Rothbaum suddenly let out a scream.

"Alexa!"

Janice pointed in horror at the house. Spinning around, Zack felt his stomach drop as his youngest sister walked up to the very edge of the moat.

"Alexa! Get back!" he called, hurrying forward to intercept.

"Oh no!" wailed Miss Guacaladilla. "She's going to jump! The poor, sad, brokenhearted little girl is going to jump!"

"She's not going to jump!" snapped Zack as he reached Alexa, who—it should be noted—had no plans to jump. Instead, she stood at the very edge of the moat, raised her head toward the shuttered window, and said simply, "Please?"

"Please?" asked Zack. "What do you mean, please? Please what?"

Rather than answer, the defiant seven-year-old took a breath, looked up at the window, and repeated, "Please?"

And Zack got it.

"Please, Aunt Gladys?" he added. Alexa smiled at him and took his hand. Together, they continued their quiet plea.

"Please, Aunt Gladys?" they asked in unison.

Janice stepped up and took Zack's hand, adding her voice to the simple question.

"Please, Aunt Gladys?"

"Oh, this is so tragically dramatic!" espoused Miss Guacaladilla. "My heart is going to burst from the pathos!"

"Please, Aunt Gladys?" they asked again, this time with the fourth and final Rothbaum temporary orphan joining in. "Please?" It was a desperate, shameless play to their aunt's emotions. Having never met her before, they had no reason to think it would work.

But it did.

"Stop that," came Aunt Gladys's voice from behind a different window.

"Please, Aunt Gladys?" they repeated in as syrupy a tone as possible.

"Go away," she grumbled from yet another window.

"Please, Aunt Gladys?" This time even Miss Guacaladilla chimed in, adding extra misery to the cause.

Suddenly, the shutters of a window on the second floor burst open and Aunt Gladys stood there wagging a finger at the five of them. "Not fair," she reprimanded. "So not fair. Shameless. Below the belt."

Trusting his gut, Zack silently led the others back a single step to leave little Alexa standing alone, facing the wavering woman.

"Please take us in, Aunt Gladys," she said.

Aunt Gladys peered at Alexa. Alexa smiled back at Aunt Gladys through eyes blurry with tears.

"You look so much . . . ," breathed Aunt Gladys in a bare whisper.

"Like our mother?" finished Zack.

"Charlotte? No! No, no, no." She waved her hand dismissively, and Zack worried he'd overplayed their hand, but his aunt softened with another look at Alexa. "Like *my* mother."

Alexa smiled.

Aunt Gladys suddenly snapped her fingers and jolted awake, all business. "Get back," she ordered, dropping from view.

"Back?" asked Zack, confused. He turned to Janice for help, but she shrugged.

"Back!" came Aunt Gladys's call from within the house. "Back, back, back!"

"Is she sending us away again?" demanded Sydney. Zack wasn't sure, but he felt it might be a good idea to do as their odd relative had asked. He ushered the frowning Sydney away from the moat while Janice took Alexa's hand and pulled her back as well. Nobody thought to urge Miss Guacaladilla, but she managed to drift back anyway, leaving a surprisingly large puddle of tears in her wake.

"Geronimo!" yelled Aunt Gladys.

There came a deep, rhythmic booming of massive chains and an ungodly squeaking noise. Then a massive chunk of the house fell forward.

"Run!" screamed Zack, who realized now that none of

them had moved back far enough. All five individuals (even Miss Guacaladilla) turned and ran as a slice of wall four stories high and easily twenty feet across fell to the ground with a resounding crash.

When the dust cleared, Zack (who found himself huddling protectively over Sydney) turned back to the house, speechless.

"That is not right," said a wide-eyed Sydney.

Zack had to agree. He'd certainly never seen anything like it in his life.

An entire twenty-foot-wide section of the house lay bare to the world, encompassing four floors. The wall that had once protected these rooms from the elements now lay across the moat, massively thick chains reaching from the farthest edge back up to the roof.

It was a drawbridge.

"Did I squish anybody?" asked Aunt Gladys.

◆ ◆ ◆

Once inside with their meager belongings, Miss Guacaladilla quickly herded Aunt Gladys off to discuss whether the Rothbaum children would be staying in the house until their father awoke from his coma, leaving the kids to fend for themselves. Before following the social worker deeper into the bowels of her home, however, Aunt Gladys ran over some basic dos and don'ts for the siblings.

"Don't scream. This is a no-scream house," she began. "If you have to go, use a potty. No eating off the floor. Wash your hands. Did I mention no screaming?"

"Yes, Aunt Gladys," replied Zack.

"Good. And don't touch the doors. That's important. No door touching."

Satisfied, the skittish little woman turned and marched past Miss Guacaladilla through an archway into the next room.

"'Don't touch the doors'?" asked Sydney incredulously. "'Use a potty'? Does she think we're three?"

"I'm seven," announced Alexa defensively.

"Guys, don't worry about it," said Zack. "She had to say something, right? I don't think she spends a lot of time with kids, so she's probably a little nervous."

"Let's explore," said Janice. Nobody objected.

Aside from the front door—or, Zack supposed, the front drawbridge—the only exits from the rather narrow front room were the archway Aunt Gladys had led Miss Guacaladilla through to the right and a similar archway on the left. Relishing a moment away from Miss Guacaladilla's waterworks, the children turned left.

They were a bit surprised to immediately find themselves in what looked to be Aunt Gladys's bedroom. As narrow as the front room—really more hallway than room—it contained a small twin bed, a side table, a dresser, and a large, open closet filled with very tacky dresses in far too many colors. Another archway beckoned on the far side of the room.

"This is weird," said Janice, frowning.

"Aunt Gladys is weird," muttered Sydney.

Zack wasn't about to disagree. He stepped up to the closet—which had no doors—and carefully pushed the clothes aside, peering at the wall behind them.

"Huh," he said.

"Huh?" asked Sydney. "What, huh?"

Rather than answer, Zack led his sisters into the next room, an equally narrow hallway/room containing a flight of stairs leading up to the next floor and yet another open archway beyond.

"Huh," repeated Zack.

"Will you stop with the *huhs*?" demanded an increasingly irked Sydney.

"Zack," began Janice. "What are you—"

But Zack held up one finger and raced into the next room, which appeared to be the kitchen. It was as narrow as the other rooms, but quite a bit longer. The inner wall was lined with a stove, fridge, sink, cabinets—pretty much all you'd need for a kitchen but in a single, extended row. Zack jogged into the middle of the room and inspected this odd "Wall of All Things Kitcheny," looking back and forth and frowning.

"I'm tired," said Alexa, dropping to the floor.

"Zack, you want to tell us why we're running around like antsy gazelles?" asked Janice.

"You guys notice anything strange about these rooms?" he asked.

"Like what?" asked Janice. "Aside from the fact that there aren't any doors in this place? Which is weird since she very specifically told us not to touch the doors."

"The rooms are all curved!" he exclaimed. "I bet if we keep going, we'll eventually run into Aunt Gladys and Miss Guacaladilla and, after that, be back at the front door. Front drawbridge. Whatever."

Janice furrowed her brow and took a closer look at the inside wall. "Huh," she said.

"Not you, too," moaned Sydney.

"We're circling something," said Janice.

"What?" asked Alexa. "What are we circling?"

"I have no idea," admitted Zack.

CHAPTER SIX

Janice Isn't Sold

MISS GUACALADILLA COULD HARDLY SAY GOODBYE THROUGH her sobbing.

"Oh, my poor, poor dears! I know your new home can never replace what you unfortunate children have lost, nor will it ever serve to soothe your broken hearts should your father never recover—which I fear is all too likely! But I pray you will find the tiniest shred of solace within these roughly circular walls."

While the rest of her siblings rolled their eyes and hid laughs behind awkward coughs, Janice shivered at the melodramatic woman's words.

She knows something, she thought. *There's something she's not telling us. Something horrible.*

The others retreated back across the drawbridge as

Janice watched Miss Guacaladilla climb into her car and drive off, taking whatever horrible thing she might or might not have known with her.

"Um . . . you there!" cried Aunt Gladys. "Girl! Niece!" She turned to Zack. "I don't know her name. I don't know your name! What's your name?"

Hiding a smile, Zack opened his mouth to answer, but Aunt Gladys held up a hand to stop him. "Later. First your sister." She spun back to face Janice. "What's your name?"

"Janice," replied Janice.

"Janice. Lovely name. Inside, please. I'm going to raise the drawbridge."

Janice dutifully complied, shuffling back across the moat into their new, hopefully temporary home. Once inside, she and the others watched in mute fascination as Aunt Gladys strained her muscles turning an iron crank on the wall. The massive chains groaned at the effort, sounding like diseased elephants wailing in misery, but slowly and surely, they pulled the massive, four-story drawbridge up until it finally clanged loudly into place and became, once again, a wall.

"Good. Okay. Well then. I have to work." Aunt Gladys spun and marched out through the archway leading to her bedroom.

"Aunt Gladys!" Janice called out. "What about us? What should we do?"

Aunt Gladys stumbled to a stop, her body turning back an instant before her feet got the message. "Oh!" she exclaimed in surprise once she had her balance. "Oh yes. Right. You can . . . you can . . ." She looked around the room as if hoping to find "How to Be a Good Aunt" instructions written on one of the walls. "You can . . . get settled. Yes. Good. Pick any room you like. Not mine. Not the kitchen. Another room. Help yourself."

She nodded, pleased with her decisiveness, and turned to go. Then her mind remembered something important, and she stumbled forward a step before her feet agreed to come to a halt. "Don't touch any doors."

Satisfied, she hurried away, leaving them alone.

"She's insane, isn't she?" asked Sydney.

Zack halfheartedly defended Aunt Gladys, saying she was "eccentric" and "scattered" and "not particularly child-friendly," but Janice had her doubts. Everything about their long-lost family member seemed sketchy. Even the way the sweaty, smelly lawyer had plucked her name out of the blue had seemed sketchy. Janice didn't like sketchy. Sketchy often led to truly doubtful, which in turn led to extremely suspicious. Which was how Janice felt about this whole deal.

Sweaty, Smelly Lawyer Guy hadn't even been able to find the actual note their mother had written. Miss Guacaladilla had done some online sleuthing and determined that their mother's maiden name had indeed been Tulving, that she had indeed had a younger sister named Gladys, and that Gladys Tulving was not currently a wanted criminal. Beyond that, there was little the Internet was able to tell them. She didn't even seem to have a Facebook account.

49

So here they were in this strange woman's strange house, and Janice felt a gerbil-sized pit in her stomach.

"Is anyone else worried about this arrangement?" she asked. "I mean, Miss Guacaladilla just leaving like that? How do we know this woman's even our aunt?"

"Gladys has to be our aunt," said Zack. "Why else would she take us in? Why else would Miss Guacaladilla leave us here? You're being paranoid again, sis."

"I'm not being paranoid!" shouted Janice. Zack raised his eyebrow at her in that really annoying way he had and she sighed. "Okay, maybe I am being a little bit paranoid. Do you blame me? Have you seen this crazy house? Who lives like this?"

"We do," stated Alexa.

"For now," muttered Sydney with serious disapproval.

"Look, Janice," began Zack. "I know you're—"

"Don't even start with me, Zack," she interrupted.

"Start what?"

"You're going to be all calm and cool and collected and make me feel like I'm overreacting, and I won't have it! I'm the oldest here, not you! I know you sometimes forget that—"

"You could stand to act like it once in a while," he interrupted.

"Oh!" Janice fumed for a moment, while Zack stood, waiting. "You're a jerk, Zack," she said finally.

"This is boring," announced Sydney. "If you two are going to have your usual fight, you don't need us. Alexa, you hungry? Let's raid Aunt Gladys's kitchen." She took her little sister's hand, and the two of them walked out of the room.

Janice and Zack watched them go. The act of their sisters abandoning them to their tussle drained all the energy (and most of the fun) out of it.

"Our usual fight?" asked Janice. "What is she talking about?"

"Who knows?" answered Zack with a shrug. "It's Sydney."

They stood in silence for a moment more, and Janice found herself running her eyes over the drawbridge mechanism. "That's a really weird front door," she mumbled, walking up to it and examining the crank.

"It's unique, I'll give it that," agreed Zack. "I suppose we should go pick our rooms?"

Not having any better ideas, Janice shrugged and followed her brother out of the room, but not before giving the drawbridge/door thing one last look. It was massive and solid and about as impenetrable as a door could be. Perfect for keeping people out.

Or keeping them in.

CHAPTER SEVEN

Sydney Finds Some Doors

"WHAT ARE YOU HUNGRY FOR?" ASKED SYDNEY AS SHE LED ALEXA into the long, narrow kitchen.

"Chocolate," answered the seven-year-old.

Sydney giggled at her sister's optimism. "I dunno," she said. "Aunt Gladys doesn't seem like a chocoholic to me." Reaching the refrigerator along the inside wall, Sydney yanked it open, ready to forage, but found herself stepping back in surprise.

"Wha . . . ?" she breathed. "Huh."

"Oooh! Something good?" Alexa bounced to her sister's side. Upon seeing the contents of the fridge, however, she became equally unenthusiastic. "Oh. Well. I like milk."

"Yeah," agreed Sydney. "Looks like that's a good thing."

The fridge was packed top to bottom with gallons of

milk. There was, quite literally, nothing else inside. Sydney carefully closed the fridge door, as if it were a bomb set to explode at the slightest jiggle.

"Maybe the pantry?" she asked rhetorically, moving on. They looked up and down the room, searching for a pantry, before Sydney just began opening cabinets at random. There were bowls, cups, and spoons, but not much else. Finally, she opened a cabinet and found rows and rows of identical boxes of cereal.

"'Honey Nut Oat Blast Ring-a-Dings,'" she read, frowning.

"For the milk," offered Alexa.

So much for a balanced diet, thought Sydney. However, the cereal seemed to be more or less fresh and none of the milk had spoiled, so she went ahead and poured out a bowl for each of them.

After gobbling hers up and admitting to herself that it was both filling and tasty, Sydney started tapping her fingers on the counter out of boredom while waiting for her little sister to finish. Unfortunately, Alexa was a notoriously slow eater, and after another minute, Sydney couldn't sit still any longer.

"Stay here and finish your cereal," she told Alexa. "I'm gonna go peek upstairs."

"Ormph-kmph!" garbled Alexa through a mouthful of Honey Nut Oat Blast Ring-a-Dings.

Sydney wandered back through the archway separating the kitchen from the . . . the . . . room that looked pretty much just like the kitchen except it had a wide set of stairs plopped in the middle of it. *This is a crazy house,* she thought.

The wooden stairs creaked slightly as she climbed, and she gripped the railing just a bit tighter than she might ordinarily have done. Though she couldn't say why, she felt more and more nervous with each step. When she finally popped her head up onto the second floor, she went from nervous to freaked out in the space of a heartbeat.

"Huh," she mouthed. "Doors."

They were stacked in piles on the floor, leaning against one another along the walls, and lying atop or across every piece of furniture in the room. They were plain, ornate, painted, sanded, large, small, and everything in between. Some looked modern and dull like a door you might find in an office building. Others seemed ancient and majestic, as if they belonged in a haunted castle or an enchanted palace. Some doors were thick, others thin, but all had two things in common. One, they were each made entirely of wood. And two, there were no knobs.

Sydney reached out to run her fingers along a bright blue door that looked like something out of a grand estate, probably French, but suddenly stopped herself.

"Don't touch the doors," she said, suddenly understanding Aunt Gladys's cryptic instruction.

Oddly enough, even with more doors than Sydney had ever seen gathered together in one place, the doorways of the room were as bare as the ones downstairs. Sydney glided softly from one room to the next, constantly shaking

her head as she encountered more and more doors tossed willy-nilly into every corner of every room. There seemed to be no pattern to the collection, no rhyme or reason. Just more and more doors.

Great, thought Sydney. *She's a hoarder.*

An unsettling chill washed over her. This was wrong. People didn't collect doors. That was just too weird. There was something else going on—Sydney was sure of it.

Then Alexa screamed.

CHAPTER EIGHT

Alexa Meets a Monster

ALEXA SCREAMED AS THE MONSTER CAME TOWARD HER.

The monster screamed right back, equally frightened.

This made Alexa pause, because she wasn't used to monsters being scared of her. Of course, she wasn't used to monsters at all, her only real experience with them being Elmo and friends on *Sesame Street*. For all she knew, real monsters were big scaredy-cats who trembled at the sight of seven-year-old kids.

Maybe that was why they hid under beds.

Alexa had finished her bowl of cereal and set out to find either Sydney or something fluffy.

It had been a fun adventure at first because (a) she rarely got to explore anywhere without one of her older siblings hanging around, and (b) she hadn't yet encountered the monster. She had passed through sitting rooms and dining rooms and rooms that were being used as closets and rooms that were being used as libraries and rooms that weren't being used at all. All of them without doors. Once she had even walked through a bathroom, with the toilet just sitting there. That had been very disturbing.

But then she came upon the weirdest thing yet.

A door.

It was on the inner wall. And big. And round. And metal. There was a big steel wheel in the center that begged to be turned. It was a serious door, guarding serious things.

Mesmerized, Alexa approached the bright, shiny door, reaching for the bright, shiny wheel sticking invitingly out of the bright, shiny center with her grubby, Honey Nut Oat Blast Ring-a-Ding–covered little fingers. Then she, too, remembered Aunt Gladys's warning against touching any doors.

She couldn't disobey Aunt Gladys on the first day.

Alexa was stuck between the absolute need to be a good girl and the equally absolute need to open the door. A lesser child might have simply imploded from indecision, but in a stroke of genius, Alexa thought up a handy-dandy solution. She would not touch the door; she would only touch the wheel. The wheel was not the door.

It was a pretty convincing argument for a seven-year-old.

Satisfied she wasn't being bad, Alexa stretched her fingers out just a little bit farther, her eyes wide with anticipation.

But before she could achieve her goal, the strangest—and, frankly, spookiest—thing happened.

The wheel began to turn on its own.

Alexa immediately pulled her arm away and stepped back, frozen in a mixture of fear and curiosity. Was Mommy behind the door? Unicorns? Something small, cute, and fluffy?

There came a quiet-yet-solid-sounding clang, and the wheel stopped spinning.

The door began to open outward.

Alexa wanted to run, convinced that whatever was about to step out of that unknown room would be terrible and horrible and evil and would probably eat her. She took a step back, then a second, then stopped. Because whatever was about to come out of that room might also be wonderful and magical and fluffy. She was torn.

Her first glimpse of the monster was the top of its head popping up from behind the door like a hand puppet. It was a strange, netlike head obviously hiding something even more hideous beneath. Alexa had frozen in terror, her little heart pounding up into her throat.

It's terrible and horrible and evil, she had thought. *I was right!*

When a slimy, rust-colored claw had reached up to grab the top of the door and push it farther open, Alexa had suddenly found her voice, letting forth a titanic scream that reverberated through every room of the house.

That was when the monster had screamed right back.

Not wanting to compete, Alexa stopped screaming. As she waited for the monster to get a hold of itself, she noticed that the slimy, rust-colored claw wasn't actually a claw. It was a big rust-colored rubber glove. And the weird, net-like white head? It was an odd hat. Over a head.

As for the voice screaming out from behind the netting . . .

"Aunt Gladys?" Alexa asked.

Aunt Gladys reached up with one shaking glove and fumbled the netting off her head. "Goodness! You startled me! I'm startled! Don't do that again!"

"I'm sorry," responded Alexa. "I got scared."

"You were scared? I was terrified!" Aunt Gladys waved the netting in front of her face for a moment, catching her breath. "No sneaking. Can't have sneaking."

"Okay, Aunt Gladys," promised Alexa. "I won't sneak."

"Aunt Gladys?" asked Aunt Gladys. "Oh! You're a child! One of'—she lowered her voice and nearly spat the word—"Charlotte's."

Alexa just nodded, feeling uncomfortable with the way Aunt Gladys had hissed her mother's name.

"Which one? Don't tell me. Starts with an *A*. Andrew. You're Andrew."

"Alexa."

"Of course! Andrew? That's silly. That's a boy's name. You're a girl. How about Alice? Is it Alice?"

"Alexa," repeated Alexa patiently.

"Yes! Good. One down, two to go."

"Three," corrected Alexa.

Aunt Gladys's face dropped. "Three? Oh dear."

"Alexa! Are you all right?" Janice ran into the room at full sprint, followed by Zack, who skidded to a less-than-graceful halt before he ran into her.

"We heard you scream," said Zack, quickly fussing over his youngest sister—a habit Alexa hated.

"I got scared," explained Alexa, awkwardly brushing Zack's hands away. "There was a monster. But it wasn't a monster. It was Aunt Gladys. See?"

The two elder Rothbaum children turned their attention to their aunt, each unconsciously taking a step back at her appearance.

"Don't tell me!" said Aunt Gladys, snapping her fingers. "Zelda and Jason. Yes? Am I right?"

Janice eyed the odd hat in her aunt's hands. "Do you have bees in there?"

"Bees? Where!" Aunt Gladys spun around, swatting the empty air around her. "Go away! Shoo! I'll fumigate again! I will! Don't test me!"

"Wait! I don't see any bees!" promised Janice, reaching a calming hand toward the flighty woman. "I meant your hat. That's all."

Aunt Gladys relaxed and held her hat in front of her face, as if seeing it for the first time. "My hat? Oh! Yes. No. I'm not a beekeeper. Do they wear these? How odd."

"Why do you wear it, then?" asked Zack.

"Why? Because I . . . well, no. I can't . . . no. Definitely not. It's for work."

"What do you do in there, Aunt Gladys?" asked Alexa. "Can I see?"

Alexa stretched her neck to the side in hopes of peering into the mysterious room beyond her aunt. Aunt Gladys followed the little girl's gaze and started, suddenly realizing she'd yet to close the hatch.

"Oh!" said Aunt Gladys, quickly shoving the large door closed. "No, you may not."

The door clanged shut with a deep, ominous boom.

◆ CHAPTER NINE ◆

Zack Injures a Stranger

"Is it a rocket ship?" asked Zack.

"No."

"Are you studying a horrible virus that turns your finger-nails to jelly?" asked Janice.

"No. Ew."

"Are there big, fluffy bears inside?" asked Alexa.

"No!" Aunt Gladys waved her hands in front of her face as if to swat away all the pesky questions. "Stop asking! Forget the room! You didn't see it. It's not here. Look away." Refusing to entertain any further questions, Aunt Gladys made to storm away but stopped as Sydney raced into the hallway (having gotten lost trying to follow Alexa's scream) and announced to everyone she'd found piles of doors upstairs. This sent Aunt Gladys into another panic attack, which didn't subside until Zack promised her that none of the kids would go upstairs and touch them.

She then made him also promise they would all clean their bowls and spoons after eating their Honey Nut Oat Blast Ring-a-Dings, that they'd use a potty every time they had to go, and that they wouldn't try to wear any of her clothes.

This last request struck Zack as a bit unnecessary.

The final thing she made him promise (and he could feel Janice glaring at him every time Aunt Gladys assumed Zack, and not she, spoke for the group) was the strangest request of all.

"You will go to school," she said. "Not now. Soon. Not tomorrow. There's paperwork. I'm not good at paperwork. Not your problem. You go to school, right? Of course. Learning is good."

She smiled.

"What about school?" asked Zack, getting used to his aunt's scatterbrained tendencies.

"What? Oh! Yes. School. You will go. And when you do"—she lowered her voice to a whisper, forcing all four kids to lean in—"do not open any doors."

The children all looked at one another, hoping somebody else understood what she was talking about. None of them did.

"But, Aunt Gladys," began Zack, treading lightly. "Why not?"

"I don't want to lose you," she replied.

◆ ◆ ◆

The remainder of the day was moderately uneventful, or at least as uneventful as a crazy afternoon spent in a crazy house with a crazy aunt could be. The children each claimed their rooms: Zack on the first floor, Alexa the room right next to his, and Janice one a few rooms down from theirs. Sydney chose a door-filled room on the third floor, which sent Aunt Gladys into a serious tizzy until Zack offered to help Aunt Gladys move some of her precious doors into another room. The rest they covered with large, flowery bedsheets.

They unrolled sleeping bags (Aunt Gladys had promised to purchase actual beds sometime soon) and laid their few, meager possessions out on the floors of their rooms. For dinner, they joined their aunt for a bowl of Honey Nut Oat Blast Ring-a-Dings (Aunt Gladys promised to purchase non–Honey Nut Oat Blast Ring-a-Dings food sometime soon, and Zack quickly offered to join her on her shopping excursion) and a glass of milk. Then Aunt Gladys, fretting about forgetting something important, mysteriously disappeared once again behind the mysterious titanium door into the mysterious central room with instructions not to be disturbed. The children were left to fend for themselves for the evening.

There was little to do in this oddly circular house. There were no televisions, no computers, no board games, no decks of cards, no pencils, no pens, no chalk, no crayons, no paper. Nor were there balls of any kind to bounce, throw, roll, fling, or toss. There also, oddly and ominously enough, seemed to be no way out of the house. The drawbridge was shut and locked tight, and the children could find no other doors. They considered letting themselves out through a window, but the yawning chasm of the moat below snuffed that idea right out. So they took to wandering about, each in their own direction.

Zack found himself absently pacing around the first floor. He considered heading for the kitchen to whip something up, because that always made him feel better, but he didn't think there was a whole lot he'd be able to do when his only ingredients were milk and Honey Nut Oat Blast Ring-a-Dings. So he wound up thinking about their father instead. Zach wondered when he'd wake up. (He knew their father would wake up eventually, because the alternative was simply unthinkable.) He wished his father were with him now. He could use a dose of the old man's parental wisdom—even though his dad often looked to be still figuring things out himself. Still, just to hear his voice would be comforting. Of course, if he were here, there'd be no need to be at Aunt Gladys's in the first place.

After a quick look in both directions to ensure he was alone, Zack slumped to the floor and placed his head in his hands. He allowed his facade of self-control to fall away, letting the grief and fear and insecurity and anger wash over him like a scalding shower.

"Why?" he whispered imploringly to the universe. "Why?"

The universe did not answer.

But someone else did.

"Hello? I am here."

Zack jumped to his feet and spun around, but no one was there. His eyes searched every nook and cranny of the room—discovering he'd plopped down next to the controls for the drawbridge—yet came up empty.

Great. I'm hearing voices, he thought.

"Hello, please? Please, hello?"

He spun around a second time. "Who's there?" he called out.

"Hello, Miss Gladys? Is Dimitri. Hello?"

The voice was coming from the drawbridge/wall contraption. Zack nervously inched forward, peering into the surprising blackness that hovered menacingly in front of the wall. He didn't think anybody was standing there in the shadows. . . .

"Miss Gladys?" came the voice yet again. "Is Dimitri. Hello?"

And he was right. Reaching the wall, he saw a black plastic walkie-talkie lying atop a series of gears that Zack figured must have something to do with raising and lowering the drawbridge.

He picked up the walkie-talkie gingerly, as if it might suddenly sprout fangs and bite him.

"Miss Gladys, is Dimitri," continued Dimitri, who struck Zack as a very persistent man. "Hello? Miss Gladys?"

Not sure what else to do, Zack pressed the Talk button.

"Hello?" he said.

A startled yelp burst through the device. A moment later, Dimitri collected himself and his voice came through again. "Miss Gladys? Your voice funny. Is bad time?"

"No," replied Zack quickly for fear of losing the man. "I'm not Aunt Gladys. I'm Zack. Her nephew."

"Oooooooooooookay," said a very confused Dimitri. "Is Miss Gladys there? I talk to Miss Gladys now."

"Actually, she's . . ." Zack stopped, not sure how much to tell the strange voice. "She's not available."

"Oooooooooooookay," repeated Dimitri. "I drop off. You open, yes?"

"Open . . . You mean lower the drawbridge? Are you outside?"

"Yes. Outside. Hello! See, I wave!"

Zack, of course, could not see Dimitri wave, as there were no windows in the room. He chose to take the man's word. "I'm sorry, but I don't know how to open this thing. Can you just leave your . . . whatever it is . . . out there?"

"No. Is fresh. Will go bad. Open, please."

Fresh? thought Zack. *She gets her groceries delivered? Does cereal go bad?*

"You open?" continued Dimitri. "I in rush. Pizza get cold."

Pizza! Now Zack was motivated. "Yeah, hold on." He quickly studied the drawbridge mechanism. Were those two gears connected? What would happen if he pulled that lever?

He pulled the lever.

Nothing. "Huh."

"You have trouble? Door tricky. Yes. Is lever," offered Dimitri. "Pull lever."

Which one? Zack ran his fingers along a series of switches, levers, and pulleys, utterly confused.

"Have you pulled?" asked Dimitri. "I think no, as door closed. Maybe try—"

He didn't get the chance to suggest anything, because Zack started pulling levers at random and got lucky.

Dimitri did not get lucky. He got squashed.

With a sickening crunch, the drawbridge fell open, raising a blinding cloud of dust that billowed out in all directions, including into Zack's face. He covered his mouth and nose with his hand while peering through almost-closed eyes at the carnage he had just unleashed.

"Hello?" he called out after a moment. "Dimitri?"

As the safari-colored fog lifted, Zack made out the sprightly shape of a tall, burly man hopping on one foot while cradling the other in his hands. After a moment, words drifted their way to Zack's ears to go along with the chaotic movement.

"Ow! Ow, ow, ow! Ow!"

Cringing, Zack stepped onto the drawbridge and called out to the suffering individual. "Are you all right?" Granted, it wasn't the most intelligent question he could have asked, but in his defense, he'd just dropped a drawbridge onto a complete stranger, which can be disorienting.

"Hello!" Dimitri let go of his injured foot with one hand long enough to wave. "Mr. Zack, yes? No. Not all right. Much pain. Very much pain." He grabbed his foot and continued hopping.

"I'm sorry!" called Zack. "I didn't mean to club you with the drawbridge!"

"Is okay," assured Dimitri without bothering to look up. "Is not first time. Give me moment, yes? Then we unload."

Unload? wondered Zack. He lifted his gaze past the flamingo-like Dimitri to a large yellow moving van parked nearby. The back doors of the van yawned open, revealing dozens of wooden doors—each one aged, worn, dusty, and looking as if it should be barring entrance to an ancient tomb of evil.

Are you kidding me? Zack asked himself. *More doors?*

Looks like it, he answered himself.

"Dimitri! I forgot!" Aunt Gladys bounded her way onto the drawbridge, appearing, as far as Zack was concerned, out of nowhere. "I knew I forgot! But forgot what? But of course! Dimitri!"

"Miss Gladys." Zack couldn't help noticing a change in the injured man's tone as he addressed the lady of the house. "Today is day. I drop."

"Of course!" Aunt Gladys brushed past Zack like he wasn't even there. "No trouble?"

"No trouble." Dimitri set his foot down gingerly. "Is good."

"You're hurt. The drawbridge again?"

"My fault. No worry."

"And the doors?"

"The best!"

"But the owners—"

"Every one."

Aunt Gladys drifted to the van in a dreamy glide. "So fresh," she commented, reaching a gloved hand toward the pile. "Vibrant. Alive."

"Maybe one—" Dimitri began.

"We can hope," Aunt Gladys finished.

"You want I—?"

"If it's not—"

"Is none. Third?"

"Second. Third to the left."

"You make progress?" Dimitri's eyes sparkled. "Is wonderful!"

Zack couldn't be sure, but he thought Aunt Gladys might have actually blushed. "I was in a groove."

Zack's head spun trying to follow the scattered, half-formed conversation. He was sure it meant something to the two of them, but from where he was standing, it was pure gibberish. "Progress with what, Aunt Gladys?" he asked. "Why do you have all these doors?"

Aunt Gladys turned around and jumped back, startled to see Zack standing there. "Oh! Zelda! I didn't see—no, not Zelda. You're a boy. Zeke? Zanzibar? It starts with a Z."

"Zack," he offered with a patient sigh.

"No, that's not it." She frowned. "It'll come to me." She shook her head clear and smiled at him.

After a moment of awkward silence, Zack asked again, "Your progress? The doors?"

"Oh! Yes!" She lit up, then quickly shook her head. "No, definitely not. It would be . . ." She turned to Dimitri. "You understand?"

"Perfectly, Miss Gladys," he replied.

"Understand what?" asked Zack.

But when Aunt Gladys turned back, she was all business. "Go inside. Stay out of Dimitri's way. He won't be long."

She stared at him with a warm-but-firm gaze, waiting.

"What's going on, Aunt Gladys?" he tried one last time.

She took a breath as if to respond, but then thought better of it and simply shook her head.

"Yes. Not long," piped a cheery Dimitri, hauling the first door out of the back of the van. "Must hurry. Pizza get cold."

Janice's Less-Than-Brilliant Idea

NOT LONG AFTER DIMITRI LUGGED THE FRESH, NEW DOORS INTO a room on the second floor and drove away, Aunt Gladys announced it was time for another dinner. Janice was confused because they'd already eaten, but also excited because Zack said the strange man had mentioned pizza. Her excitement died a quick death when bowls of cereal appeared instead.

"Cereal?" asked Zack. "I thought your friend brought pizza."

"Pizza? No pizza. Cereal. Don't like pizza," explained Aunt Gladys. "Too much cheese."

They grudgingly ate another bowl of Honey Nut Oat Blast Ring-a-Dings in silence (Aunt Gladys again promised to go to the grocery store soon and Zack again begged to accompany her), spoons bringing circles of bland nourishment to their mouths in an endless loop of boredom, until Aunt Gladys startled them all by suddenly standing up.

"Who's done? I'm done! Finished my cereal!"

She proudly showed her mostly empty bowl to the kids, then frowned, as if realizing this was odd behavior. Face slightly red, she carried her bowl and spoon to the sink. "Remember. Please clean your dishes. And put them away. When you've finished," she said. "I have work. In my . . . my room. Not my bedroom. The other room. My working room. Good night."

She turned and walked away, leaving the children to once again fend for themselves.

"She's funny," said Alexa.

"She's nuts," corrected Sydney.

"Give her a break," pleaded Zack. "She's obviously not used to company."

The children cleared and washed their bowls and spoons. It being too early for sleep, and none of them really wanting to be alone, they ended up crammed together in Sydney's third-floor room among the piles of doors hiding under floral bedsheets. Sydney sat on her bedroll, glaring at nothing in particular. Zack leaned against the opposite wall, Alexa lounging in his lap. Unable to sit still, Janice paced back and forth between uneven stacks of covered doors, fighting the desire to straighten them and mulling over the day's events.

"What does she do in that room all day?" asked Janice. "What is with her obsession with doors? Why have we never heard of her until now? How do we even know she's our aunt?"

"Miss Guacaladilla checked her out—" began Zack.

"How do we know she isn't in on it, too?" Janice interrupted, not about to let Zack deflate her suspicions. "And Mr. Groskowsky!"

"Who?" asked Alexa.

"The sweaty lawyer guy," answered Sydney.

"Maybe they're working together," continued Janice. "One big, happy conspiracy."

. "Why?" asked Zack. "Seriously, Janice. Why?"

"Who knows? We have no idea what goes on in this place! Maybe they're planning on . . . on . . . I don't know! Turning us into zombies! Or . . . or . . ."

"Or maybe Aunt Gladys is a space alien?" teased Zack. "Or a vampire? Or a diabolical gnome?"

Janice stopped pacing and glared at her brother.

"You're being paranoid, Janice. Again."

Zack let the statement hang in the air. Janice, deflated, stopped pacing and leaned against a stack of doors. Maybe she was being paranoid, but could they blame her? After what they'd all been through? The fire. Dad. A better question was, why weren't *they* being paranoid?

She looked around at her siblings and answered her own question. *They're too depressed to be paranoid,* she thought.

Suddenly, she was determined to lift everyone out of their funk. They needed a distraction. Scanning the room, her eyes settled on the stack of doors by her side. She lifted the sheet covering them and let a smile play on her lips.

"What are you doing?" asked Zack. "Aunt Gladys told us to leave the doors alone."

Janice smiled. "She did, didn't she?" With a flourish, she whipped the sheet off and flung it aside. "Who's up for a ride?"

◆ ◆ ◆

"Bad idea." Zack shook his head and crossed his arms.

"Quit being a baby," remarked Sydney as she helped Janice lug one of the doors—a simple, flat slab of wood—to the top of the stairs leading down to the second floor.

"I'm not being a baby! This is dumb and dangerous and stupid and—"

"And it's gonna be a ton of fun," finished Sydney.

Janice beamed. Her sisters, at least, liked her idea. Who cared if Zack was being a stick-in-the-mud?

"You're going to get hurt," said Zack.

"I never get hurt," replied Sydney. She and Janice eased the door just over the edge of the stairs, and Sydney jumped on.

"Hey! It was my idea!" complained Janice.

"We need to test it out," Sydney replied. "I'm a professional. Give me a push."

Janice sighed, then bent down into a shoving position.

"Guys, please," begged Zack. "You're gonna break something. Like a leg."

Janice frowned as the reality of what she was about to do—push her sister down a flight of stairs—hit home. But then she saw Sydney eagerly waiting and tossed caution to the wind.

"Torpedo . . . launch!" she yelled.

With a quick shove, the door flopped over and slid effortlessly down the stairs, crashing at the bottom and sending Sydney tumbling head over heels onto her bedroll, which they'd placed below to provide a soft landing. The entire ride took all of three seconds.

"Sydney?" asked Janice. "Sydney, you okay?"

Sydney lay on her back, staring at the ceiling, a huge grin on her face.

"That! Was! Awesome!"

Janice swelled with pride and turned to Zack. "She survived."

"Whatever. Kill yourselves if you want. Come on, Alexa. Let's go." He grabbed his little sister's hand, but she tugged it free.

"I want to ride!" she said.

"No way," he argued. "It's too dangerous."

"Sydney's fine!" countered Alexa. "Right, Sydney?"

"You bet! Janice! Help me bring this back up!"

Janice trounced down the steps to help carry the doorsled back to the top, where they found Alexa, arms crossed and face flushed, stomping on the floor.

"—I am too!" she ranted.

"You are not!" ranted Zack right back at her. "You're too little and—"

Janice winced, knowing Zack had just said exactly the wrong thing.

"I am not little!" screamed a defiant Alexa, sitting down on the door. "Somebody push me!"

Zack quickly stomped his foot down, holding the door in place. "Get off of there, Alexa!"

"Or what?" asked Janice, growing more and more annoyed at her brother. "Are you going to ground her? Send her to her room? Who do you think you are, anyway?"

"Somebody has to look out for this family!" yelled Zack.

"Give it up, Zack!" retorted Janice. "You're not Dad!"

Zack's eyes bulged, his cheeks flushed, and Janice was pretty sure steam billowed out of his ears. She stepped back, but he followed step for step, jabbing his finger into her chest. "Don't you ever—"

He never finished his sentence.

A cry of terror shook the room, and everyone watched as, almost in slow motion, the door-sled—released by Zack's foot—tore down the stairs, taking an utterly unprepared Alexa with it. Her face was a mask of pure fright, and her siblings' hearts leaped into their throats as the three-second slide felt like five hours of horror.

There was a crash. There was a tumble. There was Alexa lying at the bottom of the stairs. She looked around for a moment, stunned, before erupting in a hysterical cry, bringing all three siblings to her side.

"Alexa!" they screamed as one.

She continued to wail the wail of a young child in pain. Between gasps, she managed to inform everyone that her leg was in absolute agony. After sending Sydney off to find Aunt Gladys, Zack cradled his little sister and tried to soothe the hysteria out of her.

"Are you happy?" he snapped at Janice.

Janice could only stand there, dumb to the world.

What had she done?

CHAPTER ELEVEN

Sydney Finds THE Door

SYDNEY RACED THROUGH THE HOUSE TOWARD THE HATCH LEAD-ing to the central room. Upon reaching the imposing vault, however, she hesitated, not exactly sure what she was supposed to do. On one hand, Alexa was in pain and needed an adult to see to her injury—even an adult as flighty as Aunt Gladys. On the other hand, Aunt Gladys had left strict instructions not to be interrupted.

Sydney shrugged. She'd never been very good at following instructions.

She knocked gingerly on the partially open titanium door. *Too scatterbrained to close the door,* she thought. *Figures.*

After the briefest of pauses, Sydney decided Aunt Gladys wasn't answering her knock and more direct methods of communication were required. She inched up to the door, senselessly afraid for some reason, and peered an eye through the crack. Then the other eye wanted in on the action, so she eased the door open a bit more. When neither eye was able to make out much, the rest of her head got in on the act, followed by her arms and legs, and before she knew it, Sydney had opened the door wide enough to squeeze her whole body through.

She stood inside the room—and stared at a ratty, stained, tannish-brownish curtain hanging in front of her, blocking her view.

Loath to touch the curtain for fear of contracting an exotic disease, Sydney pushed it aside with the tip of her pinkie and stepped into the cavernous shrine beyond.

Her mind had difficulty accepting what her eyes claimed to be seeing. The room was massive. Four stories tall, circular, and wide open. The curved walls were ringed with floor-to-ceiling scaffolding, and a web of glass formed an enormous skylight that diffused the soft moonlight shimmering its way into the room. Littered about the floor were the shattered remains of dozens of wooden doors, each one cracked neatly in half.

That was all very weird.

But in the middle of the room was something even weirder.

On a slightly raised platform, perhaps a foot above the ground, stood a large, ornate wooden door like one you'd find in a royal palace. It was bolted into a brass doorframe. A series of thick black cables ran along the floor from the door to a small bank of machines off to the side. The machines were something out of a bad sci-fi movie, with blinking lights, countless dials and buttons and toggle switches, and glowing glass bulbs of every shape and size. Topping off the whole "mad scientist" vibe were the random bolts of faint blue energy whizzing and crackling around the surface of the door.

That was extra freaky.

After she'd gawked long and hard for a bit, Alexa's plight popped back into Sydney's head. Tearing her eyes away from the disturbing centerpiece of the room, she searched for her aunt. It took her less than five seconds to see she wasn't there.

"Aunt Gladys?" she whispered into the cavernous enclosure. There was no reply.

She knew she should run out of the room and keep searching for the so-called adult of the house, but instead she found herself inexorably drawn to the strange, buzzing, fancy-pants door in the center of the room. A big, bulky glass doorknob stuck out from the wood. Sydney slowly circled the platform, wary of actually setting foot upon it, and tried to imagine what in the world her aunt was up to. Nothing came to her, though at least now she knew what Aunt Gladys did with all the doors infesting her home.

Completing her ring around the platform (and noticing a lack of a doorknob on the opposite side), Sydney frowned. She had absolutely no idea what the contraption was for, which she found both bothersome and compelling. She was entranced by the mysterious puzzle of the door. She wanted to touch it. She wanted to open it.

Bad idea, Sydney, she told herself. *You'll probably get electrocuted or something. Leave it alone.*

She chose to ignore her advice.

It took some doing to persuade her feet to take a step toward the platform, and a lot more doing to get them up onto the platform itself. That accomplished, Sydney took some deep breaths to calm her jiggly nerves before reaching toward the big, bulky glass doorknob.

Which suddenly turned all on its own.

Sydney gasped and quickly sprang into "run and hide" mode, leaping off the platform and diving behind a haphazard pile of broken doors just as the one in the frame opened. Poorly hidden as she was, she concentrated on being as still and silent as she could while watching the impossible unfold before her.

The door opened wide, a burst of light erupted from within, and something stepped into the room.

Which should have been impossible.

The individual, monster, or hallucination turned back and closed the door, cutting off the burst of light. Sydney blinked a couple of times till her eyes came back into focus, and she recognized the figure on the platform.

Aunt Gladys.

She again wore the beekeeper's mesh helmet and large rust-colored gloves, and she seemed to be shaking her head.

"No," she muttered. "Amusing, yes. Helpful? No."

She stepped off the platform and approached the ominous machine with its banks of chaotic bulbs and blinking lights. "I know you're in there," she continued, slightly louder than before. "I will find you." Reaching the machine, she dropped her gloves onto the lone chair in front of the computers, sighed, and looked over the controls. "Right, on to the next—"

"Aunt Gladys? Are you in here?"

Aunt Gladys froze at the sound of Janice's voice. Not that it mattered, but Sydney froze as well. "Don't come in!" squealed Aunt Gladys in a panic, ripping the beekeeper's helmet off her head and running toward the curtain.

"Aunt Gladys?" repeated Janice. "Alexa is hurt!"

"I'm coming!" called Aunt Gladys as she passed through the curtain. "What happened? Which one is Alexa? Is that the boy?"

Sydney waited until her aunt's voice faded. She knew she should probably dash out of there right away, but all she could do was sit and stare in openmouthed wonder at the large, ornate wooden door covered in sparkling blue energy in the middle of the room.

It was beautiful.

CHAPTER TWELVE

Alexa Has a Secret

ALEXA AWOKE FEELING LIKE SOMEONE HAD DUMPED A BIG BOWL of happy juice over her head. It was dark out, so she figured it was still the middle of the night, which was just fine with her because she didn't want this night to ever, ever end. She didn't know what had woken her up this time, but she didn't care because she was still glowing from the memory of the first time she'd woken up that night.

Funny that the night would be so great so soon after almost being so terrible.

She had been convinced she'd broken something when she'd fallen down the stairs on Janice's door-sled. Her cries of pain had been real, loud, and well earned. Zack had held her close and rocked her as her sobs slowly turned into hiccups and then into quiet tears, and by the time Aunt Gladys got there, it already didn't hurt as much. Under Zack's guidance, she'd moved her ankle up and down and side to side to make sure it wasn't broken, and they'd both checked it for blood or bits of bone sticking out at weird angles. When they didn't find any, Zack announced that she'd just twisted it. That didn't sound nearly as bad as shattering it into a million pieces, which was what she'd thought she'd done.

Aunt Gladys had sort of flocked around like a confused goose until Zack suggested putting ice on Alexa's ankle. They all went down to the kitchen (Zack carrying her) so Aunt Gladys could fill a plastic bag with ice and hold it against Alexa's ankle. It was cold, but it didn't hurt and it made some of the pain go away, so that was all right. Then Sydney showed up, and Zack yelled at her for taking so long to fetch Aunt Gladys, and Sydney didn't argue or anything. That had been really strange.

Then they'd gone to bed.

Which was when everything became really great.

Alexa smiled at the memory. She'd been dreaming (something about a dog with a mustache, or was it a cat?) when a gentle rocking and an even gentler voice brought her to the surface.

"Alexa? Wake up, sweetie."

She'd opened her eyes to find the most beautiful woman in the world leaning over her with a smile. Even though she hadn't seen her since she was barely a year old, she knew right away who it was.

"Mommy?"

"That's right, sweetie. I'm here. I'm really here," Mommy had cooed. "It's so good to see you."

"Mommy!" Alexa popped right up out of her bed and jumped into her mother's arms. The movement had woken Ratty the Rat, who stirred fretfully in his cage in the corner of the room, but Alexa didn't care. Mommy held her so very tightly, and Alexa felt all her worries and problems melt away. Her ankle, which had still been a little sore when she had gone to bed, didn't hurt at all.

"Shhhhh," Mommy whispered. "It's not time to get up, sweetie. I need you to do something for me, okay?"

Alexa nodded vigorously. She would do anything for Mommy.

"Good girl. But you can't tell anyone that I'm here. It has to stay our little secret. Do you understand?"

"Yes, Mommy," Alexa answered.

"Thank you, sweetie. I knew I could count on you." Alexa burst with pride at her mother's praise. "What I need you to do, and this is very, very important, is to find my mother's door. Have you seen it? Have you seen Grammy's door?"

Alexa squinted her eyes, confused. "Door? There's lots of doors at Aunt Gladys's," she said.

Her mother smiled patiently. "Yes, dear. But I'm looking for my mother's. I know it's in that house somewhere. Can you be a good girl and find it for me?"

"You want me to find Grammy's door?"

"That's right. The original door to her bedroom. It's

rather plain, but has a large number of scratches along the bottom from when Mr. Tinkles would try to get my mother to let him into her room after one of his midnight prowls."

"Mr. Tinkles?"

"One of my mother's cats. But that's not important. Just look for the scratches, okay? Now, I don't need you to do anything with the door when you find it. In fact, don't touch it. Just find out where it is. I'll come back each night so you can tell me when you find it. Will you do that for me?"

"You're not staying?"

"No, sweetie. I have to go. Remember, no one else can know I'm here."

Alexa felt a little sad at this, but her mother gently brushed her hair out of her face and smiled. "You've grown so big, sweetie. Such a big girl," she said. "I love you so much. Find the door for me. Deal?"

Mommy stuck her hand out to shake, which made Alexa giggle. "Deal!" she squeaked before remembering to be quiet. "Deal," she repeated, this time in a whisper.

"Go back to bed now, sweetie. I love you. I'll see you soon."

Alexa had lain back down on her bed, and her mother had tucked her Pretty Pony comforter back under her chin. She had been so excited she hadn't thought it possible to fall back asleep, but she must have because she didn't remember anything else until waking up this second time.

Mommy had been here! Alexa's wish had come true!

Voices from Zack's room next door (or next doorway)

drifted into Alexa's ears. That must have been what had woken her up this time. Who was he talking to? Maybe Mommy was visiting him, too!

No, she thought. *No one else knows she's here.*

Curious and, by now, more or less awake, Alexa threw the lone sheet off and climbed out of her bedroll. She was a little surprised to find her ankle hurting again—not a lot, but it was certainly still sore. Funny how it had felt fine when her mother had woken her up earlier.

Mommy makes everything better, she told herself.

With a very slight limp (which she would be sure to exaggerate once she entered Zack's room), she made her way to the doorway to find out what was going on. She stopped before getting there, however, because she realized she was still beaming from Mommy's visit, and she didn't want to slip up and spill the beans. She took a moment to calm down and did her best to turn her really big smile into a simple grin. Once that was done, she continued into Zack's room, pushing all thoughts of Mommy to the back of her mind. For now.

She was a good girl. She'd keep their secret.

◆ ACT TWO ◆

Turning the Knob

◆ CHAPTER THIRTEEN ◆

Zack Reluctantly Follows

"Stop, Sydney," pleaded Zack. "It's bad enough you disappeared when Alexa needed you. You don't have to make up some stupid cover story."

"I'm not making this up!" insisted Sydney.

"Shhhh!" Zack put a finger to his lips. "You want to wake everybody?"

"Yes!" exclaimed Sydney before she stopped, frowning, and added, "Well, not Aunt Gladys."

Zack sighed. He was bone-tired, partly from arguing with Sydney and partly from being awake at three o'clock in the morning. Which was also Sydney's fault. She'd come down and shaken him awake with a wild story about a magic door and blue lightning and Aunt Gladys appearing out of thin air. It was all a bit much to handle at three in the morning. As much as he generally tried to be patient with her, this was pushing his limits.

"Go back to bed," he snapped, lying down on his bedroll and hoping she'd get the hint.

"No!" she insisted, punching him in the gut in such a manner as to show that she had not, in fact, gotten the hint. "Get up! You have got to see this!"

"See what?" came a little voice from the doorway.

Brother and sister momentarily halted their skirmish as little Alexa entered the room. "Good job, Sydney," Zack said, coating his voice with a thick layer of sarcasm. "You woke Alexa." He was about to try to coax Alexa back into bed but stopped short after one look at his little sister's beaming face.

Beaming? he wondered. *At this hour?*

"She's up," stated Sydney enthusiastically. "Now we just need to wake Janice—"

Zack turned back to the currently-more-annoying sister. "Stop! You're not waking Janice. You're not sneaking into that room. You're going back to bed."

"You got into the room?" asked Alexa.

Sydney spun and zeroed in on the youngest Rothbaum. "You have to see it! There are all these machines and wires and a big door in the center of the room with this weird blue lightning all around it, and it's a portal to another world!"

"Come on, Sydney," chastised Zack. "It's not a portal to another—"

"I wanna see! I wanna see!" chanted Alexa.

Zack groaned as control of the situation slipped through his fingers. "No. Guys, just no. It's the middle of the night!"

"Which is the only time we can get in!" argued Sydney. "Aunt Gladys is asleep! This is our chance!"

"Chance for what?" asked Janice, walking into the room.

"Sydney got into the forbidden room, and there's a big space door there—" began Alexa.

"It's not a space door!" interrupted Zack.

"Could be a space door," interjected Sydney.

"What's a space door?" asked Janice.

"I wanna go through the space door!" cheered Alexa.

"Everybody, stop!" yelled Zack, shoving his arms out as if to hold back the encroaching barrage of chatter. "I don't care if it's a space door or an interdimensional door or a door to the linen closet. It's the middle of the night, this whole house is creepy-dangerous, and we'll get in big trouble if Aunt Gladys catches us. What was the one rule she hammered into our heads all day?"

"If you have to go, go in the potty," offered Sydney.

"Okay, yeah," agreed Zack. "But besides that? Stay out of that room!" He folded his arms and threw his best "I'm totally serious" glare at his sisters to drive his point home.

Alexa looked down at the ground, somehow managing to look both chastised and totally jazzed at the same time. Sydney glared right back at him but for once held her tongue. Even Janice folded her arms, which Zack hoped was a mild form of agreement.

"Back to bed, people," he finished. "This conversation is over."

"I agree," said Janice.

"Thank you," said Zack, relieved.

"This conversation is over," she continued. "I'm going to go check out the room."

"Wait. What?" said Zack, no longer relieved.

"I want to know what's going on in this house if I'm gonna stay here till Dad wakes up," she declared. "Who's coming with?"

Sydney and Alexa quickly ran to their big sister's side.

Defeat looming over him, Zack made one last attempt to reason with his sisters. "Please," he said. "We don't know what's in there."

"Time to find out," replied Janice.

"It could be dangerous," he countered.

"It could be awesome," she countered right back.

With that, she turned and marched out of the room, Sydney and Alexa falling excitedly in line behind her. Zack swayed back and forth on his feet, debating with himself. He didn't want to race after them and give Janice a victory, but he also didn't want his sisters to go running headfirst into danger without him. What if something happened? Something he could have prevented?

He clenched his fists, closed his eyes, growled.

Then took off after his sisters.

The vault door was not locked. In fact, as far as he could tell, it didn't lock at all. By the time Zack caught up with his sisters, Sydney and Janice were pulling the massive hatch open, Alexa cheering them on with cries of "Go! Go!" like they were about to score a touchdown.

Zack walked past everyone and stepped through the doorway before anyone even noticed he was there.

"Hey!" burst Janice. "What do you think you're doing?"

Rather than answer, Zack shoved the truly nasty curtain aside and got his first look at the room. The sheer size of the place froze him in his tracks. It had to be bigger than every other room in the house combined, and what was with all the scaffolding? His eyes swept around the walls, taking in the piles of broken and shattered wooden doors, the weird weblike glass skylight, the strange bank of what looked to be really old computers—basically every detail of the room except for the big, fancy door standing in the center, which he was doing his very best to ignore.

Because it was covered with dazzling sparks of blue energy.

"Told you," stated a defiant Sydney, pushing her way past him.

"Huh," he answered.

"Wow!" exclaimed Alexa. "Look at the door! So cool!"

Zack did not find it cool. Truth be told, Zack found it terrifying.

"She just stepped right out of this?" asked Janice, circling the platform. "You're sure?"

"Swear to God," answered Sydney, approaching reverently.

"But . . ." Zack's voice caught in his throat. He swallowed and tried again. "But it doesn't go anywhere. It's just standing in the middle of the room."

"Like I said. A portal to another world."

The four children soon found themselves standing in a line at the foot of the platform, eyeing the slightly ominous door with varying mixtures of wonder and apprehension.

Finally, Sydney, who leaned more toward the wonder side of things, stepped up onto the platform. "Let's go," she said.

"I don't know," said Janice. Zack noted with satisfaction that, faced with an actual door that was actually covered in actual blue lightning, his older sister didn't seem so gung ho on her idea. "That actually looks kind of creepy."

Zack smugly crossed his arms. "As I said, not a good idea."

It was the wrong thing to say. Janice shook the caution away and glared at him. "You mean it's not a Zack idea," she said. "It's a Janice idea."

She marched up to the door, reached out, and grabbed the chunky glass doorknob.

The instant her hand touched the glass, the random sizzles of energy focused their wrath on the knob and, by extension, Janice's hand. There was a sudden, high-pitched, zaplike sound as Janice gave a yelp and was shot backward, tumbling off the platform.

"Janice!" cried Zack, instantly dropping any pretense of annoyance and rushing to his sister's side.

"Gah! Eeuaahh! Ow!" Janice sat on her rump, shaking

her hand in the air as if swatting an annoying mosquito away from her face.

"What happened? Can you feel your hand? Did you lose any fingers?"

"I'm fine, Zack!" she sputtered, despite faint wafts of smoke rising from her palm claiming otherwise. "It was the biggest static electricity shock I've ever felt, is all." A hush fell over the children until Janice burst into a chuckle, adding, "Did you just ask if I'd lost any fingers? Seriously?"

Zack blushed as the others shared a smile.

"Aunt Gladys wore gloves," remembered Alexa.

Sydney snapped her fingers and ran to the archaic bank of computers. "Gloves!" She held up Aunt Gladys's rust-colored rubber gloves that had been resting on the chair.

"Wait a sec," said Zack, standing. "Janice just got zapped. Let's stop and think—"

"Not gonna happen," replied Sydney, shoving the gloves over her hands.

Zack could only watch, his breath caught in his throat, as Sydney approached the door, reached out a gloved hand, and grabbed the knob.

Once again the blue sparks attacked the knob with a vengeance.

Janice gasped. Zack cringed. Alexa shrieked.

Sydney turned the knob without a care in the world. "It's fine," she said. "I don't feel a thing through the gloves."

Zack's momentary relief at his sister's well-being quickly shifted to alarm as Sydney yanked the door wide, releasing a burst of white light that nearly blinded him. Everyone turned and covered their eyes from the relentless assault of brilliance blaring into their pupils.

"Close the door!" yelled Zack.

"Don't be a wuss, Zack!" Sydney yelled back.

"This is a bad idea!"

"It's the best idea I've ever had!"

His eyes acclimating to the intense glare, Zack peeked through his fingers at his middle sister. "Please!" he begged. "Close the door!"

But Sydney did not close the door.

She walked through it.

"Sydney!" cried Zack, panic threatening to consume him.

"Sydney?" called Janice from the floor.

"Sydney?" echoed Alexa, unconsciously stepping away from the open door.

Sydney did not answer. Sydney was no longer in the room.

"Did she really just vanish?" asked Janice, struggling to her feet.

"Sydney?" Alexa's voice was catching, and Zack recognized the start of a meltdown.

A jumble of emotions poured into his head, momentarily paralyzing him with indecision. Then, through it all, a single thought swam to the surface.

My sister's in trouble.

Nothing else mattered.

Before his rational mind had a chance to talk him out of it, Zack dashed into the light.

CHAPTER FOURTEEN

Janice Remembers Something She Learned in School

JANICE WATCHED ZACK FOLLOW SYDNEY INTO THE TOTALLY creepy wall of white, feeling as if she'd just been punched in the gut. Where were they? Were they dead? She had led them into this room, made this happen—it was all her fault. What had she been thinking?

"Where are they?" asked a cowed Alexa, shuffling up to her big sister.

"I . . . I . . ." Words refused to come. Thoughts refused to come. She could only stand and stare through squinting eyes at the impossible ocean of stark white light pouring out the door.

"Janny? Make them come back," pleaded Alexa.

Janice shook her head, trying to come to grips with what had just happened. She had seen Sydney and Zack go through the door. They were gone. She didn't want that to be possible. She couldn't handle a world where that was possible.

"Janny?" Alexa's voice begged Janice for comfort.

But Janice had none to give.

Suddenly, Sydney stepped back out of the light, eyes wide with wonder. "You've got to see this!" She hopped right back through the open door before Janice or Alexa could blink.

"Did you—?" started Janice anxiously.

"Was that—?" started Alexa excitedly at the same time.

Heart in her throat, Janice allowed her little sister to grab her hand and pull her through the door.

◆ ◆ ◆

It was unlike any doorway Janice had ever experienced.

As she passed through, her skin got all tingly, the hairs on her arms stood straight up, her head felt fuzzy, and her vision blurred for the briefest of moments. Then she was through and she stopped in her tracks, flabbergasted at what she saw.

They were standing in a large room decorated in the rococo style of the eighteenth century with big chandeliers, thick rugs, mirrors on the walls, and furniture with lots of curly gold knobs. The walls were also covered with impressive portraits of both men and women in fancy ruffles between floor-to-ceiling bookcases filled with old-looking books. The place struck Janice as some sort of stuffy, lived-in museum.

"Whoa," said Alexa.

"I know, right?" said Sydney. "How awesome is this?"

Janice had to admit it was pretty awesome. Stepping farther into the room, she tried to comprehend what she was seeing. It wasn't the scaffold-filled room in Aunt Gladys's house, that was for sure. But they couldn't really be here, wherever here was. Could they?

"Why's everything look all old?" asked Alexa.

Janice was about to explain how the room was obviously made up in a style from long past, when she realized her sister wasn't talking about the furniture. Everything in the room had a yellowish hue to it, like she was looking through a filter. It was creepy with a capital C.

"All right," she said. "We went through the door. Can we go back now?"

"Are you kidding?" asked Sydney, putting her hands on her hips. "We step through a magic door into this impossible world and you want to turn tail and run home?"

"'Magic door'! 'Impossible world'!" emphasized Janice. "Aunt Gladys warned us to keep out of her room, and now we know why!"

"This was your idea," reminded Zack.

"And it was a bad one! Why did you listen to me?"

"You're afraid," accused Sydney.

"You bet I am! And you should be, too!" Janice turned and grabbed the handle of the door they'd just gone through—a

door she didn't remember closing. "Tomorrow morning we can corner Aunt Gladys and make her tell us what's going on, but right now we need to—"

She pulled the door open and stopped.

Instead of a bright white light or tons of scaffolding, the door opened into an even larger room. Equally ornate, equally old, equally yellowish.

The biggest difference between the two rooms was the butler currently setting a tea tray down on a side table next to a very plush sofa.

Janice gasped. Her brother and sisters gasped. The butler looked up, saw the children, and gasped, dropping his tray. The tea set balanced on the tray did not gasp, choosing instead to crash to the ground and shatter into tiny shards of fine china.

"Who are you?" asked Janice with what she realized was most likely a remarkable amount of stupidity.

"Redcoats!" screamed the butler, turning and running out of the room. "Redcoats in the parlor!" He waved his hands in the air as he ran, making him look like a poorly drawn cartoon character.

Sydney quickly jumped forward and slammed the door closed.

"What are you doing?" asked Janice.

She held up her still-gloved hands. "You need to open it with these, dummy." She grabbed the handle and yanked it open, only to find the exact same room as before—minus the butler, who they could still hear yelling "Redcoats!" off in the distance.

"Huh," muttered Sydney.

"I don't understand," said Alexa. "Where's Aunt Gladys's house?"

"I told you guys this was a bad idea," blurted Zack. "Are you happy now, Janice?"

Janice did not respond. Point of fact, Janice was not happy and had not been happy since she had seen the impossible blue energy whipping about the door on the platform in the first place. However, the reason Janice did not respond to her brother's question was because something the butler had said had tickled a memory, and she was very carefully scrunching her eyes together in a determined effort to draw it out. "Redcoats," she mumbled. "Redcoats."

"What did he mean by that?" asked Sydney. "We're not wearing any coats."

Janice knew that phrase. She'd heard it recently. Where? Back at school? Why would she remember anything from school? It referred to someone, or a group of someones. What had she been studying back at school? Not math. Not science. Not English. Social studies. That was it. Something in social studies. They'd been reading about the American Revolution—

Her eyes went wide.

"The British!" she cried.

"He didn't sound British," said Zack.

Janice opened her mouth to explain that *redcoats* was

what American soldiers had called the British during the American Revolution, when three angry-looking men ran into the opposite room and aimed three angry-looking muskets at the children.

"Hands up, British spies!" yelled the most angry-looking of the men.

Alexa screamed and ran from the door.

"Stop!" yelled the soldier.

"Go!" yelled Zack, slamming the door closed as all four Rothbaum children fled into the hallway.

Zack quickly looked both ways down the corridor. To the right, the hallway darkened before turning a corner, while light poured in from the left. "This way!" he yelled, taking a few steps to the right.

"No!" shouted Janice, wary of the darkness. "This way!" She grabbed Alexa's hand and ran to the left. Sydney quickly followed, leaving a frustrated Zack to bring up the rear. In moments, the siblings found themselves atop a grand, sweeping staircase leading down into a massive, two-story entrance hall. Sunlight blazed in through multiple floor-to-ceiling windows, shining off the ends of the muskets clutched by two more soldiers hurrying up the stairs toward them.

"Halt, you redcoats!" shouted one of the soldiers.

"Why do they think we're British?" asked Sydney.

Janice had no idea, but before she could admit this, the children heard the sound of their pursuers bursting through the door behind them, cutting off their escape.

Oh no, thought Janice. *We're trapped! What was I thinking, trying to lead?*

"What do we do, Janny?" asked an increasingly frightened Alexa. "Janny?"

"We . . . um . . . I . . ." sputtered Janice, her mind shutting down in the face of overwhelming responsibility.

"Are you halting?" asked the soldier. "That would be very helpful indeed."

Frozen with indecision as she was, halting was as good a description as any for what Janice was doing. Luckily, she was un-halted by an unlikely source. "Follow me!" cried Sydney, vaulting herself onto the winding banister before anyone could stop her and zipping down past the approaching soldiers with a whoop of glee.

"Careful!" said the soldier, fumbling with his musket. "You'll fall and hurt yourself before we have a chance to shoot you!"

"Come on!" urged Zack, picking up Alexa and leaping onto the banister. As the littlest Rothbaum screamed in a mixture of terror and glee, the two of them followed Sydney to the ground floor.

At the top of the stairs, Janice hesitated. She was never the most graceful individual—what if she fell? A two-story drop could break an arm or leg.

"May we shoot the spies, sir?" came a call from behind.

"By all means!" answered the sir.

On the other hand . . . Janice climbed up and let gravity propel her down. One of the soldiers on the stairs, by now ready for this trick, reached out to grab her. But a well-placed shoe thrown from below knocked him away, allowing Janice to reach the bottom unharmed.

"Look out!" shouted the shoe-battered soldier. "They're armed with footwear!"

"Dear God, no!" shouted another soldier.

"Thanks, Sydney!" said Janice upon reaching the ground.

"You owe me a shoe!" her sister snapped back with just the hint of a grin.

"This way!" called Zack, shoving the front door open to allow all four children to escape into the outside air.

Before them stood an encampment of battered tents, with bedraggled men sitting randomly on the ground in various states of boredom. Other, more official-looking men rushed from one tent to another on what looked like very important business. As inside, the entire scene seemed overlaid with a dry, dusty coat of yellowish gray.

"Where are we?" asked Janice.

"More accurately, *when* are we? And how do we get home?" added Zack.

Suddenly, the doors were forced open and the five soldiers ran out in a heady rush. "Redcoat spies!" they cried as one. "Get them!"

"That's getting old," growled Sydney.

"To the tents!" suggested Janice.

As one, the children rushed down into the sea of tents. They twisted their way through a labyrinth of yellowing gray canvas, zigzagging back and forth to throw off their pursuers. Luckily—and, Janice thought, oddly—none of the other soldiers they passed seemed interested in joining the chase. As they ran, Janice had the idea of ducking into one of the many tents and letting the soldiers run past them, but she could never find a way inside.

"Where are we going?" asked Sydney in midstride.

"Away from the guns!" answered Janice.

"My legs are tired!" warned Alexa. Zack took her hand to hurry her along.

"We're not going to lose them in here!" shouted Zack.

"You got a better idea?"

Before he could answer, a strange old man popped out of one of the canvas tents directly in their path, forcing the children to skid to a halt.

"You can't be here!" he snapped.

"We're not spies!" pleaded Janice.

"Of course not! Your knob! Quickly!"

"What are you talking about?" asked Sydney.

"You don't . . . ? Dog-eared dumplings! Of all the . . ." The old man's face turned red, and he sputtered unintelligibly as if unable to find the right word.

"Why aren't you old?" asked Alexa.

Janice's initial reaction was to point out that the man in front of them looked quite old indeed, but she then realized what her little sister had meant.

He's not yellow.

"Halt, redcoats! There's no escape! We have you surrounded!" The soldier glared at them over the barrel of his musket. "And don't even think about reaching for your shoes."

With military precision, a circle of American Revolution–era soldiers surrounded the four children, aimed their muskets, and did their best to look threatening.

"Don't shoot!" begged Janice, raising her arms. The others quickly did the same.

"Apprehend them!" ordered the soldier who seemed to be the leader. "Take them down to the dungeon! The really nasty one, not the fun one!"

"We're not spies! We're not British! Tell them!" cried Janice, turning back to the old man. "Tell them we're not—"

The old man was gone.

◆ CHAPTER FIFTEEN ◆

Sydney Gets a Chill

THE DUNGEON STANK TO HIGH HEAVEN.

It was muddy and gross and nasty, and Sydney was pretty sure somebody had gone to the bathroom in one corner pretty recently.

Brooding in the back with her knees tucked up under her arms and her unshod foot raised slightly in the air, she tried to figure out how they'd gotten here and, more important, if it was her fault. She tended to get blamed for a lot of bad things that happened, and while most of the time the accusations were spot on, this time she wasn't so sure.

"I wanna go home."

Poor Alexa was cracking. Sydney figured the only thing keeping her little sister in one emotional piece was the tight grip she had on Zack's arm. Not that Sydney blamed her.

She was pretty sure there was a meltdown in her own future if something didn't happen soon to turn this little adventure around.

It would've helped if the guy in the next cell would shut up.

"—revealing myself to General Washington," he was babbling on and on. "To do otherwise would dishonor my name, country, and king. A gentleman must remain upright and proper, even during such unseemly times of war as these. I'm sure you agree."

No one bothered to respond. They had quickly learned the man saw conversation as a predominantly one-sided affair.

"It was quite the monumental task to find the proper words with which to convey my message," he continued. "While I respect General Washington, he is, after all, rebelling against his king and, as such, beneath a proper British subject such as myself."

The man, who had introduced himself as Major John Andre, had been talking nonstop ever since the children had been thrown into the adjoining cell. Sydney had quickly tuned him out and was pretty sure her siblings had done the same. Janice, in fact, seemed to have tuned out the entire world, having spent the time since being incarcerated sitting against the wall with a blank look on her face.

What had really shaken Sydney to the core was that near as she could tell from the guy's continuous ranting, she and her siblings had somehow found themselves in the middle of the American Revolution. Since she was pretty sure that particular war had ended something like two hundred years ago or more, there was a scary-real chance that they had traveled back in time. Which freaked the heck out of her.

"Personally, I blame General Arnold," continued Major John Andre. "The man is an utter buffoon and I should never have agreed to his haphazard attempt at espionage. Did you know he constantly smells of fish?"

Aside from the self-important Andre, the only other person they'd seen since being thrown into the dungeon was the butler who had screamed when they'd opened the door. He'd come around once to offer them bread and water, managing not to scream this time.

As Andre dove into a list of everything wrong with Benedict Arnold, Sydney once again looked around their cell, trying to come up with a means of escape. She had already tested the bars of their cell as well as searched around for anything she could use to do serious damage to them. No such luck. Finally, she hopped over to Zack and Alexa, loath to step on the cell floor with her sock. "What are they going to do with us?" she asked.

Zack closed his eyes and sighed, gathering his thoughts. "We're going to be all right," he said. "What can they do? We're not spies. We're not even British. They'll let us go."

"Go where?" asked Sydney.

Zack had no answer, so she shuffled back to her corner, less than convinced. She knew her brother meant well, but she was worried.

"I do believe death at the gallows to be relatively quick and painless," mentioned Major Andre quietly.

"What?" asked Sydney.

"A swift plunge to a merciful end," he explained, relishing the thought. "The ground beneath you gives way, and you plummet straight into the abyss. But then, of course, your fall is stopped short by less-than-comfortable neckwear. I'm sure you'll find the experience invigorating."

He was smiling, but his voice dripped and drooled with an unfriendly malevolence that caused Sydney to stand and move away from the creepy spy. He followed her with eyes glistening and twinkling in the fading, flickering torchlight, but said nothing more.

A loud creaking pulled Sydney's attention to the lone door leading out of the dungeon. She held her breath as it groaned its way open. *Here we go,* she thought. Sydney was ready for anything. Firing squad. Poison. The hangman. A dancing bear. Anything.

Except for who walked through the door.

"Aunt Gladys?" cried Alexa, leaping out of Zack's lap and flying to the bars of the cell with the fervent gusto of a seven-year-old being offered free candy.

"Oh! There you . . . right. Alex, right?" asked the ever-distracted woman. "No, don't tell me. Andy?"

The other three children—even Janice—jumped up as their aunt fumbled with a large ring of keys. She wore her white beekeeper's helmet tight over her face, making it difficult for her to tell key from key.

"How did you find us?" asked Alexa.

"How'd you get past the soldiers?" asked Janice.

"How'd you get the keys?" asked Zack.

"How'd you build a time machine?" asked Sydney.

Aunt Gladys started at Sydney's question, as if physically struck. "Time machine? You think . . . ? Oh! Well, yes, I suppose . . . Time machine? How strange."

"Try another key!" offered Zack, desperate to get their aunt back on track.

"Another . . . ? Oh! Yes, of course!"

She went back to fumbling through the keys, and the four children waited as patiently as possible as she tried first one, then another, to no avail.

"You cannot unlock yourself from fate, children," crooned Major Andre. "The noose is ever patient."

Aunt Gladys looked up. "Goodness! Such negativity!" she said.

"The keys, Aunt Gladys!" prompted Zack.

"Oh! Yes. They really should number these," she muttered. "Perhaps color-code . . ."

Finally, a key slid effortlessly into the lock. So effortlessly, in fact, that Aunt Gladys was about to pull it out and try another before Zack stopped her. A moment later, the cell door was open and the children were free.

"Now, come," ordered Aunt Gladys. "It's time to return home."

"He smelled of fish!" called Major Andre. "Fish and cheese and the gallows!"

"Aunt Gladys?" asked Alexa. "Can we release him, too?"

"Seriously? The guy's way creepy!" snarled Sydney.

"Doesn't mean we shouldn't unlock his cell," said Alexa, seemingly secure in her knowledge that deep down everyone was good and deserved a second chance.

Sydney begged to differ, remembering the predatory look Major Andre had given her a moment earlier. She was about to argue for letting him rot in his cell but stopped upon noticing a strange look of amusement come over her aunt's face.

"Release . . . ?" said Aunt Gladys. "How novel. Possibly amusing. Come along."

She walked back toward the basement door.

"Aren't you going to set him free?" cried Alexa.

"Why would I do that?" asked Aunt Gladys, reaching the door and pulling something large and bulky from her pocket.

Even Sydney was a bit taken aback by her aunt's callousness.

"You're just going to leave him here?" Zack asked.

"We've got lumps of it 'round the back!" called Major Andre, making less and less sense with each passing moment.

"Oh for heaven's . . ." Aunt Gladys shook her head. "He'll be dead in less than a week."

"I beg your pardon?" asked the condemned, snapping out of his slow descent into madness.

"Aunt Gladys!" exclaimed Alexa. Sydney and the others froze in shock.

"Or, was dead, I suppose," continued Aunt Gladys without a care in the world. "Will soon to have been dead. Will once again be dead. Something like that." She returned her attention to the door and pressed the large and bulky something up against it. There was an audible click that somehow seemed to resonate more within Sydney than without, and Aunt Gladys turned what Sydney could now see was a big crystal doorknob. With a soft grunt, Aunt Gladys pulled the door wide, and a blaze of bright white light poured into the room.

"Home!" announced Alexa, who ran forward.

"Yes, yes!" agreed Aunt Gladys. "Hurry along, now."

Needing no further encouragement, Alexa bounded greedily into the light and disappeared.

"How did you do that?" asked Janice.

"Run now," said Aunt Gladys. "Explain later."

"But—"

"The polite thing to do would be to set me free!" cried the forgotten Major Andre in a voice far deeper than he had used before. Curious, Sydney peered back down the hallway, and it seemed quite a bit darker than it had a moment earlier.

"Run!" urged Aunt Gladys.

Zack shoved Janice and Sydney in front of him even as another strangled cry spilled out of the now-unseen major's lips. This one was wet, hoarse, and disturbing.

"Major Andre?" asked Sydney.

"Has been dead for over two hundred years, child!" assured Aunt Gladys. "Run!"

Another moist roar emerged from the suddenly pitch-black basement behind them, chilling Sydney to the core. With a startled squeak, Janice pushed her way past and vanished into the light.

"Go, Sydney!" urged Zack, shoving her forward.

Confused, concerned, and increasingly disturbed, Sydney gave in and launched herself into the blinding whiteness. The last thing she heard before the world wrapped itself around her was a tortured gasp of unearthly horror coming from a voice that was no longer human.

◆ CHAPTER SIXTEEN ◆

Alexa Sorts It Out

ALEXA HELD HER BREATH UNTIL EVERYONE EMERGED FROM THE blinding light pouring through the door. Only then did she finally relax. They'd made it! They were home!

The trip into the yellow world had been fun at first, but there had been something nasty lurking out of sight. Something bad. And right at the end, right after Aunt Gladys had shown up to rescue them, Alexa had felt Something Bad stepping out from the shadows. . . .

But now they were all safely back home, and everything was okay. Content, Alexa flung herself into the room's only chair—a fun, swivelly chair in front of the long bank of old-timey computers—and proceeded to twirl around back and forth, the repetitive motion helping her calm down.

Aunt Gladys was last through the door, and she quickly

slammed it closed behind her. The loss of the bright white light cast a momentary darkness until Alexa's eyes re-adjusted to the dim illumination coming from the lightbulbs scattered around the room.

"Well!" exclaimed the constantly flustered woman. "That was . . . ! Is everyone . . . ? We're all here? Zorro? Everyone's back?"

"Yes, Aunt Gladys," reassured Zack. "We're all back."

Alexa giggled. She liked how Aunt Gladys always got their names wrong.

"How did you get us out of there?" asked Sydney.

"How did I . . . ? How did you . . . !" The giggle died on Alexa's face as Aunt Gladys flipped from harmless and funny to furious and parental in a heartbeat. "What possessed you to . . . ! So dangerous! You could have . . . ! I'll never forgive myself!"

"I knew it was a bad idea!" piled on Janice, which Alexa felt was unfair, since it had been her idea in the first place.

"What just happened?" asked Zack. "Where were we?"

"The American Revolution!" exclaimed Janice. "We were actually there!"

"No!" insisted Aunt Gladys, crossing to the bank of computers. "Well, yes. But no. Definitely not."

"What was that sound? That creature?" asked Sydney.

That was the Something Bad, thought Alexa. *Duh.*

"I don't know," answered Aunt Gladys. "I don't want to know. You don't want to know. Forget you saw it."

"We didn't see it—we heard it," reminded Sydney.

"Forget you heard it. In fact, forget your entire trip," suggested Aunt Gladys as she scurried around Alexa and started adjusting knobs and buttons. "Oh! Yes. Excellent idea. This was all a dream. Nighty-night."

"I can't believe you built a time machine!" said Sydney, following her aunt. "An actual time machine!"

Aunt Gladys snorted a laugh and whirled back around. "Time machine? Of all the . . . ! Don't be silly!"

"It wasn't a dream," insisted Zack, backing his sister up. "We were there. We were in the American Revolution."

"Nope, nope, nope." Aunt Gladys's fingers flew over the immense machine, turning knobs and flipping switches. "You were most certainly *not* in the American Revolution." A single glass bulb at the top of the machine suddenly blazed bright red, and Aunt Gladys punched a big, round button sitting apart from the other controls. There was the sound of gears straining, followed by a deafening *CRACK!*

The four children turned to see the magical door they'd just ventured through snapped in half by the strange metallic frame in which it was fastened. All sparks of blue energy vanished, and silence hung in the room.

"You were in a *memory* of the American Revolution," finished Aunt Gladys.

Alexa tilted her head, trying to figure out what Aunt Gladys had meant. It didn't work. "A memory?" she asked.

"The butler's, I think," continued Aunt Gladys, walking past her dazed nieces and nephew to the now-broken door. "He seemed to be everywhere."

The four children looked from one to another, each hoping someone else understood what she was talking about. None of them did. "How . . ." began Zack, proceeding carefully. "How is that even possible?"

"Possible?" Aunt Gladys unfastened the latches connecting the door to the frame. "You went through the door. Butler's door, butler's memory. I don't fully understand. Don't have to. Hook up the door. Push the buttons."

She yanked the broken door free and let it clatter to the floor. "Forgot to shut down yesterday," she continued, stepping over the debris and approaching a pile of fresh doors stacked one on top of another. "Worried about Alice's . . . what'd you hurt? Knee?"

"Ankle." Alexa didn't bother reminding Aunt Gladys that her name wasn't Alice.

"I was distracted," admitted Aunt Gladys. "I get distracted."

"You don't say," muttered Sydney. Zack shot her a look. She shrugged at him.

"Came in here to shut down. Door was wide open. You didn't even have a knob! Well, I had to . . . I had to! So I went in. So much darker. My poor dears! If anything had happened . . . !" She shook her head sadly. "All my fault. I couldn't live . . . I wouldn't live . . . My fault."

She stopped suddenly and looked up, as if seeing them for the first time. "Heavens! Bedtime! You can't be here! This never happened! Shoo! To bed with you!"

"Are you kidding?" asked Sydney. "Aunt Gladys, this"—

she spun in a circle, taking in the entire room—"this is incredible!"

"No, it's not. It's scary," corrected Janice. "And dangerous. Not something we should mess around with. Right?"

"Absolutely. Jake is right. Very dangerous. But also wonderful," agreed the flighty woman with a pinch of pride, smiling. Then the pinch disintegrated and the smile morphed into a frown. "But so dangerous. You could have . . . you all could have . . ."

"How does it work?" asked Alexa as the tiniest beginnings of an idea began to form.

"Work? I hook up a door. To the frame. Work the controls. Just like Father taught me. Then—"

"Your father?" interrupted Zack. "Did he build this?"

"Yes. My father. Your grandfather. Marcus Tulving. Brilliant man. Ahead of his time . . ." She stared longingly at the central doorframe contraption before whispering so softly Alexa could barely hear her. "I will find you, Daddy."

"Um . . . Aunt Gladys?" prompted Zack.

She blinked and was suddenly herself again. "Yes. When you open a door—a wooden door—you leave a bit of yourself behind." She pulled a fresh door off the top of a stack and hauled it to the platform. Alexa wondered why Aunt Gladys didn't ask Zack or Janice to help, then wondered why Zack or Janice didn't offer to help Aunt Gladys. She'd help, but the door looked heavy.

"A small bit. Tiny. Insignificant," continued Aunt Gladys between grunts of effort. "But it's there. Open the door enough times, it . . . imprints . . . on you. Not the right word. Doesn't matter. *Hunnngh!*" She shoved the final grunt out while heaving the door into a standing position on the platform next to the frame.

"Every door?" asked Sydney.

"Every wooden door." Aunt Gladys carefully set the new door into the metal frame and began adjusting fasteners and latches to secure it. "Wood is organic. Used to be alive." A few more moments of fiddling and everything snapped impressively into place.

"But why does it work?" asked Zack.

Aunt Gladys turned and leaned back on the newly secured door. "Why? Don't know. Your grandfather could explain. Or your mother. She was always . . ."

"Mommy?" asked Alexa, perking up.

Aunt Gladys shook her head clear. "Not me," she said, ignoring Alexa's interest in their mother. "I was never the . . . Well, anyway."

Sydney took a step forward, mesmerized by the machine. "You just open this door and enter someone's memory? Just like that?"

"Yes. No! Not just like that! There are rules! Memory hopping is incredibly dangerous!"

"Memory hopping?" asked Alexa.

Aunt Gladys looked over at Alexa. "My own term, little Alphonse." Alexa rolled her eyes. "Yes! Rules! Safety precautions! Checklists!" She marched down off the platform and back to the bank of computers.

"First rule is simple. When you go in, make sure you can get out. Bring a doorknob." She reached down and pulled open a drawer filled with doorknobs of all shapes and sizes. "I like to use nice crystal ones. They're pretty. But any knob will do. From here. From now. It's your ticket home. Stick it on a door in the memory. Boom! Instant gateway home."

Alexa chuckled at Aunt Gladys's use of the word *boom*.

"I don't understand," said Zack. "You say we were in the butler's memory."

"That makes the most sense, yes."

"But how? He couldn't remember us—we'd never met him. We weren't even alive."

"You weren't there, Zippy. You were in a memory. Who's hungry? I'm famished." Aunt Gladys made a beeline for the ugly curtain.

"I'm confused again," announced Alexa, looking to her siblings for help.

"Don't worry," muttered Sydney. "I think Aunt Gladys is, too."

Their aunt ducked under the curtain, then poked her head back through. "Doesn't anybody else want Honey Nut Oat Blast Ring-a-Dings?" she asked.

"It's kind of late for cereal," said Zack.

"Not in France," responded Aunt Gladys, tapping her finger against her forehead for no apparent reason before ducking back out of the room.

The four Rothbaums stared at the curtain as it swayed back and forth in the wake of their aunt's passing.

"She's not all there, is she?" said Sydney.

Alexa giggled and hopped off the swively chair (though not before spinning around one final time). "I think she's fun," she announced.

"Fun?" asked Janice. "Alexa, we could have died in there."

"But we didn't," insisted Alexa.

"But we could've," repeated Janice.

"But we didn't," repeated Alexa right back. "And Sydney got her shoe back."

She pointed at Sydney's feet, and her three siblings were shocked into silence to find the shoe right back where it belonged. Then she sighed, bored of the conversation. "I'm hungry." She headed to the door.

"Hold on, Alexa," said Zack. "We need to find out what's going on. We need answers."

Alexa stopped, turned back, and put her hands on her hips in her best imitation of Sydney's "serious" pose. "And who else besides Aunt Gladys has them?"

◆ ◆ ◆

"Father had a theory," explained Aunt Gladys while pouring five bowls of cereal. "New worlds . . . new dimensions. Bubbles of reality. All from memories in the doors. He was right. Father was so smart." She emptied the cereal box, set it aside, and reached for another one.

"So we were in one of these new bubble worlds?" asked Zack.

"Exactly, Zubin! See? You're smart, too."

"But . . . but . . ." Alexa struggled to form her thoughts clearly. "But we saw the butler. He saw us. We changed what happened."

"You changed the memory, not the reality." Aunt Gladys opened the new box and finished pouring. It was more a single pour over the five bowls rather than five separate pours, resulting in quite a bit of cereal spilling onto the counter. "You can't change the actual past. You *can* change what we remember about the past. Eat! Eat!" She shoved the bowls across the counter at the children.

Alexa looked down excitedly at her bowl, then paused. "What about milk?" she asked.

"Milk? Yes. Very good for you," said Aunt Gladys. "I approve."

"We need some in our bowls," said Sydney.

"You do? You do! Oh!" Aunt Gladys rose and bounced to the refrigerator.

"Why don't I take care of that, Aunt Gladys?" offered Zack. Alexa, remembering how well Aunt Gladys had poured the cereal, thought that was a good idea.

"Oh! Thank you, Zeus." She leaned across the counter to whisper conspiratorially to Alexa. "Such a nice boy, don't you think?"

Alexa shrugged and plopped some dry Honey Nut Oat Blast Ring-a-Dings into her mouth.

"You can actually change what people remember?" asked Janice nervously.

"Oh, yes!" Aunt Gladys shifted gears so fast Alexa nearly got whiplash. "That's the danger. Of memory hopping. That's why my doors are old. Old doors mean dead people. Like that nice butler. Long dead. Who cares if we change their memories? They're dead. See? A little more, Zebulon," she said, motioning for Zack to fill her bowl to the rim with milk. "Better. Perfect! Right. I have work to do."

She grabbed her bowl and stood.

"It's four-thirty in the morning!" said Janice, pointing at the clock.

"Is it? Well, I'm up. You go back to bed. First eat, then bed." She stood awkwardly for a moment, as if waiting for something. Finally, she shrugged and sashayed around the counter toward the doorway leading to the massive steel door.

A thought popped into Alexa's head. She considered ignoring it at first because she was enjoying her Honey Nut Oat Blast Ring-a-Dings, but it wouldn't go away. "Aunt Gladys?" she asked just as the flighty woman reached the doorway. "Why did you break the door?"

Aunt Gladys's feet froze in midstep, once again a split second before the rest of her body, causing her to lurch forward like a dizzy mime. She threw her arms against the sides of the doorway to steady herself before addressing Alexa's question. "Every time someone enters a memory, it . . . sours," she explained. "Soon . . . you don't go back in. Not good. Not good at all."

She peered at each of them in turn, nodding to herself, then turned and hurried down the hallway.

"Come on, guys," said Zack, pushing his untouched bowl of cereal away. "Let's go back to bed."

Nobody argued. Alexa shoved one final, sloppy spoonful of Honey Nut Oat Blast Ring-a-Dings into her mouth and hopped off her stool, beaming with excitement. She understood now what Mommy wanted.

Somewhere in the house was Grammy's door. She just needed to find it.

CHAPTER SEVENTEEN

Zack Opens a Door

ZACK AWOKE HOPING IT HAD ALL BEEN A DREAM.

Finding himself in his bedroll on the floor with the lightly snoring Alexa curled up next to him forced him to admit that the whole "house burning down, Dad going into a coma, kids moving in with crazy Aunt Gladys" thing was real, but he still held out hope that the "traveling into other people's memories" bit had been a really whacked-out dream. Maybe he'd eaten some bad Honey Nut Oat Blast Ring-a-Dings or something.

"I can't believe you actually managed to sleep," grunted a voice he recognized as his older sister's.

"It's what I do at night," he said, squinting one eye open to find Janice leaning against the wall, arms crossed, staring at him. "You should try it sometime."

"Yeah, sure. Next time I find out I'm living with a mad scientist who hops through the dreams of dead people, I'll give it a shot."

So it wasn't a dream after all, thought Zack. *Bummer.*

"Memories," Zack corrected. "Not dreams."

"Whatever. Zack, what are we going to do?" asked Janice, kicking herself off the wall and dropping down to the floor next to Zack. "I wish Dad were here."

"Yeah," he agreed.

"Do you think he'll be okay?"

Zack paused, having no idea what to think. Seeing their father lying in the hospital . . . his whole world had been ripped open. Dad was the family's rock. A slightly scatter-brained rock that could get lost in a task and forget his kids were there, but a rock nonetheless. Zack didn't want to think about life without that rock.

"He's going to be fine," he said finally. It was the only thing he could say.

Janice nodded. "I hope he wakes up soon," she said. "This place gives me the creeps. And after what happened last night . . ."

"After what you got us into last night, you mean." Zack immediately regretted his choice of words. "I'm sorry. I just woke up. I didn't mean—"

"Yes, you did mean," said Janice, drooping. "And you're right. You didn't want to go into that room. I did. I wish to God I hadn't."

"You can't blame yourself."

"Why not? Who else should I blame?"

"Why do we have to blame anybody?" asked a third voice from the doorway. "What's so bad about what happened?" Sydney skipped into the room and joined her siblings on the floor.

"We could have died!" said Janice.

"Really?" asked Sydney. "You sure of that?"

Zack had to admit it was a good question. If you got hurt or died in a memory, did you remain hurt or dead in real life? The whole concept of these memory bubble worlds made his head hurt. "Look, let's just get up, have some breakfast, and talk to Aunt Gladys," he said. "We'll figure out where we go from there."

The three sat for a moment in silence, punctuated by a slightly-louder-than-normal snore coming from their youngest sister.

"So who gets to wake Sleeping Beauty?" asked Janice grimly.

"Don't look at me," said Sydney, quickly standing. "I gotta go potty." She hurried from the room before either Zack or Janice could stop her.

"I woke her last time," said Zack.

"Did you?" asked Janice.

"Pretty sure."

"Rock, Paper, Scissors?"

"Fine," said Zack, sitting up. "Best two out of three."

After having his rock covered by Janice's paper twice in a row, Zack gently nudged their younger sister awake. When that didn't work, he shoved her a little harder, then finally gave her a pretty serious push. True to form, Alexa immediately jolted awake with a growl and glared at Zack like he'd just tortured a fluffy bunny. With a sigh, he led her to the kitchen. Soon enough, all four children were eating their bowls of cereal.

"No sign of Aunt Gladys yet?" asked Zack.

"Duh," responded Sydney. "We've been in here with you."

"Not true," retorted Zack. "Maybe you saw her when you went to go potty."

He snickered. Sydney frowned. "I didn't say 'go potty.'"

"Yes, you did," said Janice.

"Really? Man, I'm starting to sound like her."

"Are we going to go into another memory today?" asked Alexa with the cheery innocence of youth restored now that she had some food in her stomach.

"Um . . . ," started Janice.

"We're going to talk to Aunt Gladys," said Zack. "Let's not get ahead of ourselves. Remember, we still need to go to school and all."

Alexa stuck out her tongue at this, and everyone had a good laugh.

The laugh was abruptly cut off by Aunt Gladys walking into the room and screaming.

"What?" asked Zack, jumping to his feet. "What is it?"

"You! In my house! Who are you?" cried their aunt,

stepping back and eyeing them suspiciously. "Are you robbers? Are you robbing me?"

The children traded looks of confusion. "What are you talking about, Aunt Gladys?" asked Zack finally.

Aunt Gladys whipped her hand out to grab the first thing she could find, which turned out to be an empty cereal bowl. "Keep away! I'm not afraid to use this!" She held the empty bowl protectively in front of her. "I have nothing to rob! Go away!"

"We're not robbing you, Aunt Gladys!" protested Alexa.

"You're lying! You're robbing and lying!"

"Why don't you put the bowl down?" said Zack, trying to defuse the situation. "What's wrong?"

"As if you don't know!" accused Aunt Gladys, most certainly not putting the bowl down. "What have you done with my doors?"

"What?" All four kids perked up their ears at this.

"The doors are gone?" asked Sydney.

"Are you blind? Look around! No doors! In the entire house! Why steal my doors? Is that a thing?"

"What? You took all the doors of this house down yourself," said Zack, growing more and more confused with every word coming out of his batty aunt's mouth.

"Don't be ridiculous! Remove my own doors? Why?"

Which was when Zack went from confused to worried.

Aunt Gladys's memories had been changed.

"Was it something we did during the American Revolution?" whispered Sydney to the others after the children had convinced Aunt Gladys they weren't robbers and had calmed her down enough to get her to pour some Honey Nut Oat Blast Ring-a-Dings into her defensive weapon of choice.

"I don't see how," said Zack. "She was her normal, utterly loony self when we got back. Something must have happened after we went to bed."

"Unless one of you got up and went back into that room after we went to bed," accused Janice.

"Relax. Nobody went back into that room. Right? Sydney?"

Sydney shook her head. Alexa also shook her head even though nobody had asked her.

"So, then what?" pressed Janice. "Did she alter her own memories?"

"Why would she do that?" asked Sydney.

"How should I know? Like I understand anything at all about this stupid memory hopping business. Maybe she hates us and wanted to forget she ever knew us. Or maybe she's faking it."

"This cereal is yummy," commented Aunt Gladys at the next table.

"Yeah, sounds like she's faking it to me," snarled Sydney sarcastically.

"It is a yummy cereal," agreed Alexa.

Before Zack could comment on either the possibility that Aunt Gladys was faking her memory loss or the yumminess of Honey Nut Oat Blast Ring-a-Dings, the conversation was interrupted by a voice filtering through a speaker in the ceiling.

"Hello? I am here."

Aunt Gladys dropped her spoon into her bowl, splashing soggy Ring-a-Dings all over the counter, and leaped to her feet.

"A robber!" she cried.

Zack rolled his eyes. "It's not a robber," he promised, getting to his feet. "Just the morning's delivery."

◆ ◆ ◆

Zack's previous experience opening the massive wall/door of the house allowed him to crank the drawbridge down without smashing Dimitri's toes. The husky man of indeterminable Eastern European ancestry stood proudly in front of his moving van, displaying his wares with all the fervor of a game show host showing off a new car.

"Hello, boy!" he called with a frantic wave. "Is Dimitri! I drop off! I talk to Miss Gladys, yes?"

Zack crossed the drawbridge and did his best to explain the situation, hoping Dimitri might be able to help. The smile on Dimitri's face waned a bit but never actually went out.

"Ooooooooooookay," he said finally. "I bring doors. For Miss Gladys, yes?"

"That's what I'm trying to tell you!" shouted a very frustrated Zack. "She doesn't know anything about the doors! She doesn't remember anything! Please, can you help us?"

"Oooooooooooookay. Now is not good time?"

Zack threw his hands in the air in surrender and turned to march back across the drawbridge when he spotted the others huddled just inside the wall, Aunt Gladys peeking out timidly behind them.

"Are those my doors?" she asked.

"Yes!" announced a cheery Dimitri. "Fresh doors! For you! All new!"

"New? I liked the old ones. Where are they? Who are you?"

Dimitri opened his mouth to speak, but his mind suddenly realized it was confused and didn't know what to say. He ended up not so much speaking as barking incoherently. An awkward silence stretched the length of the drawbridge as Zack waited for understanding to dawn on Dimitri's face. The usually jovial man went through a cavalcade of emotions as he slowly pieced together what was happening. Finally, he looked to Zack. "Oooooooooooookay. Miss Gladys . . . not remember Dimitri?"

Zack shook his head.

It was as if Dimitri were an inflatable balloon character at the end of the Macy's Thanksgiving Day Parade. All the air was sucked out of him in front of Zack's eyes. The man's shoulders hunched, his arms drooped, his face sagged. Even his wavy locks fell limp on his head. Quite simply, the man was crushed.

"Dimitri?" asked Zack quietly. "Can you help us? We don't know what to do."

For a long time, Dimitri did not answer. Zack nervously glanced back at his sisters, who stood waiting for him to come up with a plan and make everything all right.

"What's going on?" asked Aunt Gladys. "Who is this? Why is he bringing . . . ? They're not my doors? Good heavens! Am I a robber?"

"Zack?" called Janice. "What do we do?"

Zack looked from Dimitri to Aunt Gladys to his sisters, feeling the weight of everyone's expectations crush him down to size. Standing in the middle of the drawbridge, he had never felt so alone, so helpless. The fuzzy rug of his life had been repeatedly yanked out from under him these past few days, with each new unexpected tug flopping him back down whenever he tried to stand. It wasn't fair. Dad would know what to do, but he wasn't Dad. He was just a kid, and he honestly didn't know how much more he could take.

And then Miss Guacaladilla drove up.

CHAPTER EIGHTEEN

Janice Lies

"OH, YOU POOR, MISERABLE, FORLORN, DESPONDENT, WOE-begone children!" cried Miss Guacaladilla, choking back a flood of tears. "Amnesia! In one so sprightly as your aunt!"

"Only temporary amnesia," explained Zack in what Janice felt was a surprisingly confident tone. "The doctors say she'll be right as rain in a few days."

The siblings and Miss Guacaladilla were gathered around the kitchen table, while Aunt Gladys stood behind the long kitchen counter, hovering protectively over her bowl of Honey Nut Oat Blast Ring-a-Dings. Dimitri stood in the doorway, nervously shifting his weight from foot to foot. Zack had come up with the amnesia idea, and Janice and her sisters had jumped on board.

"A few days!" erupted Miss Guacaladilla, her lips

trembling. "Oh, the agony! The unfairness! These guardianship papers need to be signed today!"

"Why?" asked Janice, certain there was something the social worker was not telling them. "She's not our guardian. Not really. Just until Dad's better."

"Your father could be in a coma for years! Decades! Eternity!" Miss Guacaladilla raised her fists to heaven and shook them in the face of the cruel fate she apparently saw on the ceiling. "You poor, unfortunate children must be legally looked after by an adult!"

"Fine. Aunt Gladys can sign them," said Zack. "Right, Aunt Gladys?"

"Oh! Well . . . ! I mean . . . !" Aunt Gladys looked about, utterly confused. The four Rothbaum siblings smiled imploringly back at her, causing the flustered woman to be overcome by an emphatic case of "don't look at me, I'm eating my cereal."

All four children visibly sagged.

"She doesn't know who you are! Oh, if only there was something I could do!"

"We told you, the amnesia is only temporary," stressed Janice.

"Temporary or not, I cannot allow her to sign legally binding papers in her present condition. Oh, why must the law be so cruel?" pleaded Miss Guacaladilla.

Janice shot her brother a worried look. If Miss Guacaladilla wasn't going to let Aunt Gladys sign the papers, where would that leave them? "How about we call you when she's got her memory again and you can come back?" suggested Zack finally. "I know it means another trip out here, but surely under the circumstances . . . ?"

Miss Guacaladilla reached out and gently patted Zack's cheek. "Oh, my sorrowful young man, I wish it were that simple. Alas, fate seems determined to extract its pound of flesh from the four of you. You see, if I don't turn in these papers, signed by your aunt, by noon tomorrow, then she is not legally allowed to take you in. I'm so very afraid that I will be forced to scoop up your unfortunate souls and find proper foster homes for you all."

Janice's heart sank. *Foster homes?* "But Dad—" she began.

"Your father is in no condition to properly look after you," lamented Miss Guacaladilla.

"We'll have to leave Aunt Gladys?" Alexa asked with a sniffle.

"Worse! You'll be separated! Sent to the four corners of the earth!" Miss Guacaladilla let loose a torrent of tears, and the children waited patiently for her emotional storm to subside.

Finally, Zack said, "You can't separate us. We're family."

"I would never dream of separating you dear, sweet, defenseless children," moaned Miss Guacaladilla. "However, rules and regulations are cruel taskmasters that refuse to be ignored. I do so wish it were otherwise! How much better the world would be if the human race could throw off the yoke of bureaucracy and dance freely in the sunshine, each to the beat of her own drummer!"

Janice half expected the woman to burst into song. Instead, the social worker took a deep breath, sighed it out in a very nonmusical way, and returned her attention to the matter at hand. "Alas, it is not to be. Chop, chop. Pack your things. It's time to go."

The children sat, stunned. Janice looked to Zack, certain he'd come up with something to save them, but her brother was stone-faced.

"This is so wrong," spat Sydney. She kicked the leg of the kitchen table to emphasize her point.

"Life can be so horribly wrong sometimes," agreed Miss Guacaladilla. "When we return to my office, we will find you all permanent homes with proper, decent, incomplete families willing to open their doors to four total strangers in exchange for an inadequate amount of money. I believe the Uzbekistanian family with the pool is still available!"

Janice looked around, lost. Even though she was terrified of the strange world Aunt Gladys had introduced to them, she didn't want to leave. She especially didn't want to be pulled apart from her brother and sisters. There had to be some way to stay together. She looked at her siblings, each dark with resignation and defeat. She looked at her aunt, wary of everyone and everything around her. She looked at Dimitri in the next room, gazing down at his feet in an obvious attempt to ignore what was happening in the kitchen.

And she got an idea.

"Couldn't her husband sign the papers?" she asked.

"Husband?" asked Miss Guacaladilla.

"Husband?" asked Zack.

"Husband?" asked Sydney.

"Husband?" asked Alexa.

"Is there more cereal?" asked Aunt Gladys.

"Uncle Dimitri," stated Janice, as calmly and as matter-of-fact as possible. "I know he's not a blood relative, but he is family."

Upon hearing his name, Dimitri looked up, confused.

"You want doors now?" he asked.

"Yes! Uncle Dimitri!" said Zack.

"I . . . I . . . I wasn't aware . . . ," stammered Miss Guacaladilla. Janice was pleased to see the woman so obviously thrown for a loop.

"It's pretty recent," said Sydney, diving into the lie head-first. "She told us about him last night. That's why he's here this morning. She wanted to introduce us to him."

"Well!" exclaimed Miss Guacaladilla, who obviously wanted to cry but couldn't find a reason. "I had no idea."

Janice rushed to Dimitri's side and dragged him into the room. "He's very shy, and obviously crushed to find his new wife suffering from amnesia. But we think he's great. Right?"

The other children all heartily agreed. Dimitri, for his part, continued to look dazed and confused. Miss Guacaladilla collected herself and turned to the befuddled man. "I am sorry, sir. How long have you been married to Gladys Tulving?"

Dimitri opened his mouth to say something, but Janice

quickly pinched his lips closed. "Uncle Dimitri doesn't speak English," she explained. "He's from . . . Slokavaniastan. Where they only speak . . . Slokavaniastanese."

Dimitri promptly shut his mouth.

"Didn't he just say something about doors?" asked Miss Guacaladilla.

"It's all he knows," argued Zack lamely.

"They met at a door convention," said Sydney with what Janice felt was a nifty save.

"It was love at first sight," added Alexa.

"Well! This is wonderful! I think . . . I mean, I believe . . ." Unused to good news, Miss Guacaladilla fumbled for her words. "Yes. Yes, your uncle could sign the papers."

The children cheered.

"I just need to see the marriage certificate."

The children stopped cheering.

"Well, the thing is—" began Zack.

"They got married in Slokavaniastan," finished Janice. "They don't do marriage certificates there. It's against their religion."

"Oh? Oh dear. Oh dear, dear, dear." The waterworks opened up as Miss Guacaladilla was once again able to deliver bad news. "I'm so terribly afraid that without a certificate—"

"He really is our uncle," lied Zack. "Please, Miss Guacaladilla."

The misery-prone social worker hemmed and hawed, but in the end, she agreed to go back to her office and put the conundrum to her superiors. She would be back later that evening with the answer, but she warned that if her superiors said no (and she strongly-if-sadly suspected they would), the children would ride back to town with her at once to be placed in four separate foster homes with four separate families, quite possibly on four separate continents.

After shaking the new groom's hand in congratulations and shying away from the new bride, who was jealously guarding her cereal bowl, Miss Guacaladilla walked back across the drawbridge, squeezed into her car, and drove away. The children stood and waved until the car disappeared around the bend.

"Great job, Janice!" cheered Sydney as soon as Miss Guacaladilla's car had gone.

"I agree," said Zack. "Quick thinking, sis!"

"Way to go!" exclaimed Alexa, adding a joyful fist pump in the air for good measure.

"You take doors now?" asked Dimitri.

Janice glowed from the praise but quickly got down to business. "Not yet, Uncle," she said.

"Uncle?" repeated Dimitri. "Oooooooooooookay."

Janice turned to her siblings. "I got us a few hours—that's it. We need to get cracking."

"What do you suggest, Janice?" asked Zack.

"Isn't it obvious?" she answered with a shiver, dreading what she was about to say. "Someone has to go back into Memoryland and fix Aunt Gladys."

CHAPTER NINETEEN

Sydney Picks a Poor Time to Snort

"I AM TOO GOING," SYDNEY STATED DEFIANTLY, PLACING HER hands on her hips and leveling her best glare at her brother.

"It's too dangerous," argued Zack. "We don't know what's on the other side of that door." He pointed emphatically at the rather dull-looking wooden door that the children (along with Dimitri and a rather confused Aunt Gladys) had found strapped into the brass doorframe when they entered the central room of the house. It had been taken as a given that this was the last door Aunt Gladys had ventured through before heading to bed the night before. They figured whatever had happened to erase her memory must lie waiting on the other side.

"You're right. We don't know," agreed Sydney. "Which is why going in alone is stupid."

Zack frowned. Sydney knew she'd scored a point and inflated with confidence. Normally, she'd just rely on her stubbornness and the threat of a violent outburst to get her way, but in this case she was further buoyed by the fact that, near as she could tell, she was actually right.

"She has a point," confirmed Janice. "Going in alone might not be the best idea."

"Aunt Gladys has been going in alone for years," Zack pointed out.

"And look how well that turned out," snapped Sydney. "Look, Aunt Gladys can't go, Alexa can't go, Janice doesn't want to go, and you need Dimitri here."

Dimitri gave a hesitant wave from his seat at the controls. It had come as somewhat of a shock to the children when the happy-go-lucky door delivery man had confessed to having worked as Marcus Tulving's assistant a number of years previously. It was not quite clear exactly when he'd stopped working for their grandfather—Dimitri wasn't saying and Aunt Gladys no longer had a clue—but he knew how to work the memory machine. Sydney found it odd that the only clear-headed adult in the room was letting the kids take charge, but the quirky strongman was proving almost disappointingly timid and was more than happy to follow the children's lead.

"Fine," relented Zack. "Come with me. But stay close and don't run off. Deal?"

Sydney stuck out her hand. "Deal." She smiled as Zack groaned and met her hand with his own, obviously finding the act overly dramatic.

Preparations were quickly made, limited though they were. Sydney picked a doorknob out of the drawer—a particularly girlish one just to annoy her brother—and they each grabbed a pair of rubber gloves from a basket Janice had discovered against the wall. Sydney tried to think of what else they might need but came up empty.

Finally, she stood next to Zack at the foot of the platform. Although no one had said anything, there was an unspoken agreement to remain on the floor until Dimitri had the memory machine up and running.

"Whenever you're ready, Dimitri," said Zack.

"Yes. Am working on it," said an obviously stressed Dimitri. He frantically twisted dials back and forth, pulled levers, and pressed buttons seemingly at random while Janice hovered over his shoulder. "Has been while. Am bit rusty."

"You already pressed that button," mentioned Janice, obsessively following his every movement.

"Is good button!" snapped Dimitri.

"I don't understand," complained Aunt Gladys for the umpteenth time. "The door's just . . . shouldn't it . . . you know . . . ? Be on a wall?"

Sydney was surprised to find herself deeply saddened by her aunt's comment. She became more determined than ever to walk through the door and make things right.

"When will we know if it works?" asked Alexa. "Will Aunt Gladys be back to normal as soon as you leave?"

"Good question," agreed Zack. "Do you know, Dimitri?"

"Yes?" he asked, looking up from the computer bank. "Sorry, am concentrating. You have question?"

"He asked how it works," repeated Janice. "They're going into a memory of the past, right? So as soon as they go in, they'll be who knows how many years before now. So anything they change then would change instantly now, no matter how long it took them to change it then. Right?"

Everyone just looked at Janice.

"Did I say that right?" she asked.

"Not a clue," admitted Sydney.

"Does not work that way," said Dimitri. "Is not then. Is there. You spend hour there, is hour here. See?"

"I'm confused. Where is there?" asked Aunt Gladys.

"What I think Dimitri is trying to say—" started Zack.

"I remember!" interrupted Dimitri, swiveling back around to the computers. "Is this one!"

He twisted a dial that looked like any other dial, and the machine sprang to life with a mechanical cough, followed by an electric sizzle, followed by an unidentifiable sound from somewhere below. In a flash, bright blue sparks of energy wrapped themselves around the door. The entire frame buzzed excitedly for a moment before settling into a quiet drone so soft as to suggest a return to silence.

The moment past, Sydney embarrassingly removed her hand from Zack's, where it had unconsciously gone an instant before. *What are big brothers for, anyway?* she reasoned.

"Oh my," murmured Aunt Gladys in awe.

"Is good! You go now!" announced Dimitri, rather unnecessarily.

Zack looked down at Sydney. "You ready for this?" he asked.

"Quit stalling," she replied with a wicked gleam in her eye.

They stepped up onto the platform. Zack reached his gloved hand out and gingerly touched the doorknob amid the sea of crackling blue energy. When his hand wasn't zapped into cinders, he shrugged, grabbed the knob, and pulled the door open.

They walked unflinchingly into the white.

◆ ◆ ◆

"Huh," said Sydney.

"Huh," agreed Zack.

Brother and sister emerged from the whitewash of tingling fuzzy-headedness and found themselves in a dingy, dusty, dimly lit room packed with rows of floor-to-ceiling shelves as far as the eye could see. Each shelf was filled to bursting with all manner of objects, papers, boxes, and assorted knickknacks—each tagged and labeled and evidently shelved according to some chaotic system wholly incomprehensible to the naked eye. So tightly packed were they that an overabundance of seemingly useless junk littered the floor, clogging the aisles. Through the insufficient level of light coming from the sparsely placed lightbulbs high above,

Sydney was again able to make out a faint yellowish film covering the world.

"It's a warehouse of some kind," said Zack, or as Sydney liked to think of him at times like these, Captain Obvious.

"A warehouse of useless, boring junk," specified Sydney.

She was surprised when her brother snickered in response. "Looks like it," he said. "Come on. Let's find Aunt Gladys."

Sydney let him lead the way through the minefield of garage sale rejects, taking care to avoid stepping on anything breakable. "What do you think she was doing here?" she asked quietly, skirting around a stack of important-looking papers. "You know, to make her forget everything?"

"I don't know," Zack admitted, stepping over a ceramic bowl. "Hopefully we'll find out."

Hopefully we won't make the same mistake, thought Sydney, ducking under a long spear sticking out across the aisle from the shelf next to her. The thought of losing her memory terrified her. She couldn't imagine not knowing her sisters and brother, forgetting her old home, her old friends.

Forgetting Dad.

Her father's face appeared in her mind's eye, smiling in that hapless, reassuring way he had, and she had a sudden, urgent need to run up and bury her face in his arms. Zack did the best he could, but when things were really bad—like, say, now—nobody could compare to Dad in his ability to make everything okay. Without him, she didn't see how things would ever be okay again.

Sydney was jolted out of these morbid thoughts when she stumbled into a suddenly frozen Zack. "Hey! What are—"

Her brother quickly shushed her and pointed. At first, all she could see were endless aisles of junk, but then she spotted two figures up ahead. Standing as silent as possible, she was able to make out voices.

"—truly remarkable discovery!" said a small, young man in an excited, high-pitched tone. "I am aghast to think it was down here all this time!"

"Yeeeeeees. Old Stickwell will be beside himself," agreed an older, more disheveled man in an equally excited voice, rubbing his hands together like a greedy miser.

Four or five aisles away, two men in tweed were hunched over a large, wooden crate, fawning at something within. Bits of straw and splinters of wood littered the ground at their feet.

"This will make our careers!" exclaimed the young man.

"What are they talking about?" whispered Sydney, but Zack just shrugged.

"Yeeeeeees. We get to name it, of course," said the older man.

His colleague lit up. "My parents will be so proud! Let's call it a Wicklesfeltonasaurus! Our names will go down in history!"

Sydney snorted at the absurdity of the name before she could stop herself. The sound reverberated outward in an ever-expanding circle, filling the entire room with an audio eye roll. Both men immediately looked up.

"Did you hear that?" asked the small, young one, who was either Wickles or Felton—Sydney had no way of knowing.

"Yeeeeeees," replied the older, disheveled one, who was either Felton or Wickles. "You're certain we're alone?"

Sydney held her breath as the two men peered into the gloom in their general direction. She prayed her habitual disdain had not proved their undoing.

"Perhaps it was nothing," said either Felton or Wickles very slowly.

"If it was nothing," responded either Wickles or Felton, reaching into the crate. "Then it won't mind if we bash its head in."

A shiver ran down Sydney's spine as the man pulled a large, wicked-looking bone out of the crate and hefted it like a club.

"Yeeeeeees. An excellent idea," agreed either Felton or Wickles, reaching into the crate to procure his own Bone of Serious Bludgeoning.

"We should get out of here," whispered Zack. "Do you have the doorknob?"

Sydney nodded and backed away, keeping her eyes glued on the two men, who were slowly edging down their own aisle. She was thankful there were multiple shelves of junk between them.

Suddenly, she stepped backward onto a shard of pottery with an audible crack. Everybody froze.

"Got you!" cried either Wickles or Felton. He swung his bone into the row of shelving in front of him, smashing it aside with a blow far more tremendous than a man his size ought to have been able to make.

"Run!" yelled Zack.

Sydney took off, Zack at her heels. Behind them, the sound of utter destruction filled the room as the two men used their prized discovery to create their own aisle through the rows of ancient shelving.

As she approached the door—the same boring wooden door that now stood hooked up to an impossible memory machine back home—Sydney fumbled in her pocket for the knob and tried to remember how Aunt Gladys had said the trick worked. Did she just hold the knob up to the door? Did she have to attach it somehow? Did it attach itself magically? Panic swelled within her, punctuated by the crescendo of chaos chasing them. Her fingers found the knob and she pulled it out of her pocket.

"Duck!" screamed Zack from behind.

Acting on instinct, Sydney dropped to the ground as an impossibly large and just-as-impossibly real claw flailed above her head, crashing into the shelves and ripping them to shreds.

"What was that?" cried Sydney.

Instead of answering, Zack shoved her down another aisle. "Move! Move!"

She pounded her feet as hard as she could, still clueless as to the nature of this new threat. Whatever it was, it was big, and the floor reverberated with its plodding footfalls.

"Zack?"

"Keep running! Don't look behind you!"

Unfortunately—and utterly predictably—Zack's warning caused Sydney to look behind her. What she saw drained the color from her face. A mostly complete skeleton of a horrific-looking dinosaur (Sydney assumed it was a T. rex) roared with fury as it swung its claws back and forth, tossing the shelving aside in its desire to hunt down the fleeing children. The only thing keeping it from overtaking them was the fact that one of its legs was missing some bones, forcing it to shamble forward and drag that leg comically behind it. Sydney screamed all the same.

"I told you not to look behind you!" reprimanded Zack.

"It's a dinosaur!"

"No, it's the skeleton of a dinosaur!"

"We're being chased by the skeleton of a dinosaur!"

"I noticed!"

He grabbed her arm and pulled her forward as the dinosaur skeleton brought its good leg down practically on top of her. Finding her feet, Sydney ran with Zack down the aisle, only to skid to a stop as the two bone-wielding men appeared in front of them.

"Oooh!" said either Wickles or Felton. "Time to bash!"

"Yeeeeeees," agreed either Felton or Wickles.

The two men raised their bone clubs high, a look of pure evil twinkling in their eyes.

Suddenly, they were knocked aside by a large stone pillar swung at them from behind. They crumpled to the ground to reveal a huffing, puffing, grinning, wizened old

man. Their savior dropped the stone pillar—which looked far too heavy for him to have lifted let alone used as a baseball bat—and gestured to the children.

"This way!" he said. "Quickly!"

Another beastly roar from the dinosaur skeleton spurred them on, and they followed the strange man down one aisle and up the next.

"Where are we going?" asked Sydney as they ran.

"Does it matter?" answered the old man.

They turned a corner and came to a small alcove at the back of the warehouse.

"We're trapped!" worried Zack.

"Don't be ridiculous!" said the old man. "Trapped? Me? Bah!" As he rushed toward what looked like a giant furnace, Sydney realized two things. One, he wasn't faded and yellow like everything else in this memory. And two, she recognized him.

"Hey!" she began. "Didn't we—"

Ignoring her, the old man yanked the door of the furnace open. "Get in! Hurry!"

"Inside the furnace? Are you crazy?" asked Zack.

The floor shook with the approach of the skeletal T. rex.

"Most likely! Hurry!" urged the old man, gesturing toward the door. Within was not the red-hot fire and coals one would expect to find in a furnace, but complete blackness.

"What's in there?" asked Sydney.

"Gluttonous gum balls, just go!" yelled the old man, pointing behind them.

Another chilling roar of rage from the impossible beast chasing them sealed the deal, and Sydney quickly spurted forward and dove into the darkness.

◆ ◆ ◆

She landed face-first in a pile of sand.

Not a pile, she corrected herself. *An entire beach.*

There was a sudden popping sound, and Zack practically ran her over. He leaped to the side at the last instant and fell to his knees, panting heavily.

"What . . . where . . . ?"

A second popping sound, and the old man walked past them and took a deep breath.

"That was a close one," he said, shaking his head and pacing. "Did you see that dinosaur? That was a dinosaur! Fascinating! What would have happened had it caught us, I wonder? It would chew us up, certainly, but without a stomach, what then?"

"Who cares? We'd be dead!" interjected Sydney.

"Very true. Quite dead." The old man turned and jumped back a step as if seeing Sydney and Zack for the first time. "You're kids! Of course I knew you were kids, but I didn't know you were actually kids! Why is she sending kids? What is she thinking?"

Sydney scrambled to her feet. They were on a wide, peaceful, yellow-tinted, sandy beach. The sun shone down, birds sang, waves tugged at the shore. Behind her was a small tent, out of which they had evidently emerged. There was neither sign nor sound of any rampaging dinosaur—skeletal or in the flesh.

"Where are we?" asked Zack, standing and brushing himself off.

The old man wasn't listening. "She should know better." He was muttering to himself. "Much too dangerous. It's not a toy. What is Gladys thinking?"

Sydney's ears perked up. "You know Aunt Gladys?" she asked.

The old man looked up in shock. "Aunt . . . ? You mean you're . . ." He took a step forward, peering at them as if through a magnifying glass. Sydney stumbled back a step in the face of such intense scrutiny. "That would mean . . . Are you . . . You're Charlotte's children?"

"You know our mom?" asked Zack. "What's going on? Where are we? Who are you?"

Sydney had to hand it to Captain Obvious—those were all very good questions. She also wondered what was going on and where they were. However, she had a sneaky feeling she knew the answer to Zack's final question.

"Simpering sunspots!" stuttered the old man awkwardly. "I never . . . Well, I guess I'm . . ." He took a deep breath before confirming Sydney's suspicions. "I'm your grandfather."

CHAPTER TWENTY

Alexa Goes Exploring

ALEXA WAS BORED.

She had assumed the moment Zack and Sydney went through the door that everything would just snap back to normal. She had asked Janice what was taking so long, and her sister had told her they needed to be patient, stay calm, and wait.

Seeing as how Alexa—being all of seven years old—was not very good at being patient, staying calm, or waiting, this wasn't a very satisfying answer.

She would have asked Aunt Gladys, but her aunt just stood there, staring at the now-closed door, jaw open wide like she was waiting for a small airplane to land on her tongue. "What . . . ? How . . . ?" the poor woman had tried to say, her totally confused brain unable to find the words to express how totally confused she was.

It hadn't helped Alexa's mood when the weird Dimitri guy had jumped out of his seat and bolted from the room the moment Zack and Sydney were through the door. He had hesitated a moment as he passed Aunt Gladys, but in the end his need to get out of the room overcame his desire to help the dazed woman.

So Alexa had begun to wait. To her credit, she had paced silently around the room for over thirty seconds before she couldn't take it anymore.

"Where are they?" she asked.

"It's been, like, five minutes, Alexa," answered Janice. "Relax."

Relaxing was not one of Alexa's strong suits.

After ten or fifteen more seconds, Alexa found herself wondering if this big, dirty, cluttered, old room contained any small, cute, furry animals. Then she remembered her aunt saying something about not having any pets because her mother had kept cats and they had scared her. Still, she imagined there had to be rats somewhere around the house at least, maybe even a vole or a groundhog or—dare she hope—a bunny. So she spent an impressive fourteen minutes and seventeen seconds searching the circular room for rodents and other assorted vermin. She looked under all the scaffolding ringing the room, behind all the neatly stacked piles of doors waiting to be used, and among the tattered remains of those already broken. No luck. Whatever else went on in the room, it didn't involve cute little animals.

Frustrated, she approached her aunt. "Aunt Gladys?" asked Alexa.

Aunt Gladys tilted her head toward Alexa without taking her eyes off the door. "That's me? Yes?"

"Do you have any rats or possums or cats or hamsters or anything?"

"How should I know?" answered the wide-eyed aunt. "I don't know what to think. Not anymore." With a final shake of her head, the tired woman turned and walked out of the room, muttering about needing some rest.

Alexa sighed as she watched her aunt shove her way through the heavy curtain, then returned to pester Janice.

"Do you think they'll be much longer?" she asked.

"Please stop asking," her sister replied. "I don't know any more than you do. We just have to wait."

"But I'm bored!"

"Go explore or something. Anything. Just leave me alone!"

The last words came out with a bit more venom than Janice had probably intended and knocked little Alexa back a step. "Janice?" she asked.

Her sister's shoulders drooped and she folded her head into her arms on the computer console.

So Alexa went exploring.

At first she wandered aimlessly around the first floor, not really looking for anything. Halfway around the ring of rooms, she started looking for cute little animals but didn't find any. When she got to the stairs leading to the second floor, she shrugged and climbed up, continuing her search.

These rooms, with their many piles of unused doors, seemed more promising but proved just as empty of furry things as the rooms below. She was halfway around the third floor when she realized there was something else she should be looking for.

Her grandmother's door.

Mommy had said it was plain with scratches on the bottom. That wasn't much to go on. Was it big? Flimsy? Painted a fun color, like pink or turquoise? There was no way to know. Especially now that the one person who would have known—Aunt Gladys—probably didn't know anymore.

Alexa sat crisscross-applesauce on the floor—her back to yet another stack of wooden doors—put her elbows on her knees and her chin in her hands, and tried to figure it out. Grammy's door would have been one of the first ones Aunt Gladys collected. It'd be someplace special. Like her bedroom. Except it wasn't in Aunt Gladys's bedroom. So where else? If Alexa wanted to store a very special door, where would she put it? Someplace safe, where no one else would find it. The big room in the middle of the house? No. She'd put it as far away from that room as possible.

Alexa lifted her head and looked up at the ceiling.

She'd never been on the fourth floor before and didn't know what to expect. Of course, once she'd climbed the stairs, she found the same thing she'd found on the second and third floors—endless piles of doors.

The fifth floor, however, was different.

First, it wasn't so much an entire floor as it was a small landing at the top of a set of stairs.

Second, there weren't any piles of doors lying on the floor or leaning against the walls.

Third, there were no windows, so the room was pretty dark.

Most important, it had something none of the other floors had—a closed and locked door.

This has gotta be it, thought Alexa. *Grammy's door's gotta be behind this one!* She couldn't wait to tell Mommy the next time she saw her. Maybe she'd give Alexa a treat for being such a good girl.

Pleased as punch, Alexa retraced her steps to the first floor.

It was somewhere between the second and third floor that she suddenly remembered Zack and Sydney had come back.

She remembered that Dimitri had stuck his head in while Alexa had been sitting on the third floor, trying to figure out where Aunt Gladys kept Grammy's door. He'd told her that her brother and sister were back and had asked her to tell Janice, who had fallen asleep in front of the computers. He also said they should be sure to snap the door in half because too many people had gone through and it was getting bad.

With the new memory fresh in her mind, Alexa was eager to see her siblings as she ran into the central room. Sure enough, there was Janice, asleep at the computer board, head in her arms.

"Janny! Janny, wake up!" Alexa bounded over and shook her big sister awake. "Wake up, Janny!"

"Wha—?" exclaimed a bleary-eyed Janice, lifting her head. "Where . . . ? What—"

"They're back!" explained Alexa, not having the patience to wait for Janice to be fully awake. "Zack and Sydney are back!"

"They are? Where . . ." She let out a huge yawn. "Right. Right. I remember. Where are they?" She pushed the swivelly chair away from the computers.

"Wait!" ordered Alexa. "You have to break the door. It's gone all bad."

"Break the . . . ? Oh, right. That makes sense." Janice returned to the computer bank and stared at all the buttons and levers. "Um . . . how do you . . . ?"

"The big round button over there," said Alexa, remembering when Aunt Gladys had cracked the door to the American Revolution in half.

"Got it." Janice reached over and pressed the big round button. Once again there came the sound of gears groaning against a lifetime of neglect, followed by a booming *CRACK* as the door on the platform was snapped in half like a stale graham cracker.

CHAPTER TWENTY-ONE

Zack Uses Bad Grammar

ZACK'S LEGS THREATENED TO TURN TO JELLY AT THE OLD MAN'S words, but they settled for a thick marmalade. *Grandfather?* He was pretty sure that was impossible, wasn't it? Not impossible like he can't possibly have a grandfather, because of course he had a grandfather. It was just that . . . but they were . . .

In a memory.

"Cool," said Sydney, taking a seat on the sand. "I kinda figured."

"Did you?" asked Marcus Tulving. "What gave it away? My beard? I've been meaning to shave."

"You sound like Aunt Gladys," answered Sydney with a smile.

"I do? Ah. That explains it. Though I should point out it

is far more likely that she sounds like me," replied Marcus with just the slightest hint of sarcasm.

"But you're dead!" exclaimed Zack.

The old man (his grandfather, Zack reminded himself) lifted his left eyebrow. "Am I? How unfortunate. Nobody tells me anything."

"Nobody said he was dead, Zack," reminded Sydney. "Just that he was gone."

Thinking back, Zack realized his sister was right. They'd all just assumed their grandfather was dead, and Aunt Gladys hadn't bothered to correct them. He wondered why.

"Where have you been all this time?" asked Zack. Sydney rolled her eyes as if Zack had asked the dumbest question in the history of dumb questions.

"Right here," answered Marcus.

Zack looked around the empty beach. The cry of a lone seagull punctuated the air. "Where are we?" he asked finally.

"In a memory. Duh," snapped Sydney.

It was all proving too much for Zack, who plopped down next to his sister with a resounding "Huh."

"How does it work?" asked Sydney. "Can you go anywhere?"

"What are you talking about?" asked Zack.

"We're not in the same memory we were when we were being chased by that dino-skeleton monster. Unless you think there's a secret passage leading from the furnace to this beach?"

Zack's face flushed as his sister pointed out what should

have been obvious. He cast a glance at their grandfather, who was eyeing them quizzically, as if they were a pair of goofy lab rats being studied under a microscope.

"Fictional fruitcakes!" Marcus exclaimed. "You're an amazingly astute young girl."

Amazingly annoying, you mean, thought Zack automatically even as he mulled over the implications of this new revelation.

"Can you control where you go?" Sydney asked. "What memories you jump into?"

Marcus scratched his beard in thought. "I think we're done here," he stated. "Time to go. For you, not me. I stay. You go."

"We just got here!" protested Sydney.

"And almost died," reminded Marcus, tossing a blanket on her burning excitement. "The MemorySphere is a dangerous place."

"MemorySphere?" repeated Zack.

"My own term. Now, go. Shoo. While you still can. You brought a knob this time, yes? Please say you brought a knob."

"We brought a knob," repeated Zack. "But we can't leave."

"Sure you can. It's easy. I'll show you." Marcus twisted his neck back and forth, searching the shore. "We just need a door. . . ."

"No, it's not that," corrected Zack, "We're here for a reason."

"We need to save Aunt Gladys!" declared Sydney.

Marcus took in a quick breath. "What's wrong with my daughter?" he asked in a rush.

"She doesn't remember anything," explained Zack. "Not us, not your machine, not the fact that she's a serial door-hoarder. Nothing."

Their grandfather's face turned very pale. "They didn't," he muttered. "They must have. They couldn't? I guess they could. But why now? Why now . . . ?" Slowly, his eyes came to focus on his grandchildren sitting on the sand in front of him. Suddenly, he gasped and brought his hand up to his mouth. "Oh, portable potbellies!"

Zack wasn't sure if they were supposed to be alarmed by their grandfather's outburst or not, but he got to his feet and dusted himself off nonetheless. "Who did what?" he asked. "Is that bad?"

Marcus quickly covered Zack's face with his hand, then pulled his hand back and snapped his fingers nervously a number of times. "No time. There's no time. You must go." He looked down at Sydney. "You too. Now. Quickly. Come!"

"What is it?" asked Zack, picking up on Marcus's sudden anxiety.

Marcus set off across the beach at a brisk trot toward a large house set back from the shore. Zack and Sydney hurried to keep up.

"Grandfather! Wait! We need to fix Aunt Gladys!" repeated Zack. "She must have made some sort of change the last time she was in here—"

"Your aunt? No. Not your aunt," said Marcus, leading

them around the back of the house to a small storage shed under the front porch. "This was done to her. Deliberately."

"By who?" asked Zack.

"By whom," corrected Marcus, who then groaned at himself and waved the comment away. "Not your problem. Well, yes. It could be your problem. But not yet. Just . . . we need to get you home."

"We're not going anywhere until you start answering some questions," said Zack, puffing out his chest and trying to look serious.

"You can and you will!" shouted Marcus. The outburst took Zack by surprise, and he flinched at the cold strength suddenly on display. A moment later, Marcus blinked the harshness away and was once again the doddering old grandfather. "Children. Grandchildren . . . grandchildren? Who would have thought . . . Never mind. The Memory-Sphere is not a playground. Not meant for children. Not meant for anyone. Now, give me your knob."

He held out his hand to Zack.

"Go on, Sydney," said Zack.

"Sydney? Nice name. I had an aunt named Sydney. Now I have a granddaughter. Symmetry. The knob?" He held out his hand to Sydney.

Zack watched his sister squirm under the old man's kindly-but-not-to-be-disobeyed gaze. Finally, she relented and reached into her pocket.

"Does Aunt Gladys know you're in here?" asked Zack.

A flicker of doubt twitched across Marcus's face. "Unfortunately, she does," he said with a sigh. "That's why she keeps opening doors and expanding the MemorySphere. She's trying to find me."

"Really? But . . . why . . ." Zack stuttered out of confusion. "Why not just pop up and say hi the next time she opens a door?"

"You're assuming I want to be found."

Zack didn't quite understand what his grandfather meant, but before he could ask for an explanation, Sydney gave a desperate gasp.

"It's gone!" she cried.

"What?" asked Zack. "Did you drop it when we were being chased?"

"No! It was in my pocket!" She looked up at Zack, her eyes pleading. "I swear it was."

"What is in your pocket now, child?" asked Marcus.

"Um . . ." Confused, Sydney nevertheless shoved her hand back into her pocket. "Nothing. Hold on. . . ." She pulled her fist out of her pocket and opened it to reveal a handful of what looked like bright white sand.

"Sand?" asked Zack.

"Feathered ferrets! No!"

"Is sand bad?" asked Sydney.

"It's not sand," answered Marcus with a heavy, weary, suddenly exhausted sigh. "It's what's left of your doorknob."

Zack's heart sank. "Our doorknob?"

"Has been destroyed," confirmed Marcus, nodding. "The door you used to enter the MemorySphere has been broken."

That made no sense at all to Zack. Why would Janice have broken the door before he and Sydney returned?

"But . . . but . . . how do we get home?" asked Sydney.

Marcus's jovial face turned incredibly grim.

"You don't."

◆ CHAPTER TWENTY-TWO ◆

Janice Has a Sinking Feeling

A LESS AND LESS GROGGY JANICE FOLLOWED A VERY EXCITED AND bubbly Alexa to the kitchen. She couldn't believe she'd slept through Zack and Sydney returning from . . . from . . . from over there. More than that, she couldn't believe they'd just left her asleep when they returned. Well, okay, she could see Sydney doing that, but not Zack.

Hopefully, they were both simply too excited after restoring Aunt Gladys's memory to notice her snoozing at the computer. She'd been sitting off to the side of the room and was pretty sure she didn't snore, so she supposed it was possible they'd just missed her.

Unlikely, but possible.

She shoved her suspicions aside as Alexa led her into the kitchen, shouting, "Did you guys fix her?"

Janice scanned the room while waiting for either Zack or Sydney to reply. The place was exactly as they'd left it, complete with the remnants of Aunt Gladys's bowl of Honey Nut Oat Blast Ring-a-Dings sitting out. The dirty dish gnawed at Janice's need for things to be neat and orderly, and she grabbed it and moved it to the sink.

"Guys?" Alexa's voice interrupted Janice's thoughts. She looked again around the room, finally noticing it was empty.

"Where are they?" she asked her little sister.

"I dunno," answered Alexa.

"Did they say to meet them in the kitchen?"

"Um . . . Dimitri didn't say where," admitted the little girl.

"Dimitri?" asked Janice, her suspicions once again brandishing the mighty sword of doubt. "You didn't see Zack or Sydney yourself?"

"Well . . . no."

A very dark cloud began to creep into Janice's mind. "Where is Dimitri?" she asked.

"I dunno."

The dark cloud flexed its tendrils threateningly. "Come on," she ordered, quickly rinsing the dish out before walking past her sister and continuing through the ring of rooms.

"Janny? Is everything all right?" asked Alexa, her voice still ridiculously perky, yet tempered with a touch of apprehension.

Janice squeezed her sister's hand and lugged her from room to room. Where was everyone? Had they actually come back? She refused to think about what it might mean if they hadn't returned. If they were still inside . . .

Ducking through yet another empty doorway, they arrived in what amounted to the entry hall—the drawbridge/wall thing stretching out across the moat, leaving four floors of the house open to the elements. Janice breathed a sigh of relief upon spotting the lanky form of Dimitri pacing back and forth. Now, at least, they would get some answers.

"Dimitri!" she called, trudging across the drawbridge.

The man with the unplaceable accent flinched upon hearing his name called, nearly tripping over his feet. Once he regained his balance, he looked back at Janice and asked excitedly, "Miss Gladys is fixed? Miss Gladys is Miss Gladys?"

"Is that what Zack said?" asked Janice. "They fixed her?"

Dimitri cocked his head to the side like a confused puppy. "Zack? Ooooooooooookay. I no talk Zack. Please, Miss Gladys is Miss Gladys?"

"You didn't talk to Zack?" The dark cloud scratched at the door of her consciousness with its terrible claws. "Did you see him at all? Or Sydney?" Behind her, Alexa shifted excitedly from one foot to the other.

"Zack? Sydney?" repeated Dimitri defensively, sinking his head into his shoulders like a little boy being scolded for eating paste. "Is in memory, yes?"

"You said they came back!" accused Alexa.

Dimitri shivered slightly and shook his head. "I outside. Is seeing nobody."

Janice's dark cloud tore out chunks of the protective shield sheltering her mind. Spots formed in front of her eyes. "You didn't . . . ? You haven't . . . ?"

"You told me they came back!" cried Alexa. "You said! You said!"

"Did you tell Alexa that they'd returned?" asked Janice very slowly, her voice shaking.

Dimitri's entire body crumbled under the interrogation. "I see nothing," he insisted, his voice rising to a panic. "Nothing! Where Miss Gladys?"

"That's not true! You said they were back!" Alexa's lips quivered as tears began to flow.

"I no talk little girl!" Dimitri backed away, waving his hands. "I no talk anyone!" Incredibly agitated, he tripped over his feet once again, this time falling to the ground beside his van. Still, he continued waving his hands back and forth. "I no talk! I no talk!"

Janice whirled on her sister. "Alexa! Did you really see Dimitri?"

"He told me!" she cried through a deluge of tears. "He told me! He told me!"

"I no talk! I no talk!"

"You said they were back!" yelled Janice at her little sister.

"He told me! He told me!"

"Do you think this is a game, Alexa?"

"He told me!" repeated the shell-shocked little girl. "He told—"

"WHAT HAVE YOU DONE?"

Janice had never let loose with such a force of raw emotion in her life. Her words struck her sister like a lightning bolt straight from the hand of Zeus, sending Alexa sobbing into the house.

Behind Janice, Dimitri continued to babble about "no talking," his voice rising in panic. She ignored him, as well as her weeping sister, as the enormity of what she'd just done punched her in the gut.

She'd broken the door, trapping Zack and Sydney inside the memory.

Possibly forever.

◆ CHAPTER TWENTY-THREE ◆

Sydney Meets Another Monster

AT FIRST, SYDNEY FIGURED SHE'D HEARD HER GRANDFATHER wrong. They weren't stuck in here. That would be wrong. There were other ways out of this place. All they had to do was . . .

"Whenever a new door is opened, that memory becomes part of your MemorySphere, right?" she asked.

"Yes! Absolutely!" agreed Marcus enthusiastically. "Such a smart girl!"

"So all we have to do is wait for Aunt Gladys to open another door."

Her grandfather sighed and displayed his sad-puppy face. "Ah. No. You still need a doorknob. They don't grow on trees."

Sydney flushed, embarrassed. She should have realized that.

"Aunt Gladys doesn't remember how to hook up a door in the first place," interrupted Zack.

"So you say." Marcus nodded sagely.

The unfamiliar feeling of hopelessness descended upon Sydney. She didn't like it. "So what do we do?" she asked, determined to find a course of action. "There's something we can do, isn't there?"

Their grandfather first shook his head, then nodded, looking more than anything like an out-of-control jack-in-the-box. "For now, I think—"

He gasped and froze in midsentence at the sound of a screen door sliding open above them. "Waggling wombats! Hide!" he hissed, true fear sweeping over his features. He pulled Zack and Sydney down behind a pile of old beach furniture stacked up against the house.

"What—" began Zack.

"Zip it! Zip! Zippity-zip!" Marcus ran his finger across his throat, either telling them to stop talking or indicating that they were going to be beheaded soon. Sydney figured the former.

She tried to imagine what sort of horrific monster stalked these beachside memories. A hideous sand beast? A giant crab? A multitentacled sea monster?

She started momentarily as Zack placed what he probably thought was a reassuring hand on her shoulder. She let him keep it there. He liked to feel he was protecting her, and, to be honest, it was slightly comforting.

The three waited in silence, Sydney straining her ears for signs of the incoming menace. From the look on her grandfather's face, it was something truly evil.

Eventually, the rhythmic, tranquil beating of the waves against the seashore was finally broken by the oddest of sounds—singing. Someone was singing a sweet, innocent little tune that vaguely reminded Sydney of something she'd heard in a Disney movie. Then the singer came closer, and Sydney could make out the words.

"*. . . with the big red knife that she chopped, chopped, chopped till the teddy bear popped and the head fell, plop!*"

Marcus Tulving's face turned white as the abomination skipped into view.

"*Sally the silly clown, liked to chase the children down, chase them all around the town, chase them with a . . . hatchet!*"

It was a little girl, maybe Alexa's age. She wore an old-fashioned blue-and-white dress, had bright pink ribbons in her hair, and was smiling from ear to ear. She didn't look evil; she didn't look monstrous. She looked adorable. She sang out loud and proud the way children do when they can't carry a tune, and from the look on Sydney's grandfather's face, it was obvious that this sweet little girl was, for him, the stuff of nightmares. She clutched a stuffed animal of some sort in her hands—maybe a bear, maybe a dog, maybe an armadillo. It was hard to tell exactly what it was because it was missing all of its limbs.

"She took the hatchet to the store, and she dipped it in the gore. . . ."

The girl skipped lazily past their hiding place and disappeared behind the corner of the house, her chilling tune mercifully fading away until it could no longer be heard over the roar of the surf.

Only then did Marcus relax.

"Close," he muttered. "Too close. We should leave. Before she comes back."

He stepped up to the door of the storage shed.

"That was the most horrible song I've ever heard," said Sydney.

"Yes. It's worse each time I hear it," admitted Marcus. "It used to be about planting flowers. Still excruciating, mind you—she can't sing a lick—but nonviolent."

"Is she a crazy killer or something?" asked Zack.

"No," their grandfather replied absently. "But if she sees you . . . nasty. You have to join her tea party. Or she starts screaming." He shivered. "Horrible little girl." He pulled the storage shed door open to reveal another wall of absolute blackness. "In we go. Quickly. Before that ribbon-haired monstrosity returns. Trust me. You don't want to drink her tea."

"I don't understand," said Zack, peering into the void in front of him. "There's nothing there. It's just . . . black."

Marcus opened his mouth to respond but was interrupted by an uncomfortably near, out-of-tune voice singing

at the top of her lungs. "... *to chase the children down, chase them all around the town, chase them with a ... a bazooka!*"

"Go!" spat Sydney, giving her brother a helpful shove. He staggered forward into the blackness, vanishing in an instant. She followed right on his heels. . . .

◆ ◆ ◆

Sydney found herself in a dingy corridor that might once have been painted white but whose walls had long ago given up the fight against systemic decay. Zack was leaning against the wall, catching his breath.

"Not cool, Sydney," he said. "Pushing me like that."

"Actually, it was really cool," she argued. "And surprisingly satisfying."

"Ah, sibling rivalry," commented their grandfather behind them. "As charming as ever."

Sydney was confused for a moment until she realized he was probably referring to their mother and Aunt Gladys. She wondered what they'd been like as kids.

"Where are we now?" asked Zack.

"Not sure. Probably a hospital. Or a very boring hotel. Never could tell."

A series of numbered doors littered the hallway, a few rusty lightbulbs flickered on and off in the ceiling, and from somewhere below came the ominous sound of laughter.

"Why did you bring us here?" asked Zack.

"Duh," teased Sydney. "This is where the storage shed under Evil Little Girl's beach house leads. Right, Pop-Pop?"

Marcus raised an eyebrow at Sydney. "Pop-Pop?" he asked.

"You mean like how the furnace led to that tent on the beach?" asked Zack. Sydney was impressed to see him putting it all together. "They're like . . . secret passages within the MemoryWorld—"

"MemorySphere," corrected Marcus.

"MemorySphere, right."

"Terminology is important."

"Got it."

"I discovered it, I named it."

"Okay, yes. I get it." Zack was amusingly flustered. "The connections are permanent?" he continued.

Marcus nodded.

"How many are there?" asked Sydney. "Memories, I mean."

"Hundreds," said Marcus. "With more added all the time. Gladys keeps opening doors."

"And in all those, there's no other way out?" asked Zack.

"Zack," reasoned Sydney, "if there was another way out, don't you think the guy who created this place would know?"

Marcus gave a little cough. "Well . . . not that I . . . I mean yes. Of course. Still . . . I wonder . . ." His voice trailed off as he gazed up at the ceiling as if truly impressed by the crown molding.

Sydney and Zack waited for him to finish his sentence.

When he didn't, Sydney finally poked him in the belly. "Wonder what?" she asked.

Their grandfather frowned. Looked away. Looked back. "Well, the thing is . . . ," he began.

"You know a way out?" challenged Zack.

He shook his head. "No," he said, momentarily dashing their hopes. "However," he said, flaming their hopes back to life, "there may be someone in here who does."

"Who?" asked Zack and Sydney together.

Marcus's mouth twisted into an embarrassed smile. "Me."

◆ ◆ ◆

"The first door, memory, what have you. It was mine. My door, my memory. It was my closet. From my lab at the university." He was leading them down the hallway of an old library. "It was an absolute disaster."

They had followed him through one disturbing patch of blackness after another, traveling from the hospital to a school to a palatial estate to an old sweatshop to a simple country home to another hospital to a pirate ship to a cemetery to an estate even more palatial than the first one to a very ugly barn and now a library. More often than not, they entered and exited these memories not through normal doors, but in obscure and unexpected ways. A pantry. An oven. A treasure chest. Their grandfather had explained that portals between memories only appeared behind doors the memory's creator never opened.

"The pirate never opened his own treasure chest?" Zack had asked.

"Wasn't the pirate's memory," had been Marcus's response. "Scullery boy, I think."

The deeper they traveled into this strange world, the more uneasy Sydney became. At first, the memories had been seemingly normal, but each new vista was just a little bit creepier than the last. The curious looks from those they passed became menacing. The skies darkened. Unseen things whispered behind their backs.

More and more inanimate objects had teeth.

The library was the creepiest memory yet. Sydney sensed an uncountable number of eyes leering at her from just beyond her range of vision, felt the narrow aisles closing in on her ever so slowly, and heard a sound that could only be described as paper being sharpened.

This was not a happy library.

"Why was your first door a disaster?" asked Zack, snapping Sydney's attention back to the present.

"I learned the first rule of the MemorySphere." Marcus paused in front of a rickety, rusting metal staircase. Flecks of black paint flaked off flimsy-looking railings, and the steps groaned under the weight of the empty air. Sydney couldn't imagine a less inviting set of steps.

"What is the first rule of the MemorySphere?" prodded Zack.

"Don't enter your own memories." He placed a foot on the first step and started climbing.

Zack quickly followed Marcus up the stairs. When the stairway failed to collapse under either of them, Sydney braved the climb. The sound of their footsteps echoed in the gloom.

At least she hoped she was only hearing echoes.

Stacks of neglected and disintegrating books welcomed Sydney at the top of the stairs. The smell of fresh decay stung her nose, making her eyes water. She buried her face in the crook of her arm and studied the offensive tomes lining the shelves.

Is it my imagination, or are these books breathing? She took pains not to touch anything.

"When I returned, I remembered. Everything. From both sides of the conversation," Marcus continued. "It was . . . disorienting." He pulled a single string dangling from above, causing a section of the ceiling to swing down as a small metal ladder expanded to the floor.

Yet another patch of utter blackness beckoned.

"This is where I leave you," he announced. "Up there is that memory. The first bubble of the MemorySphere. I'm in there, somewhere. Find me. Hopefully, I can get you home."

"Why would you know in there if you don't know here and now?" asked Zack.

Their grandfather sagged and leaned back against the bookshelf. "He knows more than me. The truth is . . ."

He paused as one of the books behind him stretched its cover toward him. "Stop that," he commanded. The book retracted its cover and, Sydney was pretty sure, gave off a disappointed whine.

"The truth is," continued Marcus, as if having a book reach out to him was an everyday occurrence, "I was forgetting things. Little things at first. Where I'd put my glasses. A conversation with Gladys or Dimitri."

"Old people always forget stuff," Sydney pointed out.

"True," he admitted. "But no. It was more. I forgot how my machine worked. Oh, I knew what it did, just couldn't remember why. That's when I realized my memories were being altered."

"You were changing your memories?" asked Zack.

"What? Me? No. Don't be silly. It wasn't me."

Sydney felt a panic rise in her throat. "But if you weren't doing it, who was?"

"Good question. A very good question." He shifted uncomfortably against the shelving. "Don't know. Yet. But I will. I entered the MemorySphere to save my mind. Before I lost everything. In here, you keep your memories. Change all you want, you'll still remember it all. In here, I know who I am. My mind is my own."

"But if you left . . . ?" prompted Sydney.

Marcus closed his eyes and shook his head. "I have changed so many things. Manufactured my own, selfish world. To leave now and face reality . . . I would go mad."

He smiled at them with such sadness, Sydney was nearly moved to tears. "You can't go home," she said.

He shook his head, then turned it into a neck stretch. "Now, go," he said, gesturing toward the imposing ceiling of black. "If anyone can help you, I can. I'll be in my lab. Big door at the end of the hallway. My name on the front. Can't miss it. Oh, and be careful."

"Careful?" asked Zack.

"This is the oldest memory in the MemorySphere. It may have . . . soured."

◆ ◆ ◆

Walking through a door into a darkened hallway knocked Sydney for a loop because she was pretty sure that a moment before she'd been climbing a ladder. She wasn't exactly sure how this was possible, but then traveling through a series of other people's memories shouldn't have been possible, either, so what was one more crazy detail?

"I don't like the look of this place," said Zack.

Sydney only avoided rolling her eyes because she agreed. They stood in a narrow hallway lined with a series of classrooms on either side. That would have been bad enough, what with schools in general being evil and all, but this felt more evil than usual. For one thing, the hallway seemed to go on for way too long. For another, the frosted panes of glass in each door leered at them hungrily.

Which was just totally wrong.

"It's just a hallway," said Sydney, trying to convince herself as much as her brother.

They inched forward, the overhead lights somehow managing to flicker in perfect time with their footsteps. At one point, Sydney could have sworn she heard a stomach growl, but she convinced herself it had been Zack's.

"This place goes on forever," commented Zack.

Their speed down the corridor slowed with each intimidating step until they were almost paralyzed with fear. They were one or two steps away from simply freezing in their tracks when a door banged open and Dimitri burst into the hallway.

"What you doing?" he squawked. "You no be here!"

"Dimitri!" cried an elated Zack. "You opened a new door!"

"I call security!"

"Security?" asked Zack.

But Sydney understood. She quickly put a hand on Zack's arm to stop him before he said anything else. "He's yellow," she pointed out.

"Yellow? What do you . . . oh. Oh, right."

Disappointment colored Zack's voice. Sydney didn't blame him. The Dimitri in front of them was covered in the same, faded, yellowed filter as everything else in the MemorySphere—he was a memory.

"Out! Out!" Dimitri stormed forward, waving his hands in front of his face.

"Hold on! We need to see our—" started Zack before Sydney elbowed him in the ribs. "I mean, Professor Tul—"

"Too busy!" interrupted Memory Dimitri. "Nobody see your grandfather. Go away! Shoo! Shoo!"

"We have to see him!" insisted Sydney. "It'll only take—"

She was interrupted by a flurry of sudden and unexpected activity. First, something unseen at the far end of the hallway gave a mighty roar. This was instantly followed by the sound of industrial devastation on an unimaginable scale. Next, a large section of wall came flying down the hallway toward them, along with a door recently ripped from its hinges. Finally, the glass panel on the door in question let out a cry of utter terror as it hurtled toward its impending doom.

Seeing the flying door speed toward them like a flat cannonball, Sydney dove into her brother, knocking them both to the floor. Memory Dimitri also managed to avoid the deadly projectile by quickly flopping down like wet spaghetti. The screaming, rectangular object crashed into the wall behind them, letting loose with a final, high-pitched "Why?" before shattering into a gazillion pieces.

"Sydney! Are you all right?" asked Zack. Sydney found the question ironic as she was currently lying on top of him, having saved him from being flattened.

"What was that?" she asked, standing and peering back at the source of the carnage.

In response, Memory Dimitri screamed like a little girl and ran past them down the hallway a ways before running into a classroom and barricading himself inside.

"Sydney?" asked Zack, eyes glued to the rather shocking entity clomping down the corridor toward them. "Is that—?"

"Pop-Pop!" finished Sydney.

Sure enough, Marcus Tulving—the one man who might have known how to send them home—stomped forward, eyes blazing red, muscles bulging out of his sleeves, steam pouring out of his ears. His body filled the entire hallway, as if he were an overinflated balloon animal. Rivulets of drool fell from a jaw filled with large, sharp—and, for some reason, humming—teeth.

"Door!" hollered the Hulk-like behemoth. "Need door!" His teeth accentuated his roar with a very musical hum in three-part harmony.

I'm guessing this memory has soured, thought Sydney, her mind oddly calm in the face of the deranged monster charging toward them.

"Run, Sydney!" cried Zack, grabbing her hand and yanking her backward down the hall.

Seeing his prey retreat, Monster Marcus roared with even more fury and bounded into a canter, his feet pulverizing the linoleum floor with each step. Exciting, up-tempo chase music thrummed in his mouth.

It was enough to spur Sydney into action. Her legs pumped like they'd never pumped before. Behind her, the booming, crushing, humming carnage closed on them in a most unfair manner. Zack and Sydney needed four or five steps to cover the same distance the abomination took in a single bound. Sydney very quickly saw they would reach neither the door back to the creepy library nor the one Memory Dimitri had hid behind in time, so she altered her plan and rammed her shoulder against the nearest classroom door.

Zack sped by her a step before stopping. "What are you doing?"

"Hoping Pop-Pop never entered this classroom!" she answered, giving the door another shove. Zack instantly understood and lent his shoulder to the task. Together, with the hungry pane of glass ogling them from above and the charging, slobbering monster grandfather bearing down on them, they forced the door open and stared into a welcome expanse of black. Without any hesitation, Sydney grabbed her brother's hand and charged into the darkness.

◆ ◆ ◆

Their urgent momentum carried them forward three steps before they both tripped and fell onto a soft, queen-sized bed.

Sydney lay facedown a moment, catching her breath. "What is it . . . ," she wheezed, "about the Memory-Sphere . . . and huge, freaky things chasing us?"

When Zack didn't answer, she lifted her head and tried again. "Zack?"

"We're home," he said quietly.

Confused, Sydney sat up and looked around, her jaw slowly dropping. Zack was right. It was impossible, but he was right. They were in their father's bedroom. The one that had burned down just a few short days ago.

"We can't be in our own memories!" she said.

"It's not my memory," answered Zack. "I've been in Dad's closet."

She turned to see a gaping maw of blackness just inside the sliding closet door. "Me too," she said. "That's where he keeps the Christmas presents."

Zack got off the bed and frowned. "We're not in my memory and we're not in yours," he announced, once again stating the obvious. "And it's not Dad's," he added unnecessarily.

"Janice showed me where the Christmas presents were kept," offered Sydney, ruling their big sister out. She met Zack's gaze, eyes wide. "Alexa?"

Without another word, they opened the bedroom door and entered the hallway. All was quiet, the ever-present yellow filter giving the familiar passageway a pleasant, late-autumn feel. They walked slowly in a daze of nostalgic awe until stopping in front of a plain wooden door decorated with a poorly drawn snowflake and the word *Alexa* scribbled in the middle.

"She made this just before Christmas break," said Sydney. "This memory is recent."

Zack nodded, placed his hand on the doorknob, and opened the door.

A faded, yellowed Alexa sat with her back to them, talking to a small, wounded chipmunk Sydney remembered her rescuing just a few months ago. It sat in its cage while Alexa sat cross-legged in front of it with an open picture book in her lap.

". . . is a tree. That's where you live, Chippy. You live in a tree. I think."

"Alexa?" asked Zack reverently.

Their little sister turned and gave them a huge smile. "Hi, guys! I was reading to Chippy. You wanna listen? Does he live in a tree? I think he lives in a tree, but I'm not sure."

"I . . . I don't remember . . . ," mumbled Zack, overcome with shock at seeing his sister sitting happily in front of him. "Maybe they live in burrows in the ground. Do you remember, Sydney?"

Remember, thought Sydney, chewing on an idea. *Remember.*

"Remember!" she shouted, the idea blossoming in her mind. "Alexa, we need you to remember something for us. Can you do that?"

Alexa twisted her face, confused, but Zack caught on right away. "Yes!" he said. "Alexa, tell Janice to open another door. We can travel between memories!"

"Huh?" she responded.

"We're trapped, Alexa!" continued Sydney. "Tell Janice to open a door! Any door!"

"And bring a knob!" added Zack.

"A door and a knob!" repeated Sydney. "Tell Janice to— OW!"

Sydney's startled cry of pain stemmed from a sudden pinching on the tip of her ear. The pinching turned into pulling, and she was hauled backward out of the room. Next to her, Zack was similarly dragged backward by his similarly pinched ear.

Once out of the room, they were tossed to the floor and the mysterious ear-puller slammed Alexa's door closed. "Just what do you think you're doing?" demanded their tormentor.

Sydney was about to confront their attacker but stopped short upon seeing a middle-aged woman holding her hands on her hips in disapproval.

She was not yellow. "Mom?" asked Zack in wonder.

♦ CHAPTER TWENTY-FOUR ♦

Alexa Remembers

ALEXA WAS TORN.

On one hand, she had just remembered something very important and needed to tell Janice right away. On the other hand, she was angry at her sister for not believing her about Dimitri—that big, dumb liar—telling her Zack and Sydney had got back. She didn't know why Dimitri—that big, dumb, liar—was lying about telling her, or why he had told her in the first place if it hadn't happened. Maybe because he was a big, dumb liar.

And Janice had believed him over her, and that wasn't fair, and so she was mad at her big sister as only a little sister can be. The last thing she wanted to do was go and find her and talk to her, but she was pretty sure that was what she should do because she remembered Zack and Sydney being very specific when they told her a few months ago. She knew it was a few months ago because it was after she'd found Chippy but before she'd found Ratty the rat.

She did not stop to wonder how they could have given her a message a few months ago that she needed to deliver today. To think about that would be confusing, and she was not in the mood to be confused.

But neither was she in the mood to talk to Janice. So she was torn.

After thinking it over, she got up and walked purposefully around the first floor of the house. She had made a decision. It was a good decision, or at least she thought it was, and she wanted to follow through before something happened to change her mind. If she couldn't talk to Janice, but needed Janice to know, then she would tell someone else and let them tell Janice. Since she wouldn't talk to Dimitri, the only person left was Aunt Gladys.

She found her aunt where the poor, confused woman had spent most of her time since waking up totally not remembering anything—in the kitchen in front of a bowl of Honey Nut Oat Blast Ring-a-Dings.

"Aunt Gladys?" she asked.

"Am I?" asked Aunt Gladys. "I don't remember brothers or sisters. Or parents. Or, really, much of anything." She sagged and dropped her head into her hands.

Alexa gave her a second to be sad before asking, "What do you remember?"

Aunt Gladys lifted her head and looked out at something only she could see. "Ice cream," she said. "There was a circus. A man offered me ice cream. He had a large mustache."

She drifted off, squinting her eyes as if trying to peer at something just out of sight. Alexa figured that was all her aunt was going to say, so she got right to the point of her visit. "Zack and Sydney are trapped, and they need Janice to open a new door so they can get out. But I'm not talking to Janice, so I thought you could talk to her. So will you? You need to tell Janice that Zack and Sydney need Janice to open another door so that they can get out."

With great difficulty, Aunt Gladys turned her gaze away from the cloudy past and looked at the littlest Rothbaum. "I have no idea what you just said," she confessed.

"Adults!" huffed Alexa, who gave up on her aunt (she really missed the old Aunt Gladys) and stormed out of the kitchen.

Once she'd stomped through a few rooms in frustration, Alexa slowed and considered her options. She could ignore what she had just remembered about Zack and Sydney needing a new door. No, that didn't seem right. She could tell someone else. Yes, that felt better. But who? Aunt Gladys had been a flop. Dimitri—the big, dumb liar—was out of the question. And she wasn't any less angry with Janice. There wasn't anyone else to tell.

Fine, she decided. *I'll do it myself.*

She circled back to the central room, slipped through the vault door and under the heavy curtain, and walked up to the platform. The broken door still hung in the frame, a huge crack running down the center.

Step one, get rid of the old door, she thought. *Easy-peasy.*

She'd seen Aunt Gladys switch out the doors last time. It hadn't looked that hard. There were big gold latches on the frame at each of the four corners. She hopped up onto the platform and toyed with the bottom two latches until she figured them out, twisted everything the right way, and got them to snap open with a satisfying *sprong!*

The upper latches were out of her reach, so she dragged the swivelly chair over, shoved it onto the platform next to the doorframe, and climbed on. By stretching out on her tippy-toes, she was just able to reach. She carefully twisted the first latch-knobby thingy while the chair beneath her threatened to roll away from the door and send her crashing to the floor. It was a delicate balancing act, and Alexa was quite proud of herself when she heard the *sprong!* of success. Next, she moved the chair over a bit and climbed back up to unlatch the final doohickey and release the door. It was again slow going, and at one point, the chair jerked over just a bit, enough to get Alexa windmilling her arms to keep from toppling over. But she steadied herself, reached up, twisted the thingamajig, and was rewarded with one more *sprong!*

"What on earth are you doing?"

Janice's sudden outburst caught Alexa by surprise. She instinctively leaped back off the chair, and her momentum shoved the chair forward, where it crashed into the newly released door. The door toppled over with a deafening crash at the same time Alexa herself landed on her rump with a resounding *thump*.

"Alexa!" cried a suddenly worried Janice, rushing forward. "Are you all right?"

Alexa took a moment to answer that question. She had every right to be howling in pain and/or shock after her dramatic tumble—and she considered doing just that—but in the end, her mission was more important than a well-deserved tantrum. She staggered to her feet and was about to tell Janice that she was fine when she remembered she wasn't talking to her sister. So instead, she shrugged, dusted herself off, and walked around the brass frame to start hauling the broken door out of the way.

"Wait! What's going on? What are you doing?"

Alexa ignored her sister and dragged the heavy door as best she could. Which was not very well.

"That's way too heavy for you," said Janice. "Just stop, okay? Tell me what you're doing."

"What does it look like I'm doing?" answered Alexa, in as sassy a tone as she could muster for a seven-year-old. If she was going to talk to her sister, she'd at least be nasty about it.

"Why are you dragging, or trying to drag, that away?"

Alexa stayed silent, huffing and puffing against the weight of the door.

"Alexa? Why won't you talk to me?"

"Because you don't believe me!" snapped Alexa, finally giving up both on moving the door and not talking to her sister. She gained a moment's satisfaction at the startled look of guilt on Janice's face, then decided this was all way too much emotion for her to handle at once, so she went ahead, fell to the floor, and burst into tears.

Surrendering to her big-sister instinct, Janice rushed forward. "Oh, Alexa! I'm so sorry!" She dropped to a knee at Alexa's side and cradled the crying girl's head in her arms.

"Yoo-ooo di-id-n't be-le-ee-ee-eve me-ee-ee," hiccuped Alexa through her tears. "Yoo-oo thi-ink I—I—I'm a bi-ig, du-umb li-i-i-ar!"

"No!" protested Janice. "Never! You're not a liar, Alexa. I never thought that."

"Yoo-oo be-ee-lee-eve-d Di-mi-i-i-tri-i," continued Alexa, who felt she might as well get it all out. "You-oo ye-elled at me-ee."

"I did," admitted the eldest Rothbaum. "I know I did. I shouldn't have done that. Please forgive me?"

Alexa paused in her whimpering and peered up at her sister. "You're not mad at me?" she asked without a trace of misery in her voice. "You don't blame me?"

"I don't blame you."

"Really?"

"Really."

"Really really?"

"Really really."

"Really really really?"

Janice raised an eyebrow quizzically. "Weren't you crying a moment ago?"

"That was then." She pushed herself out of Janice's lap and leaned back down to grab the broken door. "Help me move this?"

"Why did you disconnect the door? What are you doing down here?"

"Oh." Alexa bit her lip. "Right. I didn't tell you. Because I wasn't talking to you. Because you yelled at me. So it's your fault." She planted her hands on her hips like she'd seen Sydney do when placing blame, but it didn't feel right, so she let her hands drop.

"Didn't tell me what?" asked Janice.

And Alexa told her. She told her about remembering how Zack and Sydney came into her room when she was reading to Chippy, about how they were trapped in the memory, about how they could travel between memories, and about how they needed someone to open another door and bring them a knob so they could get home. When she was done, Janice just stared at her in utter amazement, her mouth hanging open like it was trying to air out a particularly bad smell.

Alexa waited for her sister to say something. Janice, for her part, gave no indication that she was planning on doing anything but gawk endlessly at her little sister until the sun went supernova in a few billion years.

"Did you get all that?" asked Alexa finally. "Or do you need me to say it again?"

Janice shook herself out of her daze. "No. I got it. I'm good."

Alexa didn't think her sister sounded good, but she chose to ignore the matter and get back to work. "So will you help me?" she asked, indicating the broken door at their feet.

To Alexa's great relief, Janice spun into action, grabbing the door and quickly shoving it out of the way. "You're sure about this?" she asked.

"I'm not a big, dumb liar."

"I didn't say you were."

"You thought it."

"I never thought it."

"You yelled at me!"

"Didn't we already do this?"

Alexa giggled.

"Did they say anything about what kind of door they need?" asked Janice, looking around at the countless piles of doors ready and waiting to be hooked up and explored.

"Nope."

"Right. Okay. So we just . . . pick one?"

Alexa marched up to the nearest pile of doors and patted the topmost door with the palm of her hand. "This one."

"Are you sure?" asked Janice. "It looks a little flimsy."

"A door's a door," answered an increasingly impatient Alexa. "Let's go!"

With Alexa functioning as project manager and offering moral support, Janice lugged the chosen door over to the machine. Under her little sister's direction, she stood the door on its end and latched it into the brass frame. Then the two girls retreated to the bank of computers, and Janice fumbled with the controls.

"Do you know what you're doing?" asked Alexa.

"I watched Dimitri pretty carefully, then asked some questions after Zack and Sydney went in. I'm pretty sure—"

She interrupted herself by twisting a dial that looked like any other dial on the board. The machine instantly jolted to life with a mechanical cough, followed by an electric sizzle, followed by an unidentifiable sound from somewhere below. The now-familiar bright blue sparks of energy wrapped themselves around the door once again, and the entire frame buzzed excitedly for a moment before quieting into the soft, ever-present drone that meant everything was working.

"Is good! We go now!" shouted Janice, mimicking Dimitri.

"Don't mimic that big, dumb liar," said Alexa.

"Sorry."

The two sisters turned their attention to the flimsy-looking door cracking with blue energy in the middle of the room.

"Now what?" asked Janice.

"I think we go in," answered Alexa. She waddled over to the drawer and pulled out a doorknob. "You ready?"

"You realize we have no idea what's on the other side of that door, right?"

"Zack and Sydney."

Alexa grabbed a pair of rubber gloves and handed them

to her big sister. Then she took Janice's hand and led her, somewhat reluctantly, up onto the platform. At her prodding, Janice pulled on the gloves and reached out to gingerly touch the plain doorknob currently sparking with unidentifiable blue energy. When touching the knob failed to kill her, she went ahead and gave it a good grasp. A serious twist followed the grasp, a forceful yank followed the twist, and the two girls walked blindly into the light.

◆ CHAPTER TWENTY-FIVE ◆

Zack Learns an Unhappy Truth

"What's wrong with you?" hissed Charlotte Rothbaum to her children. "You can't just throw yourselves into your sister's memories! Do you have any idea the damage you could do? You could . . . You might . . . !" Her exclamations faded into growls as she fought for the right words.

Zack, who hadn't seen his mother in over six years, stammered a nonreply. She seemed hard and severe—the opposite of her father and Aunt Gladys. Most of all, however, she looked kind of crazy, with her hair all disheveled and her eyes bulging just the slightest bit from her head.

Truth be told, she looked like she'd just stuck her finger into a light socket.

"Are you really . . . our mother?" asked Sydney, sounding

so meek Zack did a double take to make sure it was still his sister next to him and not some impostor.

"You can't be here!" continued Charlotte, waving her arms. Zack noticed one of her hands was covered by what looked like a thick rubber gardening glove. "I don't know how you found this memory, but you need to leave! Now! Before you . . . It's not . . . !"

"We can't leave," said Zack, finding his voice. "They closed our door."

"They what? Of all the stupid, brainless . . . My sister is such a . . . !" She quickly reached into her pocket with her gloved hand and pulled out a plain brass doorknob. "Someday I'm going to knock some sense into that woman!"

With a violence Zack didn't really think was necessary, his mother slammed the brass knob onto the back of Alexa's door. The knob instantly melded itself onto the door, spitting out a number of bright blue sparks of energy in the process. She turned the knob and pulled the door open, releasing a world of intense white light.

"Well?" she prompted. "Go on!"

Zack tried to process the ridiculous amount of impossible that had been dumped into his lap in the last five minutes. Finally, his brain chose to toss it all out his ear and focus on the most important question.

"Where have you been for the last six years?" he asked.

"Get moving!" ordered Charlotte.

Zack and Sydney quickly leaped into the merciless blaze of illumination.

◆ ◆ ◆

They emerged in a way-too-cluttered one-room apartment.

Boxes of wires and gears and widgets and switches littered the floor, the lone couch, both tables, and two of the three chairs. Piles of paper lay scattered everywhere, mixed in with old pizza boxes and takeout containers. Zack was pretty sure if his room had ever looked like this, he'd've been grounded for a week.

There was a soft pop followed by a loud slam, and Charlotte pushed her way past her children. "Sorry about the mess," she muttered as she flung her glove off her hand and leaned over a collection of old laptops to pound some buttons. "I wasn't expecting company."

"Where are we?" asked Sydney.

Charlotte's fingers flew over multiple keyboards. Zack tried to follow the readouts on the various screens, but none of them made any sense. Finally, his mother stabbed the Enter key on one of the laptops, and the soft, magical drone he hadn't even realized he'd been hearing suddenly fizzled out with an erratic burst of static.

Zack turned around to see a plain wooden door—which he recognized as belonging to his sister, which was weird because he'd thought it had burned down with the house—give off a wisp of smoke.

"My apartment," said Charlotte with a weary sigh. "I never was much of a housekeeper, as I'm sure your father has probably mentioned."

She sat in the only available chair and peered at them, as if studying an unusual species of mollusk.

"Actually, Dad never said much about you at all," said Zack.

"No?" She seemed disappointed for a moment. "I suppose I deserve that. Actually, I deserve worse. Far, far worse." She said this last part more to herself than to them, causing Zack and Sydney to exchange inquisitive looks.

"Why?" asked Zack.

"Why?" She jumped up and paced through the mess of her apartment, wringing her hands together as if washing them under an invisible sink. "Have you seen him lying there? He's just . . . And you ask . . ."

"Lying there? You mean in the hospital?" asked Sydney. "You visited Dad?"

"Of course I visited your father! It's the least . . . After what I . . ." She stopped and bit her lip.

The color drained from Zack's face. "Mom?" he began, afraid to even ask. "Did you have . . . Did you . . . the fire . . . ?"

"He wasn't supposed to be home!" snapped Charlotte, throwing her hands in the air and marching away from her children. "He had a very important meeting! And you four . . . in school . . ." The invisible hand washing became incredibly frantic as she stumbled to get her words out. "Nobody was supposed to be there!"

"You started the fire?" asked a shocked Sydney.

"No one was supposed to get hurt! I even saved Alexa's hamster!" She gestured wildly to the kitchen counter, where there was a wire cage containing a rather disheveled-looking creature currently buried in shredded newspaper.

Zack was so devastated over his mother's revelation that he didn't bother telling her the "hamster" in the cage was actually Ratty the rat—though he was mildly relieved for Alexa's sake to learn the disgusting thing had survived.

"When I saw his car pull into the driveway, I was furious!" continued Charlotte. "What was he thinking? Didn't he know I was burning the house down? Once he came home, I assumed he'd see the fire and put it out, and I'd have to try again another time, but did he? Of course not! He just rambled in, oblivious to the flames already flickering out the kitchen window! Of all the stupid . . . Can't even . . . !" She tore at her hair in frustration.

At a loss for words, Zack could only shake his head.

"He's punishing me. He's still angry I left. That's why he made me go in there and drag his sorry butt out of the house! That's why he's in that coma! He's punishing me!"

She sank into her chair with a moan and tossed her head back, staring up at the ceiling. Nobody spoke, each lost in their own tumultuous thoughts. All the revelations had pulled the rug out from under Zack's entire world. He didn't know what to think.

"Why . . . ," whispered Sydney. "Why did you burn our house down?"

"Why?" Charlotte parroted, only slightly crazy-like. "I needed your doors, of course!"

"Our doors?" Overwhelmed, Zack plopped down on the edge of the couch.

"I couldn't ask your father for them," she explained, as if this should have been obvious. "And if they disappeared, he'd wonder where they went. He's nosy like that. But if the house burned down, he wouldn't know they were missing. Nobody would know!"

Seeing a slightly obsessive glint in his mother's eye, Zack scooted back against the cushions. "Why did you need our doors?" he asked carefully.

"Because your grandfather's an idiot!" she spat. "He just left her there!"

"Left? Who?" Utterly confused, Zack looked to Sydney for help, but she just shrugged.

"My mother! She's trapped inside! But my father gave up! He closed the door and locked it away! Well, I never gave up. It took years to duplicate his work. But . . . look!" She spread her arms, indicating all the machinery and gadgets and papers crammed into the tiny room. "I finally got in! I accessed the MemoryVerse!"

"MemorySphere," mumbled Sydney automatically. "Pop-Pop calls it the MemorySphere."

"He does?" She frowned. "What is that supposed to mean? MemoryVerse is much better. Memory universe. MemoryVerse. Dad was always rotten with names. Thank goodness my mother named us, or we'd've been called Pigwort and Boomshakalaka."

"I thought Grandma died," said Sydney. "You say she's trapped in there?"

Charlotte popped out of her chair and lunged toward her daughter. "She's in agony! Every time I visited she was worse. She needs to be saved!"

Seeing a look of true fear creep into his sister's eyes, Zack gently tugged his mother away from Sydney and sat her back down in her chair. "You went into her memories?" he asked.

"She's trapped, Zack. She's been trapped for so long. . . ." She trailed off, her head drooping in exhaustion.

"But what does that have to do with our doors?" asked Sydney. Zack could see her struggling with the intensity of her emotions. This was not the mother any of them had remembered or imagined.

Charlotte lifted her head. "I knew you'd end up with my sister," she said conspiratorially. "I was going to travel into your father's memories through his bedroom door—our bedroom door—and plant the idea. With the house a pile of ashes, where else would you go?"

"You wanted us to go to Aunt Gladys's?" asked Sydney.

Their mother nodded. "But then your father was caught in the blaze, so I had to improvise." She jerked a thumb behind her to indicate a plain office door against the wall with the name *Fletcher Groskowsky, Esquire,* stenciled on a small pane of glass near the top. "And it worked! You're in! I can't get in. Gladys locks up tight and yells at me from a window if I get within fifty feet. She's still angry about some of the things I said when I left. But you're in! And when you get back, you'll find my mother's door for me. I'm thirsty."

She popped up and maneuvered her way through the clutter and debris to the kitchen. Zack found himself sifting through what she'd just said, trying to make sense of it, but Sydney beat him to the punch.

"You're sending us back?" she asked. "We just found you! We don't need to live with Aunt Gladys. We can live with you!"

"Here?" Charlotte guffawed awkwardly and grabbed a glass pitcher from the fridge. "Out of the question." She poured herself some unidentifiable brown liquid from the pitcher and gulped it down.

"But you're our mother!" cried Sydney.

"And she's mine!" roared her mother right back, slamming the empty glass on the counter. Zack and Sydney flinched, and Charlotte closed her eyes and took a deep breath. "I'm sorry, Sydney. Maybe when this is over . . . after I save her . . ."

Zack came forward to put his arm around his sister's shoulder. She absently shoved it off, but he didn't mind. "So you planned on, what?" asked Sydney. "Traveling into our memories to trick us into finding Grandma's door for you?"

"Not all of you," she answered, eyes cast down in shame.

"Alexa," said Zack. His mother nodded without looking up. "Why take the rest of our doors?"

She lifted her head, and Zack was surprised to find tears in her eyes. "I missed you."

Nobody spoke, and this simple confession hung in the air for a moment. Finally, Charlotte cleared her throat. "Either of you thirsty?" she asked, holding up the pitcher.

"What is it?" asked Zack.

"Guava-prune-carrot-soy energy drink with egg and protein powder," she said. "My own mix."

They passed. She shrugged and poured herself another glass. "By the way. Don't tell my sister about meeting me. We have a history."

"Not anymore, you don't," said Zack.

Charlotte lowered her eyebrows suspiciously. "Not any . . . What do you . . . ?"

"She doesn't remember you," he explained. "She doesn't remember us. She doesn't remember anything."

Her eyebrows remained lowered even as her eyes themselves scanned left and right as if looking for someone else to explain what Zack was talking about. When she failed to find anyone, she pressed forward with her best guess. "My sister's memory has been altered?"

Her children nodded. Her eyes widened. Her hands shook.

She dropped the pitcher of guava-prune-carrot-soy energy drink with egg and protein powder onto the kitchen floor.

CHAPTER TWENTY-SIX

Janice Beats a Hasty Retreat

JANICE AND ALEXA FOUND THEMSELVES SURROUNDED BY WHITE tile walls and sterile metallic sinks. A row of mirrors lined the wall above the sinks, and opposite them were six swinging doors, each a few inches off the ground.

"We're in a bathroom," said Alexa.

Janice chuckled at her sister's observation. "Do you have to go potty?" she asked jokingly.

"No!" answered Alexa very seriously.

Janice hid a smile and looked around the room. Suddenly, she gasped and pointed. "Look!" she chirped. "Look, look, look!"

Alexa turned and looked.

"What are those?" she asked, confused.

Alexa might have been stumped, but Janice knew full

well what a line of urinals against the wall meant. "Boys' bathroom! This is a boys' bathroom!"

"What!" Alexa was scandalized.

"Ew! Ew, ew, ew!" Janice couldn't help but flap her hands in agitation. "Out! Go!"

The two girls nearly trampled over each other in their rush to exit the men's room.

They emerged in an old movie theater lobby. The scent of popcorn invaded their nostrils as they skidded to a stop.

"Hey!" sniped the pimply faced boy behind the counter, his voice bouncing up and down between octaves. "What are you doing in there? That's for boys, not girls!"

"Sorry," said Janice, tensing up. "We're sorry. We didn't . . . I mean . . ."

"I had to go," said Alexa, putting her hands on her hips. "You got a problem with that?"

Pimply Faced Boy flinched and backed down. "No. Enjoy your movie." He shuffled away to pump some fake butter flavoring into the popcorn machine.

Janice breathed an uneasy sigh of relief while marveling at her little sister's ability to intimidate a teenager. She knew a dorky kid working at a movie theater probably wasn't going to be their most difficult challenge in searching for Zack and Sydney, but she'd take a win any day. She wasn't thrilled to be back inside this weird world of memories where everything was covered in a faded yellow wash. She hoped they found their siblings quickly.

"Where do we meet them?" she asked.

Alexa squinted her face together in thought for a moment, then relaxed. "I dunno," she admitted. "They didn't say."

"Think back. What, exactly, did they say to do?"

"Open a new door."

"We did that. What next?"

"I dunno," repeated Alexa. "They didn't say."

Janice felt the first inklings of panic creep into her belly. "Do we just wait for them? Do we have to find them? How do we go from one memory to another? How do they know we opened a new door?"

Alexa shrugged. "I dunno."

The panic made itself right at home in Janice's belly, sending tendrils of uneasiness worming through her body. "You have that doorknob, right?" she asked.

Alexa reached into her pocket and held it up with a smile. Janice was overcome with an urge to take it out of her sister's hand, march up to a door—any door—and get out of there that very moment. She was only able to hold out because she knew if she tried to swipe the knob from her sister, it would turn very ugly very quickly.

"Good. Put it back in your pocket," she said. "Keep it safe."

Alexa did as asked, then turned toward a pair of dark doors leading from the lobby into one of the theaters. "Maybe they're already here," she announced, walking forward.

"No, they can't be," said Janice, taking another scan of the room. "We just opened this door. This memory. It

225

doesn't work like that. I think. Does it? I'm not really sure. I don't really understand how any of this—Alexa!"

The little girl, tuning her bigger sister out, tugged the door open and slipped into the darkened theater.

"Alexa! Wait!" Janice rushed in after her sister.

The theater seemed about half full, though it was hard to tell since it was so dark. On the gigantic screen in front was a ten-foot-tall cartoon pelican dancing with quite a bit more expertise than is generally found in that species. Janice sort of half recognized the movie, but her attention was more focused on the little form of Alexa calmly marching down the aisle, yelling, "Zack! Sydney! Are you here?" at the top of her lungs.

"Quiet yer trap, little girl!" barked someone in the audience.

"Zack? Is that you?" Alexa called out.

"Hush up!" yelled someone else in the audience.

"I'm looking for my brother and sister," announced Alexa. "Zack? Sydney?"

"For crying out loud, we're trying to watch the movie!" shouted a third individual.

Janice caught up with Alexa, quickly grabbed her arm, and pulled her down into a crouch. "You can't just yell out like that in a crowded theater," she said.

"But it's not real," said Alexa. "They're just a memory."

"They're still people," countered Janice hurriedly. "Well, memories of people. I mean . . . well, they . . . huh." She was stumped.

Alexa pulled her arm free and stood up. "Zack! Sydney! Where are you?"

"Will somebody shut that little girl up?" hollered someone in the audience.

"They're obviously not here, Alexa," whispered Janice. "Let's get out of—"

Before she could finish, she was smacked in the head by a well-thrown shoe.

"Ow!" she cried.

"Keep it down!" screamed a very menacing voice from the audience.

"Did you throw a shoe at that girl?" asked someone else in the audience. "How dare you?"

"I can throw whatever I want at whoever I want, lady!" barked the shoe thrower. "It's a free country!"

"Somebody should throw a shoe at you!" responded the woman.

"If you two don't shut up, I'm throwing shoes at both of you!" snapped someone else a few rows back.

"Go ahead and try it!" yelled the initial shoe thrower, standing. "I'll turn that shoe right around and send it straight up your—*hey!*"

The man lurched forward as a large boot clonked him in the back of the head. He swiveled around, furious. "That was a boot! Who threw that?"

Accusations flew and tempers rose as more and more people began yelling at one another and throwing various items of footwear back and forth. Janice took hold of Alexa's wrist and bolted up the aisle. "We've got to get out of here!" she hissed.

Alexa did not disagree.

The two girls emerged from the darkened theater into the seemingly blinding glare of the theater lobby to find Pimply Faced Boy snarling at them. "You guys are trouble-makers," he announced. "I'm gonna call the cops!"

"Alexa! Run!" cried Janice.

Her sister turned on the afterburner and ran ziggedy-zaggedy through the lobby like a flustered moth. Janice heeded her own advice and also broke into a run, slowing just long enough to steer Alexa toward the front door.

"Hey!" cried Pimply Faced Boy. "Get back here! I'm making a citizen's arrest!"

In less than a heartbeat, they were out the door.

"What do we do, Janny? Where do we go?" Alexa clung tightly to her sister's hand, all hint of bravery gone.

"I don't . . . We should . . . ." Janice looked up and down the street. There were no signs of life anywhere, no indications where they should run next. *We should just get out of here,* thought Janice. *This is too dangerous.*

She was about to ask her sister for the doorknob when Alexa squeaked like an excited helium balloon, let go of Janice's hand, and rushed toward one of the shops.

"Alexa! Wait!" cried Janice, but she soon saw it was pointless. The store to which Alexa ran was a pet shop, and the front window was filled with small, fluffy, unbelievably soft bunnies. The gravitational mass of this overwhelming cuteness was a pull Alexa simply could not resist. Janice quickly hurried after her sister.

Approaching the store, Janice saw Alexa pull open the front door and stop, momentarily frozen upon seeing a blank wall of darkness within. Something about this darkness made the hairs on Janice's head stand on end, and she called out to her sister, warning her not to enter.

Too late.

Alexa skipped into the darkness, instantly vanishing from view.

"Alexa!"

Janice reached the storefront and pulled the door wide. Abyssal darkness confronted her, sucking the yellowed light of the street into its void of nothingness. "Alexa?" called Janice timidly. She was torn. She in no way wanted to pass through into the black, yet she couldn't abandon her sister. She took a deep breath, reached out her arms, stepped forward . . .

◆ ◆ ◆

And found herself in an old, rickety, long-abandoned upstairs hallway.

"Janny? Where are the bunnies?"

Alexa was turning in circles, utterly confused. This was obviously not a pet store.

We must have entered a different memory, reasoned Janice. From the look of things, however, it wasn't a very nice one. The wooden flooring was rotting and warped, paint was peeling off the walls, and cobwebs abounded. A sickly smell hung in the air—a mixture of rotten fruit and body odor. Janice shivered.

"There were bunnies in the window," repeated Alexa. "They were super cute."

"I don't think there are any bunnies here," said Janice, trying to figure out how this whole thing worked. She supposed they could go out through the door they'd just come through, but that would drop them right back on the street in front of the movie theater and the increasingly angry crowd, not to mention Pimply Faced Boy, who wanted to arrest them. Not an option.

"This place is creepy," announced Alexa as she wandered down the hallway, the floor creaking with every step.

Creepy doesn't do this place justice, thought Janice. Every fiber in her being screamed to get out of there, even though there didn't seem to be any obvious threat. Still, when had her fibers ever been wrong? She looked up and down for another door to pass through—another gateway to another memory—but there were none. None intact, anyway. Plenty of half-rotten doors hanging by a single hinge or leaning against the doorframe, but nothing you could open and close.

Alexa stopped at the top of a flight of steps. "What's down there?" she asked.

Janice joined her sister and peered down the stairs. There looked to be no end, no ground floor. Nothing but darkness. Total, absolute darkness.

The fear that had thus far been lightly tapping at the back of her mind started thumping madly. Looking into that abyss, Janice felt her blood turn to ice. She unconsciously stepped away, eyes glued to the emptiness yawning before her.

We have to leave, she thought. *Now.*

"Alexa, give me the doorknob."

Her sister, equally terrified, nodded and slowly fumbled in her pockets for the promise of delivery. Janice felt a momentary pang of guilt for abandoning Zack and Sydney like this, but (a) she wasn't sure she was actually abandoning them, and (b) they had to get out of this hallway.

"Alexa?" she asked as her sister continued to search her pockets.

"I got it. . . . Hold on. . . ."

A sound erupted from the chasm of inky blackness below. A sound at once terrifying and familiar. A sound that caused both girls to freeze in their tracks. The sound of a door. A very creaky door.

"What was that?" asked Alexa, her voice starting to tremble.

"The doorknob, Alexa," implored Janice. "Please."

But a new sound assaulted their ears. Footsteps. Deep, heavy footsteps.

"Janny?"

"The doorknob. Hurry!"

As the footsteps rose, growing louder and more ominous, Alexa finally scooped the doorknob out of her pocket.

She shoved it into her sister's hands with such ferocity it slipped and clattered to the floor at the top of the stairs.

"No!" cried Janice, dropping to her knees to grab the knob before it rolled off the top step and began a one-way journey toward the source of those horrible footsteps.

"Hurry, Janny!"

Clutching the precious doorknob in her fist, Janice got to her feet and reached for Alexa.

"A supremely pleasant good morning to you, urchins," croaked a wispy, high-pitched voice. "Have you journeyed forth to my humble abode in need of medical ministrations? I do believe an opening can be procured."

Climbing out of the darkness came a decrepit old man dressed in the blackest of black. His hands were gnarled and knobby, his face pockmarked and ancient, and his head covered by a top hat so purple even the yellowish filter of the memory itself failed to dull the purity of the color. Evil pulsated from his body with a physical force that knocked the two girls back a step even as their eyes were drawn to the wolflike smile on his face.

"Janny . . . ?"

Janice couldn't move. Couldn't talk. Couldn't breathe. She remained mesmerized with terror as the old man reached the top step and leered at them, seeming larger than possible.

"What I mean to say is . . . ," he rasped, "the doctor will see you now." From out of his black, black jacket he

withdrew a long, long needle. "Mayhap a prick or two shall cure what ails you. Shall we commence?"

He came forward, holding the needle out like a jousting lance, his eyes twinkling with malice. The girls stood frozen in place as he approached, unable to react, unable to run. Janice watched the rusty tip of the immense needle come closer and closer to her face. To her eye.

Suddenly, something large sailed over their heads and struck the old man's top hat, knocking the purple monstrosity from his head. The creepy stranger staggered back a step, momentarily stunned, and dropped the impossibly long needle to the floor.

"What in tarnation . . . ?" he cried.

Confused, Janice looked down and saw what had knocked the hat off his head.

A shoe.

Again with the flying shoes? thought Janice.

"Run, girls! Run!" yelled a voice Janice did not recognize. It seemed, however, to be giving good advice, so she grabbed Alexa by the arm and ran down the hall.

"And just where do you think you're—ow!"

A second shoe smacked the old man in the face, knocking him down the steps. He stumbled momentarily before regaining his balance.

"Second room on your left!" called the voice. "Hurry! I'm out of shoes!"

Not bothering to question their unknown savior, Janice bolted toward the second room on the left. They were just about to slip inside when the voice called out once more. "Other left! Other left! My left! Oh, galloping Gorgonzola! Turn around!"

Alexa actually figured out what the new voice meant before Janice, and she pulled her sister across the hallway into the correct room.

"How dare you interfere with an urchin's proper medical care!" screamed the creepy old man from the stairs. This was quickly followed by a thunk and another cry of "Ow!"

A moment later, a second old man ran into the room. He looked vaguely familiar. . . .

"Forgot I had an extra shoe," he said, stopping to catch his breath.

"You're the not-old man!" exclaimed Alexa.

It took Janice a split second to understand what her sister was talking about, but her own memory returned just as the rest of her mind pointed out the fact that whoever this man was, he wasn't yellow.

He wasn't a memory.

"Yes! Although no, I'm quite old. I'll explain later!"

"Who are you?" asked Janice.

"Moistened muttonchops! I'm your grandfather! Now, go!"

Grandfather? thought Janice.

"Go where?" asked Alexa. Janice took a quick scan of the room. Her sister was right—there did not appear to be any other doors.

"The laundry chute! Quickly!"

"You are growing children!" The taunt oozed with malignant purpose. "Neglect not your health and vitality!"

Janice quickly spotted the lip of a laundry chute against the wall. "Over there!" she yelled. Alexa ran to the wall and struggled to lift the lid. Before she could stop and think, Janice picked her sister up and dumped her, feet-first, into the chute.

"I do not believe I gave either of you permission to leave my office!"

Janice turned to see the horrible old man now grown so large he barely fit through the doorway. His eyes were red and demonic, and huge fangs poked out of his mouth. He reached his clawlike hands into the room, and his fingers stretched forth like serpents, writhing their way toward her.

"Go!" screamed the not-creepy old man who had just claimed to be their grandfather.

She leaped head-first into the laundry chute.

◆ CHAPTER TWENTY-SEVEN ◆

Sydney Feels Left Out

"ARE WE FAR ENOUGH BACK? THAT DRAWBRIDGE CAN KILL! MOM lost so many cats that way! Maybe we should . . . just in case . . ."

"We're fine, Charlotte," droned Sydney with a slight eye roll.

"Maybe just another few feet," suggested her mother. "I wouldn't want to . . . The drawbridge might . . ."

"Is coming! No squishing!"

Dimitri's cheery-if-scattered disembodied voice interrupted Charlotte's hemming and hawing. There was a groan, some clanking, and lots of gearlike sounds. Once Dimitri had agreed to let them in, he had sworn up and down that he could lower the drawbridge slowly and safely.

All the same, they had retreated behind Charlotte's car.

Their caution was rewarded when the massive wall plummeted down in one swift crash, sending out billowing folds of dust in its wake. When the air finally cleared, Dimitri poked his head out and waved.

"Hello? No squishy?"

"No squishy, Dimitri," said Zack. "Ready, Mom?"

Sydney scowled inwardly. Zack might have welcomed their mother back with open arms, but Sydney wasn't yet sold. To be safe, she was keeping her emotional distance: calling her Charlotte rather than Mom, refusing any offers of a hug. "Let's go see if your plan works, Charlotte," she said. "I'll bring the rat."

She lifted Ratty's cage by the handle and walked past Charlotte into the house.

"That's a rat?" asked Charlotte, alarmed.

Behind them, Zack wrestled with the plain wooden door their mother had made them stop and purchase from a local House Depot on their way here. She hadn't explained why they needed a new door, but Sydney had her suspicions.

"Zack? Sydney? Outside?" Dimitri's face was a mask of confusion as the siblings approached. "You go through door. Inside. Now outside. I confused."

"We . . . sort of found a window," said Zack.

"Window? Now I very confused."

Charlotte regained her composure and hustled forward. "Right. Where's my sister?" she asked.

"Ah! Miss Gladys! Yes!" The man welcomed the change of subject. "In kitchen."

"The kitchen. Good. I can make a smoothie," announced Charlotte, though Sydney felt she was in for a disappointment. "Are my . . . my daughters with her?"

"Janice and Alexa," explained Sydney. "We brought Alexa's rat. She'll be thrilled." She indicated Ratty's cage. Dimitri's eyes widened, and he took a step back.

"Ah. Rat," he said. "Very nice. Yes. No. They no here."

"Where'd they go?" asked Zack.

"They no tell Dimitri," confessed the oddly accented man. "But I think they in memory. Looking for you."

◆ ◆ ◆

"That's not the door we went through," said Zack.

"Duh," interjected Sydney. "They cracked that one in half." She motioned with Ratty's cage toward the broken door lying a few feet away from the platform.

"You disappeared," mumbled Aunt Gladys from the curtained doorway. She hadn't been able to take her eyes off Zack and Sydney since they'd entered the kitchen, causing her to fall to the floor with a yelp of surprise. "I saw. You vanished. Into thin air. Very upsetting. I ate two bowls of cereal."

A wave of sympathy washed over Sydney. She hoped Charlotte's idea worked.

"What is it with you kids?" griped the woman Sydney refused to call Mom. "The MemoryVerse is not a playground! I swear, when they get back, I'll . . . I'll . . . I'll ground them! Yes! I can do that. I'm the mother."

Sydney felt that was still up for debate, but let it drop. "Do we go in there and get them?" she asked, setting the cage down.

"Under no circumstances!" stated Charlotte, stomping her foot because, Sydney guessed, she'd seen an angry mom stomp her foot once on TV.

"They could be dozens of memories away from this one by now," added Zack. "We'd never find them."

"This is incredibly upsetting." Charlotte paced back and forth in front of the platform, once again wringing her hands together as if struggling to properly clean them. "We can't switch out the door until they return, which means we can't fix my sister, which means we can't find my mother's door."

"Will you shut up about Grandma's door?" Sydney was on the verge of a RAGE. "Janice and Alexa are in danger! Your daughters! But why should you care? You don't care about them! You don't care about Dad! You don't care about any of us! You're not my mother!" She gave the platform a solid boot—though the platform, in its defense, really hadn't done anything to deserve such violence—and ran into Zack's arms, who covered her protectively and rubbed her back, calming her down.

"Not your mother?" asked Aunt Gladys. "Does that mean she's not my sister? I'm so confused."

"Is done!" announced Dimitri, shoving his way into the room. He cast his proud face about, taking in the gloom and misery dripping off everyone's chin, and jerked back as if physically struck. "Is bad time. I come back."

Charlotte stopped pacing and stood, trembling slightly. "You're right, Sydney," she whispered. "You're absolutely right. I left you. I'm so sorry. I thought I had to . . . I just wish . . ."

They never learned what it was she wished for because her confession was suddenly interrupted by a blast of dazzling light pouring forth from the door as it was opened from within. Everyone looked away, shielding their eyes, until a telltale *slam!* rang out with the clarity of an all clear siren.

"Zacky! Sydney!" cheered a tiny voice both siblings knew well.

Sydney had barely forced her eyes open before little Alexa barreled into her and Zack, nearly knocking them to the floor.

"How did you guys get back?" asked Janice. "Gramps said your doorknob disintegrated."

"You met Pop-Pop?" asked Sydney.

Janice nodded. "Pop-Pop. I like that."

Zack pulled her into the group hug. "It is so good to see you," he said. "Why'd you go in there?"

"To find you, silly," said Alexa. "You were trapped."

"Which leads back to my earlier question," said Janice. "How'd you get out?"

"I got them out."

Four heads turned as one, and Charlotte looked for all the world like she was about to have a heart attack. Or maybe bad indigestion.

"Guys," said Zack, clearing his throat, "this is—"

"Mommy!" declared Alexa, jumping up and racing to Charlotte's side. She wrapped her arms around her mother's legs, a look of ultimate bliss lighting up her face. "I love you!"

Charlotte awkwardly patted her youngest daughter on the head. "Hello . . . honey," she said.

Alexa poked her head out from between her mother's knees. "Guys, look! It's Mommy!"

Sydney nodded, not trusting herself to say anything. She looked at Janice, curious to see how she was taking the unexpected reunion, and was amused to find her older sister's eyes bugging out of her head like she was on the moon without a helmet.

"Mmm . . . Mom?" Janice muttered.

"In the . . . er . . . flesh," said Charlotte, blushing slightly.

"What are you doing here?"

Rebuked, Charlotte swallowed a reply, giving Alexa's hair an extra pat as if it were a security blanket. "I used to live here, you know."

"You used to live at our house, too," reminded Janice. Sydney swelled with sisterly love.

"Now that Janice and Alexa are back," interrupted Zack, all too obviously changing the subject, "we can try Mom's plan."

"Plan?" asked Janice.

Charlotte turned back to the curtained entryway. "Is everything ready, Dimitri?" she asked.

Dimitri sprang to life like somebody had just plugged him into an electrical outlet. "Yes. Is ready."

"We think we have a way to bring Aunt Gladys back," explained Zack.

"Did I go somewhere?" Aunt Gladys asked.

"Now that you guys are here, we can—" He stopped midsentence. Wondering why, Sydney turned back to look and found Janice scowling. Their older sister gave the stiffest of head shakes in answer to Zack's raised eyebrow, so he coughed and continued. "We can hopefully get to the bottom of this."

Everyone followed the cheerful Dimitri out of the room. As she ducked under the curtain, Sydney cast a quick glance back and caught Janice whispering something into the ear of a wide-eyed Zack.

◆ ◆ ◆

The group congregated once again in the kitchen. Aunt Gladys immediately gravitated to the cupboard, almost unconsciously pouring herself a bowl of Honey Nut Oat Blast Ring-a-Dings. Sydney's eyes, meanwhile, were drawn to the true oddity that now stood in the doorway—a door.

"The first step is simple," began Charlotte. "Gladys, if you'll . . . Gladys? Put the spoon down."

"I'm nervous."

"Fine. Just set it . . . Zack, can you . . . ?"

Zack walked over and took the spoon out of Aunt Gladys's hand. "It's okay, Aunt Gladys," he said. "This is the easy part."

"There's a hard part?" she asked.

"Somebody want to explain what's going on?" asked Janice, who—Sydney noticed—was looking more at Dimitri than at Charlotte.

"Someone messed with my sister's memory," stated Charlotte. "We need to find out who. And when. And how."

"And why," added Sydney.

"Yes. Good one. Okay. Gladys, you said the last thing you remember is a carnival?"

"Oh! It was lovely. There were elephants. I wanted to ride one. Father said no." She pouted.

"What else do you remember?"

"Um . . . I'm not . . . It's all so . . . Oh! Oh!" She lit up. "A girl was sick on me! Right on my dress! It was nasty!"

Charlotte looked around guiltily. "That was me."

"You? No, it was a little girl. Bigger than me. Not as big as you."

"I used to be smaller." She turned to the others. "I was eight. Had way too much cotton candy. Lifelong weakness. All right, Gladys, go ahead. Walk through that door." She pointed to the new door separating the kitchen from the front hall.

Nervously, Aunt Gladys stood and approached the door. "Just open it and walk through?" she asked.

"It's all right, Aunt Gladys," encouraged Sydney.

Hand trembling, Aunt Gladys twisted the knob, opened the door, stepped through, and closed it behind her. "Did I disappear?" she asked from the other side of the door.

"No, Gladys," said Charlotte with just a hint of sarcasm. "You did not disappear."

"Oh. Will I ever see you again?"

"Oh, for the love of . . . !" cried Charlotte. "Just open the stupid . . . !"

The door opened and Aunt Gladys walked back into the kitchen. "I don't feel any different," she said.

"It's just a door!" Charlotte clenched her teeth in frustration.

"We need to go into your memories," explained Sydney. "The only way to be sure we enter yours instead of anyone else's is to use a brand-new door. Right now, you're the only one who's ever used that door. According to Charlotte, when we hook it up, we're guaranteed to enter your memories."

"Who's Charlotte?" asked Alexa.

Sydney paused. "Mom," she finally said.

"Why do you call her Charlotte?" asked the innocent little girl in her most innocent-little-girl voice. Sydney just shook her head, feeling no desire to explain.

Charlotte had Aunt Gladys walk through the new door a dozen more times until she felt it had absorbed enough of

Aunt Gladys's ethereal essence (whatever that meant) to be of use. Then she had Dimitri take it down and lug it back to the central room.

The whole time, Sydney kept noticing Janice and Zack looking suspiciously at Dimitri. She wasn't sure why. As near as she could tell, the odd, jumpy man wasn't doing much more than standing around, waiting to be told what to do.

Somebody had better clue her in soon. She didn't like being left out.

Once the new door was in place, Charlotte worked the controls on the big banks of computers (all the while muttering about old, archaic technology) until the machine groaned to life, sending the now-familiar blue sparks of energy racing around the door. Then she grabbed a doorknob from the drawer and stepped onto the platform.

"Father was wrong about one thing. Well, many things, but one in particular. These doors can take you to any point in someone's memories. You can control it. Guide it. I'm going back to that carnival."

Charlotte had already explained all that to Sydney and Zack on the ride over, so Sydney figured her mom was just showing off. It was actually a pretty basic trick, once you got past how absolutely impossible the whole business ought to have been.

"You shouldn't go in there alone," said Zack.

"Yes, I should," she disagreed. "The MemoryVerse is dangerous. You know that."

"MemoryVerse?" asked Alexa.

"I'll explain later," promised Sydney.

"Gladys," continued Charlotte, "a man gave you ice cream?"

"He had a big mustache," confirmed Aunt Gladys. "Very nice man. I had Rocky Road."

"Fine. A man with a mustache." She pulled on a pair of rubber gloves. "Everybody, just stay here. Do not follow me." She opened the door and stepped into the blinding white light.

Sydney was tempted to say sarcastically *What are you, my mother?* but held back.

◆ CHAPTER TWENTY-EIGHT ◆

Alexa Screams Real Loud

"Is Mommy back?" asked Alexa for the four zillionth time.

"No," answered her grumpy brother yet again.

Alexa bopped around the room to stand next to Janice, who sat by the big computers, glaring out at everyone. "What's taking her so long?" she asked her big sister.

"I don't know," repeated Janice through her teeth.

Undaunted, Alexa set off once again around the room and plopped herself on the floor by the platform next to Sydney. "Do you think she'll be back soon?" she asked. "I gotta pee."

"Go pee," said Sydney, before quickly adding, "In the bathroom."

Well, duh, thought Alexa. *I'm not a baby.* But whether to use a potty wasn't the issue. "I don't want to miss anything," she admitted.

"You won't," said her sister.

"I might."

"Will you just go already?"

Alexa didn't take Sydney's sudden snap personally. Everyone was all tense and on edge and stuff. It was boring. "Come with me?" she asked. "I don't want to go alone."

"No," growled Sydney, getting up and walking away.

Alexa crossed her arms and considered pouting, but decided against it. Instead, she called out to the whole room. "Somebody has to come to the potty with me," she announced.

Everyone looked down and shuffled their feet. Finally, Dimitri raised his hand. "I go," he said.

"No!" burst out Janice and Zack at the same time. Dimitri froze, hand still in the air, looking like a chastised puppy.

"She's . . . a girl," continued Zack.

"Yes!" agreed Janice. "And there aren't any doors."

"I no look," assured Dimitri.

"No," said Janice. "Out of the question."

Alexa didn't know what the big deal was, but she could see Janice was in one of her bossy moods, so she moved on. "Aunt Gladys, will you go to the potty with me?" asked Alexa.

"Me?" Aunt Gladys looked up, startled. "I suppose . . . I mean . . ."

That was enough for Alexa. She skipped over to her aunt, grabbed her hand, and pulled her through the curtain.

◆ ◆ ◆

As nervous and jittery as waiting for Mommy was making her feel, Alexa was glad to be back at Aunt Gladys's house. She and Janice had dropped through the laundry chute and walked out into a really nasty-looking hallway. How they had gone from falling straight down to walking calmly through a door, Alexa hadn't known and hadn't really cared. They had gotten away from the horrible old man with the big needle. That was all that mattered.

A moment later, Grampy had come through the door. "Boisterous bunions, that was close! When I saw you'd stumbled into that particular memory, I was afraid I wouldn't get there in time!"

He had then led Alexa and Janice down the nasty, smelly hallway toward another door, first making sure they had a knob with them. He'd gone on to tell them all about his visit with their siblings before asking why that particular door had been destroyed. This had been a little awkward for Alexa, since she still kind of felt it was a little bit her fault, but Janice had been good and blamed it all on Dimitri. This had gotten Grampy's attention and he'd taken Janice aside and said a few things Alexa couldn't hear. Then he'd taken the knob, attached it to the door at the end of the hall, and ushered them through.

Alexa had been needing to go pee pretty much ever since.

"Are you excited to get your memory back, Aunt Gladys?" called Alexa from the bathroom. As Janice had mentioned, there weren't any doors, but Aunt Gladys was helpfully hanging out in the next room.

"My memory? Yes. I think. Also a bit nervous," admitted Aunt Gladys. "I don't really know . . . what I'm like. Well, no. I know who I am. But do I? What if I'm another person? Do I like that person?"

"I liked her," said Alexa.

"Oh."

Aunt Gladys sounded sad. It took Alexa a moment to figure out why, but then she got it. "I like you, too!" she said.

"Oh! That's nice."

"Do you think you'll feel anything? You know, when you change?"

"Change what, dear?"

"You know . . ." Alexa tried to find the right words. "Change back into Aunt Gladys."

It was a couple of seconds before her aunt replied. When she finally did, she sounded even more confused than normal. "Who else would I . . . ? Where are you? Are you going? You're using a potty, yes? Hello? Arthur? No, not Arthur. You're a girl. The little one. Abraham? Where is everyone?"

Alexa clapped her hands excitedly. Mommy had done it!

◆ ◆ ◆

They returned to the central room to find it in chaos.

Mommy was screaming at Dimitri, who was hiding behind Sydney, who was screaming at Zack and Janice, who were screaming right back at Sydney.

Upon entering the room, Aunt Gladys joined in the screaming.

"Charlotte! In this house! How dare you?"

"Miss Gladys!" cried a desperate Dimitri, grasping at a possible lifeline. "Tell sister I no go! I no go!"

"It was you!" accused Mommy, jabbing a finger at the frenetic foreigner. "I saw you!"

"I no go!"

"Out of the way, Sydney!" shouted Janice.

"You're keeping secrets from me!"

"I saw you!"

"Get back, Sydney!"

"I no go!"

"How dare you!"

It was all too much for little Alexa, who couldn't even tell who was screaming at whom anymore. So she went ahead and did the one thing she could think of to calm everybody down.

She screamed herself.

It was louder, higher-pitched, and far more piercing than anyone else's scream, and caused them all to duck down and throw their hands over their ears.

When she was done, Alexa surveyed the scene with satisfaction.

"Better," she said.

"I think you burst my eardrum," muttered Sydney.

"You guys were yelling," she responded.

"Dimitri's been wiping memories!" said Zack.

"Charlotte cannot be in this house!" said Aunt Gladys.

"Zack and Janice are keeping secrets!" said Sydney.

"It's my house, too!" said Mommy.

"We're not keeping secrets!" said Janice.

"I no go!" said Dimitri.

"Do I have to yell again?" warned Alexa.

Everybody was quiet. Alexa enjoyed her little moment but was already feeling uncomfortable, so she walked over to Zack. "What's going on?" she asked.

"Mom did it," he explained. "She went into Aunt Gladys's memory and saw the mustached man luring her away at the carnival. Mom stopped him."

"And Aunt Gladys got her memory back!" deduced Alexa.

"I got a good look at that man, honey," said Mommy. "It was Dimitri, wearing a very obvious fake mustache."

"No! I no go in memory!"

"I know what I saw, Dimitri!"

"It's true, Alexa. Pop-pop warned me about him before sending us back," said Janice. "He'd been having suspicions."

"Is mistake! I no go!"

Alexa frowned and shook her head. It made perfect sense for the big, dumb liar to be the big, dumb bad guy. She crossed her arms. "What do we do with him?" she asked.

"Lock him up and throw away the key," said Sydney, walking away from the condemned man. "Why didn't you guys tell me about this?"

"We weren't sure," said Zack. "We didn't have any proof. I'm sorry."

Sydney nodded, accepting the apology.

"Charlotte?" asked Aunt Gladys, stepping forward. "Is this true? You went into my memories?"

"To save you, Aunt Gladys," said Janice. "To help bring you back."

The two sisters faced each other, years of mistrust lying heavy in the air between them.

"Well, there's that," said Mommy, nodding nervously. "But also . . . Still, it's good . . ." Flustered, she put out her hand.

Aunt Gladys eyed it like it was a venomous snake. "I know why you helped me," she said. "You want Mother's door."

Mommy dropped the hand, not bothering to deny the truth.

"Can we get back to the real issue?" asked Janice. "Locking up Dimitri?"

"Yes!" agreed Alexa. "Put the big, dumb liar away!"

"One question," commented Zack. "Behind what door do we lock him?"

◆ ◆ ◆

In the end, they simply tied Dimitri to a chair in the kitchen.

Bowls of Honey Nut Oat Blast Ring-a-Dings were passed around, and everyone enjoyed a quiet lull after the madness of the past few hours. Alexa, however, was in serious pouting mode. It had become clear that even though Mommy was sitting right next to her (Alexa hadn't let her out of her sight since she'd returned), Alexa and her siblings were still going to live with Aunt Gladys. This did not make Alexa happy.

Now they were all sitting around, more or less waiting for Miss Guacaladilla to show up so Aunt Gladys could sign the papers and make everything official and nobody would have to go live in Uzbekistan.

"Sorry about the cereal," Aunt Gladys was saying. "I'll go to the store. There's a store nearby. I'll go. Buy something besides cereal."

"I'll go with you," volunteered Zack quickly. "I know what my sisters like to eat."

Alexa smiled. She knew Zack just wanted to go shopping. He loved food and was not going to pass up an opportunity to stock the kitchen.

"Char . . . Mom?" asked Sydney timidly. "What was it like? Going into Aunt Gladys's memory?"

"And how did that fix her?" asked Alexa, curious.

"I unblocked her memories," explained Mommy. "When Dimitri entered my sister's memory of the carnival—"

"I no go!" pleaded the condemned.

"He took her home with him so that she wouldn't be able to remember going home with us. When that happened, her mind chose to cut off access to the rest of her life's memories."

"The mind can't handle a paradox, little Abner," interjected Aunt Gladys. "It blocks any memories that might cause one. They're still there. Just blocked."

"And that's why you couldn't remember anything after the carnival?" Alexa asked, close to sorting it out in her head.

"Everything after the carnival was dependent on Gladys coming home with us," confirmed Mommy. "So her mind cut off access to those memories. When I went in there and stopped Dimitri from kidnapping her, she was free to come home with the rest of us, and her mind released the rest of her life's memory because the paradox was gone."

"Was it weird being back there?" asked Sydney. "Did you see yourself?"

Their mother swallowed a mouthful of cereal and set her spoon down. "No," she replied. "I had just thrown up all over my sister's dress—"

"Oh! I remember that!" exclaimed Aunt Gladys.

"And Father had taken me to the first aid tent. I wasn't around. Thankfully."

"Why thankfully?" asked Janice.

Charlotte didn't answer. Alexa looked up to find her staring off into space.

"Is it dangerous?" asked Alexa.

"Is what dangerous?" asked Mommy, blinking back into the present.

"Meeting yourself in somebody else's memory," said Janice.

Mommy stared at Janice in confusion. "What are you talking about?" She looked around the room, quite obviously growing more and more alarmed.

"When you went into Aunt Gladys's memory a few hours ago," said Janice.

"Who?" she asked.

Alexa looked over to Janice, worried. Janice, in turn, looked at Zack.

"Mom?" he said. "Are you okay?"

"I'm your mother?" she replied.

"Mommy? Mommy!" Alexa tugged at her mother's sleeve, her heart sinking.

Mommy climbed off her chair, shaking her head and growing agitated. "Who are you people? Where am I? What's going on?"

"No, no, no!" Sydney jumped off her chair. "Aunt Gladys! They got Mom! What are we going to do?"

In the silence that followed, all four Rothbaum children swiveled their heads about to stare in horror at their aunt, who stared back, equally horrified.

"Who are you?" she whispered. "What are you doing in my house?"

Alexa allowed a single tear to fall from her eye. Both her mother and her aunt were gone.

◆ ACT THREE ◆

Opening the Door

◆ CHAPTER TWENTY-NINE ◆

Zack Drops the Bomb

"MOM? AUNT GLADYS?" SYDNEY'S VOICE ROSE WITH EACH syllable, and Zack watched the imminent RAGE build to a head. "You know us, right? Tell me you know us!"

"I've never seen you!" said their mother, raising her hands up as if to stop a slobbering puppy from licking her face. "Leave me alone!"

"How is this possible?" asked Janice. "They were fine five seconds ago!"

Sydney lurched over to Dimitri. "What did you do to them? Bring them back!"

"I no go!" cried the hysterical man. "I no go!"

"Bring them back!" repeated the increasingly frantic girl. The RAGE was boiling over. Zack knew they were moments away from it turning ugly.

"Sydney," he called, trying to stuff the genie back in the bottle. "Sydney, stop. It wasn't him!"

"Bring! Them! Back!" She shoved Dimitri hard in the chest, her pent-up anxiety giving her just enough strength to tip the poor man backward.

"Sydney! No!" Zack ran forward to catch Dimitri before he fell.

Too late.

The chair balanced on its back legs for an instant, before slowly teetering to the ground with a solid clunk.

"That looked painful," said Aunt Gladys.

"You kids are monsters!" cried Charlotte, taking another step away from everybody.

Zack kneeled down next to the now-prone Dimitri, who was still tied to the chair. "Dimitri, are you all right?"

"I fine," assured the accosted man, bringing a sigh of relief from Zack. "I lie down now. Is comfortable."

"Are you happy, Sydney?" Zack snapped.

"He took their memories!" she accused.

Zack stood and glared at his headstrong sister. "No, he didn't! He was right here the whole time," he said, gesturing down at Dimitri.

"But he went back and . . ."

"That's not how it works," said Janice. "Time passes in there the same as it does out here. Whatever happened to take their memories, it just happened. Just now. While we were all sitting in here, including Dimitri. So Dimitri couldn't have done it."

"I no go," repeated Dimitri from the floor.

"But he's a big, dumb liar," protested Alexa.

"Maybe," agreed Zack. "But he didn't take their memories. Not this time, at least."

"Then who did?" asked Sydney.

No one had an answer.

"Sorry to interrupt," said Aunt Gladys after a moment. "I have some questions. Little things. Who are you? Where am I? What's going on? Finally, may I eat this?" She pointed down at the bowl of Honey Nut Oat Blast Ring-a-Dings in front of her.

Zack nodded, then turned to his mother. "You probably have the same questions?" he asked.

"Aside from eating the cereal, yes," she admitted.

"What are we going to do, Zack?" asked Janice.

It was a good question. Did they go back into the MemorySphere and try to fix everyone again? How? They had no idea where to look, what door to hook up, whose memory to enter. For that matter, how did both their mother and aunt go blank at the same time? Didn't changes in the MemorySphere only affect the owner of the memory?

Fortunately, Zack was spared the need to answer Janice's question right then.

Because a more immediate problem arrived.

"Hello? Hello? Is anybody home or has something absolutely terrible happened?"

"Oh, no," breathed Sydney. "Miss Guacaladilla."

The ever-tearful social worker rounded the corner,

followed by two very large, very burly, and very grim-looking men. "I'm so, so sorry to have entered without an invitation, but the wall was open." She tried to smile at everyone, but the effort proved too difficult for her to manage. Dropping her gaze to the floor, she spotted Dimitri. "That man is lying on the floor, tied to a chair," she stated matter-of-factly. "Have we come at a bad time?"

Zack could only gawk, jaw hanging open and mind empty. He soon became aware, however, that most, if not all, of the eyeballs in the room were pointed more or less in his direction. So he carefully closed his mouth and said the first thing that came to his head.

"Huh."

"We found Mommy!" exclaimed Alexa, weaving through legs to reach her mother's side.

"Oh?" Miss Guacaladilla's eyebrows rose along with her voice.

Charlotte, however, stepped away from her youngest daughter. "Oh, no you don't!" she said. "I'm not anyone's mother."

"But . . . but . . ." Alexa's lips quivered.

"She . . . has amnesia," explained Zack.

"Another one?" asked Miss Guacaladilla. "First your aunt, now your own mother doesn't remember you? How horrible! How tragic! You children have been chosen to suffer!" Tears dribbled uncontested down her cheek.

"Not to mention the fire," added Janice quietly. Zack

threw Sydney a look, realizing they'd yet to tell their sisters exactly who had started that fire. Sydney shook her head slowly, her meaning clear.

"Oh, the fire! The fire!" screeched Miss Guacaladilla. "You mentioned it!" She dissolved into hysterics and had to be comforted by one of the two very large, very burly, and very grim-looking men who pounded on her back, apparently not very good at comforting people.

Alexa, meanwhile, continued to look up at her mother, her lips still quivering. "Please, Mommy?" she breathed. "Please?"

"I'm . . . sorry," responded Charlotte, seeming to melt just a little in the face of Alexa's shockingly heart-wrenching plea.

"Well!" Miss Guacaladilla gave one huge sniff and dabbed her pinkies under her eyes. "Do you have the marriage certificate?" she finally asked, addressing Dimitri on the floor.

"Dimitri tied up right now," he answered.

"Yes, I see that. It's horrible!"

"Is okay," he said.

"We haven't had a chance to find it yet," said Zack, stepping in. "Things have been a little crazy around here."

Miss Guacaladilla's face scrunched up sadly, her lips thrusting out into official pouting position. "Oh no! Without that certificate . . . I can't . . . legally . . ." She squeezed out a few squeaks of misery. Behind her, the two very large, very burly, and very grim-looking men shuffled their feet impatiently.

"But they're married! Really, they are!" claimed Janice.

"Without proof . . ." The waterlogged social worker shook her head. "I can't legally leave you children here to live among strangers."

"This is our family!" stressed Sydney.

"But they don't know that, dear," said Miss Guacaladilla as patiently as if she were trying to explain algebra to a confused ferret. "And with your father still in a coma, I'm afraid there's no one else to take care of you."

"But Dimitri—" began Zack.

"Is not legally family. Not without a marriage certificate. Plus he's currently tied to a chair, which, frankly, is not proper parental behavior. I'm afraid you four will have to come with me."

Zack's stomach dropped. This wasn't happening. A few minutes ago, they had been reunited with their mother and gotten their aunt back, and their fortunes had seemed on the upswing. How had it gone so bad so quickly?

"Are you sending us to Uzbekistan?" asked Alexa.

"I'm so sorry, but the Uzbekistanian family has been scooped up by a lucky little orphan from Barberville who lost her parents in a blimp accident. I'm afraid there will be no pool for any of you." She closed her eyes and shuddered, as if not going to live in Uzbekistan was the worst thing to have ever happened to them. "However, there is a new family who lives in the jungles of Uruguay. They are near a river. Which one of you is the strongest swimmer?"

"You're sending these children to South America?" asked Charlotte.

"One of them. If we act quickly. This Uruguayan family is a hot property and won't be on the market long."

Zack watched his mother struggle internally with the situation. He knew deep down she was a good person, and he could see the wheels turning. Unfortunately, he knew they wouldn't turn fast enough.

"We should be going," declared Miss Guacaladilla. "Children, collect your things. If you've anything heavy, ask Gonzo or Pixie to carry it for you." She gestured to the two very large, very burly, and very grim-faced men. Neither of whom looked like either a Gonzo or a Pixie.

"No!" screamed Sydney. "No, no, no!" She ran forward and kicked one of the very large, very burly, and very grim-faced men in the shin. He didn't react.

"Sydney, stop it!" snapped Janice, pulling her sister away.

"Let go of me! I don't want to go to Uruguay!"

"I'm so sorry to hear that, dear!" sobbed Miss Guacaladilla. "But we can always send one of your siblings down there instead. Perhaps little Alexa. I think she'd enjoy the jungle."

Alexa crossed her arms defiantly in response to the suggestion that she'd like to live in the jungle.

"You can't take us away!" shouted Sydney. "This is our family!"

Zack was impressed by the strength of Sydney's passion

but saw determination in the tear-soaked eyes of the social worker. She was not going to be dissuaded.

"They really have to be taken away?" asked Charlotte again.

"I'm afraid so," answered Miss Guacaladilla. "Though it pains me to no end. Though my heart breaks for these unfortunate urchins. Though every fiber in my being tells me that ripping them away from one another is wrong. The law is, sadly, the law."

"Zack!" cried a very desperate Janice. "Do something!"

And there it was. The plea. Zack's mind churned into overdrive. There had to be a way to fix this. A way to save his sisters.

A plan slowly took shape.

"Gonzo, Pixie, would you please help these miserable little darlings?" asked Miss Guacaladilla. "They may need some encouragement."

Gonzo and Pixie smirked in a very un–social worker way. Zack quickly held up his hand.

"No, it's okay. We'll go," he said.

"What?" asked Janice.

"What?" asked Alexa.

"Are you crazy?" asked Sydney.

"She's right," continued Zack, slapping the pieces of his plan together on the fly. "We're just kids. We need adult supervision."

"I don't need—" began Sydney.

"Yes, you do," interrupted Zack. "Now we're going to go

gather. Our. Things." He looked Sydney in the eye and narrowed his brow, praying she'd play along.

"Gather . . . our things," she repeated.

"Exactly," he said, breathing a slight sigh of relief.

"Oh, I am so, so pleased to hear you say that," said Miss Guacaladilla. "Gonzo and Pixie will help—"

"We don't have anything heavy," said Zack, walking backward to the refrigerator. "First, we should probably empty the fridge."

"Huh?" asked Janice, fully aware that the only things in the fridge were dozens of large jugs of milk.

"Yes," continued Zack. "Sydney, could you come here and help me? Janice, too."

"I'll go outside and make some calls," said a very relieved Miss Guacaladilla, who nonetheless somehow managed to still be crying. "I get no reception in this place. If I act quickly, I should be able to put a hold on Uruguay."

She pulled out her cell phone and left the room, making Zack's plan that much easier to implement.

Janice and Sydney joined him at the fridge, as did Alexa, who was no dummy and figured something was going on. Aunt Gladys remained sitting at the counter, and their mother stood against the wall, frowning. Gonzo and Pixie had stepped back and were very blatantly guarding the doorway leading to the entry hall and outside. No child was going to slip past them and escape.

Which was fine with Zack, because he wasn't planning on running in that direction.

He pulled the fridge door open just as his sisters joined him.

"What are we doing?" whispered Sydney.

"Grab jugs," whispered Zack right back.

Zack, Janice, and Sydney each crouched down and grabbed two large milk jugs, shielding their action with their bodies. Zack had worked everything out in his head. There was one loose end, but time had run out, so all he could do was hope. He took a breath, let it out, then nodded.

"Now!"

As one, the three children hurled their milk jugs at the feet of Gonzo and Pixie. The jugs burst upon impact, sending waves of creamy milk splattering all over the two men's severe-looking black slacks.

"Hey! No fair!" yelled one of the men.

"Milk bombs!" yelled the other.

"To the central room!" yelled Zack. "Go!"

His sisters ran out of the kitchen at full speed.

"No you don't!" yelled Gonzo and Pixie in unison. They each took a menacing step forward in preparation for breaking into a run, but their feet slipped out from under them with their first step on the milk-covered floor, and they fell down on their bums.

"Mom! Aunt Gladys! Come on!" yelled Zack, hoping against hope.

Charlotte Rothbaum and Gladys Tulving looked up, surprised at Zack's urgent cry.

"We need Dimitri!" he said. "Please!"

"Yes. Is sticky now," said Dimitri from the floor.

Gonzo and Pixie were struggling to their feet. Time was running out. Would the two women help?

Yes.

Without another word, the sisters hurried to Dimitri's side and picked him up—chair and all. Zack soared in elation. This was going to work! "This way!" he cried, leading the two women down the hall toward the hatch and the portal room beyond.

Behind them, the two very large, very burly, very grim-faced, and now very milk-splattered men managed to get to their feet.

The chase was on.

Luckily, Zack's milk bombardment had given his family enough of a head start. He ushered his mother and aunt through the door, then quickly pulled it closed. "There's no lock!" he cried. "Mom, Aunt Gladys! We need you to hold this door closed!"

Not bothering to argue, they set Dimitri down (sitting up) and returned to the door, grasping the wheel and planting their feet.

"Zack, what now?" asked Janice.

"We go back in!" he answered, running over to the computers.

"Finally! Some action!" said Sydney, clapping her hands together eagerly.

"Dimitri! Which buttons do I press?" asked Zack.

"Blue lever left! Press black button! Third row! Second from right! Twist knob!"

Zack's hands froze above the endless rows of dials, knobs, switches, and buttons. "I don't . . . I don't understand!"

"They're pulling the door open!" yelled Charlotte as she and Aunt Gladys strained against the combined strength of Gonzo and Pixie.

"Black button!" continued Dimitri. "Fourth knob! Is clockwise!"

It was no use. Zack couldn't figure it out. His plan was going to fail after all.

And then Janice was there.

"Move," she grunted. Zack gladly stepped away as she went to work on the controls, guided by Dimitri's instructions.

"That's still Aunt Gladys's door," observed Sydney. "Won't it just take us to that carnival from years ago?"

"There's no time to switch it out for a different one," said Zack. "Besides, as soon as we enter, Gramps will know. He'll find us."

"We can't hold them much longer!" warned their mother.

"This is so exciting!" yelled Aunt Gladys.

And then Janice twisted the dial that looked like any other dial, and the machine sprang to life with a mechanical cough, followed by an electric sizzle, followed by an unidentifiable sound from somewhere below. There was the expected flash, followed by bright blue sparks of energy wrapping themselves around the door, followed by the entire frame buzzing excitedly for a moment before settling into a quiet drone so soft as to suggest a return to silence.

"Is good! You go now!" urged Dimitri.

Janice grabbed a rubber glove, ran to the platform, and pulled the door open. Blinding white light poured forth from within, searing everyone with its intensity.

"Go!" yelled Zack. Sydney grabbed Janice's hand and dashed through.

"Wait!" Alexa ran back to the bank of computers, pulled open a drawer, and grabbed a doorknob.

"Good thinking, Alexa!" commended Zack gratefully.

There was a sudden crash and the door was yanked open, sending the two valiant women to the floor.

"Stop!" yelled one of the very large, very burly, very grim-faced, and very milk-covered men.

"I don't think you're collecting your things!" yelled the other.

Zack grabbed Alexa's hand, and together they raced into the dazzling white.

◆ CHAPTER THIRTY ◆

Janice Gets Cozy with a Foot

THE CARNIVAL WAS NOT WHAT JANICE HAD EXPECTED.

She had imagined sunshine, brightly colored tents, and carnival barkers offering to guess her weight. Instead, the four children walked into a dark, misty labyrinth of canvas and plywood that smelled like a mixture of Zack's gym socks and a rotting pumpkin.

"I thought this was a happy place," commented Alexa.

"I think it's safe to say this memory has spoiled," answered Zack. "We should get out of here as quickly as possible. Look around for any doorways a young Aunt Gladys wouldn't have walked through."

They inched their way through the ominous maze of carnival trappings. Janice's sense of neatness rebelled at the truly haphazard way the canvas flats bordering the lane hung just slightly off-kilter, and she found herself itching to straighten them as she crept along, the way twisting and turning back on itself like a confused snake. A number of tent flaps beckoned, but none presented the telltale blankness signaling a way out of this oppressive memory. It seemed as though Aunt Gladys had ducked into every tent she came across all those years ago.

"Is anyone else thoroughly disgusted by how squishy this ground feels?" asked Sydney.

Janice yanked her attention away from the uneven walls to look down at her feet. Her sister was right—the ground seemed to almost swallow up the soles of their shoes. Yet it was not muddy. Rather, the dewy grass seemed to wrap itself around their feet as they walked, each step causing them to sink just a little bit farther into the earth.

The children continued their search until the narrow track spat them out onto the larger, main thoroughfare of the carnival. Suddenly, the unending and unyielding walls of canvas and plywood gave way to a horrific vision of pure circus evil. Patrons lurched along like eager zombies, even emitting a subconscious moan or two as they walked. Large tents that might once have been brilliantly colored punctured the landscape, the faded browns and greens and purples of their former glory bleeding down their sides. Vendors cackled from behind moldy, fungus-encrusted carts offering who-knew-what.

In the midst of it all, a loudly dressed man wearing a

huge bow tie stood in a large wooden tub of water, calling out to anyone and everyone. "Step right up, ladies and gentlemen! Let your dreams become reality! Be ye young or old, short or tall, fat or thin, living or dead or in between, your destiny awaits!"

"Why are you standing in a tub of water?" asked Janice, whose eyelid twitched at the very thought.

"A better question," said the man, flashing a toothy smile at her, "is why aren't you?"

Janice didn't think that was a better question at all. "Which way?" she asked her siblings, glancing up and down the fairway and trying to ignore the man's shiny, overly energetic smile.

"Should we split up?" asked Sydney.

"Absolutely not," answered Zack.

"That way looks more kid-friendly," said Janice, pointing toward the sound of what could only be a merry-go-round, though its song was slightly slurred, as if it was playing just a bit too slowly.

"Right," said Zack. "Then that's not the way we want to go."

The others agreed and shuffled away from the siren call of the demented merry-go-round. Behind them, the man in the tub of water called out, "Venture forth, young ones! The carnival awaits! I can already tell you will make excellent additions to the gallery!"

Janice stopped and turned around. "What does that

mean?" she asked. Something in the way the man stood in his tub of water smiling at them sent a shiver down her spine. "What gallery?"

"The Glorious Gallery of the Grotesque!" replied the man with a flourish, his hands rolling and waving in the air. "Where all the carnival's oddities are stored! In my experience, there is little in this most marvelous world more gloriously odd than four miserable orphans! I can't wait to see you on display!"

"Wait. What?" asked Janice.

The odd man made a motion as if tipping his hat toward them—though he wasn't wearing one—then sank down into the tub with a small splash. Janice blinked, quite certain she hadn't just seen what she had, in fact, just seen.

"Uhhh . . . guys?" she warned.

The others turned around. "Where'd the circus dork go?" asked Sydney.

Janice didn't trust herself to answer that particular question, so she stuck to what she felt was even more disturbing. "He said something about putting us all on display."

"Display? What, like an attraction?" asked Zack, confused.

"A permanent attraction!" yelped a frizzy-haired guy popping up from behind a garbage can directly in front of them.

"Folks will line up for miles to see ya!" sneered an old woman who suddenly appeared behind a small cart to their left selling something called a Fro-Yo-Blo.

"You'll be famous!" cackled an impossibly flexible woman

hanging upside down from the branches of a tree on their right.

Alexa, who had backed toward the tree when the Fro-Yo-Blo crone had appeared, gave a yelp and dashed away just as the freaky upside-down lady made a swipe for her hair.

"Alexa!" yelled Zack, grabbing her and sweeping her up into his arms.

"Awwww," purred the voice of the man in the tub of water. "Is someone being bashful? This is your big break!"

Janice spun around, searching for the source of his voice, then stopped and stared in abject horror as he slowly rose up from the ground directly behind them, like some Greek god rising out of the ocean. Except he was rising out of the disturbingly squishy grass, which should not have been possible.

"You were born to die here," he said, the toothy smile never wavering from his newly formed face.

Janice screamed.

"Run!" yelled Zack.

The Rothbaum children ran.

With fully grown carnival freaks on either side and in front of them, the children chose the path of least resistance and ran back the way they'd come while the loudly dressed carnival barker was still only a head and torso. The man/creature/nightmare snapped at them with his teeth as they passed but was easily avoided. Sydney even went out of her way to step on the top of his head as she ran.

"Gumph!" he complained. "How rude!"

The children ran past the labyrinth from which they'd come and hurtled toward the ominous sound of the lethargic merry-go-round. Around them, the carnival came alive, snarling and growling at them. Arms rose up from the grass to grab at their ankles. Faces formed just long enough to stick out their tongues and blow raspberries at them. Legs popped up and sort of flailed uselessly in the air.

Still the children ran.

"Look for doors!" cried Zack. "Anything we can attach the knob to! We have to get out of here!"

Though she couldn't argue with his logic, Janice worried that if they left the MemorySphere now, they'd never get a chance to come back. Miss Guacaladilla would be waiting for them on the other side, and they'd be trucked off to the four corners of the earth.

There had to be a better way.

Think, Janice, she implored herself, easily dodging a hand rising up from the grass, hoping to snatch her heels. *Where would little Aunt Gladys not go?*

Her attention was diverted when Sydney gave a sudden yelp, her foot having crashed into a half-formed forehead in her path. Janice's usually graceful little sister gyrated her arms wildly in an attempt to keep her balance while stumbling forward. (The forehead she'd kicked was left behind to quietly develop a serious lump, not yet having formed a mouth with which to cry out in pain.)

The others could only watch in horror as Sydney awkwardly lost the battle with gravity and slid face-first into the grass, skidding forward a foot or two until yanked to a stop by dozens of hands suddenly growing out of the earth. "Sydney!" Zack yelled, doubling back.

Janice joined her brother, and they began stomping on an unending supply of fingers (and, here and there, the odd toe), trying to give Sydney a chance to get back to her feet. But for every thumb they squashed, two more sprang up around their prone sister.

"Looks like we have our first specimen!" cheered a set of lips off to the side in what sounded like the voice of the guy in the tub of water.

"Let my sister go!" snarled Alexa, stomping on the lips with all her might.

As satisfying as it was to see her little sister squash those lips (they very quickly swelled from the blow), Janice was growing desperate. Despite all that she and Zack were doing, more and more hands and arms, a couple of legs, and, for some reason, one pair of buttocks were yanking Sydney down into the grass. Her arms pinned to her sides, Sydney could only cry out in a muffled scream of RAGE, which unfortunately wasn't helping to set her free.

Suddenly, Janice looked up, eyes alight with inspiration. "Keep stomping!" she ordered.

Before Zack could ask what she was doing, Janice dropped to her knees, grabbed one of the feet sticking out of the ground, and began tickling the bottom.

The reaction was instantaneous.

"Oooh! Ha-ha! Stop! Ooooh, stop! Gaaa!"

A number of different mouths sputtered and laughed, and the leg in her hands spasmed, kicking out.

"Brilliant, Janice!" cheered Zack. "Keep going!"

Janice held on and grimly continued tickling with a fevered intensity. One by one, the hands let go of Sydney and flailed about in response to Janice's tickling.

"Gah! Stop! Oooh! No fair! Gee-hee!"

Zack grabbed Sydney by the arm and dragged her out of the grasp of the few fingers still holding her. "Got her!" he cried.

"Go!" yelled Janice, dropping the foot. All four ran with a renewed urgency, while the twitching hands and fingers sank into the earth behind them.

"That was not nice!" crooned the creepy tub man, popping up from behind a clump of balloons, his voice far more menacing than before. "We were hoping you'd join us willingly, but if you're gonna be nasty, two can play at that game!"

A massive wall of grotesque, half-formed people rose out of the grass as the children reached a central courtyard. Four lanes dumped into the circle, and the sickly, demented merry-go-round sat in the middle, its haunting melody getting under their skin and giving each child a serious case of the willies. The grass-formed creatures cut off all avenues of escape, and slowly but surely closed in on the Rothbaums. Not having any other choice, the children hopped up onto the disturbing merry-go-round.

"What do we do?" asked Alexa.

Zack opened his mouth to answer, but one of the horses

on the merry-go-round bent its head and snapped its jaws at him. Everyone screamed as more and more of the supposedly inanimate animals came to life around them. Janice ducked as a unicorn whipped its horn above her head, then she rolled under a newly animated ostrich and found herself staring at the center of the ride.

And she got an idea.

"Guys! Over here!" Janice hopped into the center of the ride and out of reach of the various merry-go-round animals, which, amazingly, remained locked in place by the poles attaching them to the ride. Seeing this, her siblings quickly joined her in the center. "There's always a room in the middle! Aunt Gladys couldn't have gone in there!"

Without a word, the others quickly scoured the central base of the ride, running their hands along the walls in search of a hidden door. Finally, Zack shoved on a painted tiger and a section of the inner wall swung inward, revealing black nothing beyond.

"Here!" he cried.

With the merry-go-round animals' snarls and growls echoing in their ears, the four Rothbaums squeezed through the narrow opening and escaped the cacophonous carnival once and for all.

High atop the tallest tent of the carnival, someone watched them disappear.

CHAPTER THIRTY-ONE

Sydney Readies a RAGE

SYDNEY DID A FACE-PLANT IN THE DIRT.

It hurt, but not as much as when Zack landed on top of her a moment later.

"Ahhrgh!" she hollered. "Get off!"

"Sorry, Sydney," said Zack, rolling off and getting to his feet.

Sydney sat up and wiped the back of her hand across her face. "Where are we?" she asked.

"Who cares?" said Janice. "It's not that carnival."

Sydney agreed. That place had been terrifying. And totally, utterly wrong.

She took in their new surroundings. They were in a pleasant-looking meadow surrounding a peaceful little lake. The sun shone down, warming the grass (normal-looking grass rather than that soul-sucking stuff in the carnival memory) and making the normal yellowish film over everything seem a little brighter. Looking behind her, she noted that their entrance into this memory had been through a weathered old window missing its glass, which explained the short fall onto the dirt. The window belonged to a rambling old wooden shack sitting in the middle of the meadow.

"Everyone okay?" asked Zack.

The girls all mumbled in the affirmative, dusting themselves off and taking a moment to enjoy the feel of the sun on their faces—a nice change from the gloomy, oppressive darkness of the carnival. The children ambled away from the shack, unconsciously putting as much distance as they could between themselves and the entrance to the most recent memory. Soon, they found themselves at the edge of the lake. It was small, clear, and placid. Sydney was surprised to see her reflection in the water so clearly. She hoped it was somewhat distorted, because she didn't look very good.

"Do you think we can drink this?" asked Janice.

"Probably shouldn't," said Zack. "And I'd say that even if this wasn't a memory."

Alexa, meanwhile, had removed her shoes and was carefully dipping her toes in the water. "It's cold!" she exclaimed.

"Yeah," said Zack, carefully grabbing her arm and pulling her out of the water. "Let's stay dry for the moment, okay? Put your shoes back on."

Sydney smiled to herself, observing Zack watch over Alexa. It was a refreshing, if small, slice of normal amid this impossible madness.

"Hey, guys," said Janice. "Who's that?"

She pointed across the lake, where a small figure could be seen waving his or her arms, trying to get their attention.

"It's someone real," observed Sydney. "They're not yellow."

"Grampy!" squealed Alexa, breaking out of Zack's grasp and racing around the edge of the lake in her bare feet.

"Alexa! Wait!" called Zack. "We don't know if it's him!"

"Of course it is!" she called back.

Zack, Janice, and Sydney raced after their youngest sister (Zack first grabbing Alexa's shoes). Across the lake, the figure stopped waving and started circling the water as well, though in more of a quickened walk than a run. Before long, it became apparent that Alexa's hunch was correct, and the others breathed a little easier. Marcus Tulving lumbered along the shore, finally stopping and bending over to catch his breath as Alexa reached him.

"Grampy!" she cheered, jumping up into his arms. Unfortunately, he had not actually extended his arms, so she ended up knocking him over. "Oops! Sorry!"

"Breakfasting baboons, girl!" he muttered, sitting up. "You'll give an old man a heart attack!"

"Hey, Pop-Pop," said Sydney as she and the others arrived. "It's good to see you."

"Is it?" he asked. "That's a first. Why are you here? You shouldn't be here. The MemorySphere isn't a play—"

"They got Mom," said Zack.

"Charlotte?"

"And Aunt Gladys. Again," added Sydney.

The four of them took turns filling their grandfather in on all that had happened out in the real world. When Janice told him about Dimitri's innocence, he frowned and rubbed his chin absently.

"You're sure?" he asked. "That's very strange. Very strange, indeed."

They finished bringing him up to speed with the story of their adventure in the carnival. When they were done, their grandfather stood and paced away for a moment, grumbling to himself and shaking his head. The children waited patiently for him to gather his thoughts. Finally, he gave a big harrumph and rejoined them.

"You're certain Dimitri isn't involved? I could have sworn . . ."

"He was tied to a chair when Mom and Aunt Gladys lost their memories," assured Zack.

"Securely?"

"Double knots," added Sydney with a modest amount of pride. Marcus grunted in approval.

"He's actually been very helpful," said Janice. "Without him, we wouldn't have been able to escape Miss Guacaladilla."

"And he's been taking very good care of Aunt Gladys since she forgot everything," added Zack.

"Yes, he was always fond of her," said their grandfather, rubbing his chin. "My daughters lost their memories at the same time? That's odd. Shouldn't be possible."

"A shared memory?" suggested Sydney. "Something that happened at the same time to both of them?"

"You mean like how Dimitri was in Grampa's memory?" asked Zack.

Marcus looked up sharply. "Wait. What memory?"

"That first memory of yours that you sent us into," explained Sydney. "The one that turned out to be a total death trap." She glanced up at Zack for confirmation that it had been, indeed, a total death trap. He nodded.

"My university laboratory?" pressed their grandfather, suddenly narrowing his eyes and sounding almost spooky.

"Yeah." Sydney didn't like the look crossing her grandfather's face. "What?"

Marcus Tulving leaned back, his face a mask of puzzlement. "Dimitri did not work for me at the university," he said. "He should not have been in that memory."

The kids froze.

"Huh," said Zack.

Sydney struggled to wrap her head around what her grandfather had just announced. "You mean . . ." She failed.

"You're sure it was a memory of Dimitri?" asked Marcus. "Not Dimitri himself?"

"He was yellow," said Zack.

"As yellow as everything else," agreed Sydney, thinking back. There had been something else, too. Something else that hadn't been right.

"That can't be right," stated Marcus, shaking his head. "You must have already jumped into another memory."

"We hadn't left that hallway," said Zack.

Suddenly, Sydney remembered. "Grandfather!" she shouted.

Everyone jumped, startled. "Yes?" asked Marcus.

"That's what he said. In the memory. He called you our grandfather," she explained. "But how could he know that? No matter which memory we were in?"

Sydney watched as everybody digested the implications of her discovery. Zack looked severely troubled. Janice was even more confused. Alexa had given up paying attention and was cautiously dipping her toes into the water.

Suddenly, their grandfather erupted excitedly. "Hibernating hedgehogs!" he cried. "Is it possible?"

"Is what possible, Pop-Pop?" asked Sydney.

Shushing her, Marcus rose to his feet and started mumbling and pacing again.

"Don't shush me," complained Sydney.

"Relax, Sydney," admonished Zack. "We're all stressed out here."

"He shushed me!" she answered defensively, a stress-induced RAGE beginning to boil.

"A lot of good it did," remarked Janice.

"What is that supposed to mean?"

"Don't be such a snot!" said Janice.

"A snot? Seriously?" She turned to Zack. "You're going to let her call me a snot?"

"If the shoe fits," he answered.

The RAGE was about ready to blow. "I am not a snot!"

And that was when Alexa screamed in terror.

◆ CHAPTER THIRTY-TWO ◆

Alexa Dips Her Toe

ALEXA HAD QUICKLY GOTTEN BORED WITH THE CONVERSATION. Grampy had been saying all kinds of nonsense and her brother and sisters had been following along like they understood what he was talking about, so Alexa had figured she might as well duck out and go play in the water.

At first, she settled for getting her toes wet, but when that failed to grab anyone's attention, she decided to roll up her pant legs and wade in ankle-deep. The water felt nice and cool as it lazily lapped against her leg. Mud oozed up between her toes, giving the whole experience a nice, squishy feel. She heard the others fall into a bicker session and had been about to distract them with a good splash when she noticed they weren't alone.

On the other side of the lake, back near that ugly, broken

shack they'd come from, stood a yellow man. Normally, Alexa would have found it odd to see a yellow man on the edge of a small lake, but of course by now she knew his coloring only meant he was a memory. Since he wasn't real, Alexa didn't give him much more thought and again prepared to splash her siblings. But then he did something strange.

He waved.

Do I know him? she asked herself. *He looks a bit familiar.* Not having an answer, Alexa remained curious, watching as he pulled something about the size and shape of a flattened football out of his jacket. She was pretty sure it was not, in fact, a flattened football. It made the hair on the back of her neck stand up, and Alexa immediately felt repulsed. The memory man carefully set the flattened football down at the lake's edge, shooed it into the water, then stood, looked directly at Alexa, and put his finger to his lips in the age-old sign for "Don't tell Mommy."

Alexa, being a big girl and smart enough not to listen to strange memory men when they tell you not to tell Mommy, had been about to turn and yell out to Zack (who would have done just fine as a Mommy stand-in) when she noticed ripples in the, until now, still waters of the lake.

The ripples had started close to the far shore, where the memory man had lowered the flattened football into the water, but they had very quickly expanded outward, growing in both size and intensity. Fascination had held Alexa in place as the edge of the ripples approached. She had been pretty certain about the need to say something or do something or run somewhere but had been unable to resist the oddly soothing effect of watching the ripples float atop the lake.

It wasn't until she'd caught sight of the Nasty, Slithery Something just under the surface of the water at her feet that she broke out of the spell, and it wasn't until the Nasty, Slithery Something had wrapped itself around her ankle that she had the presence of mind to scream.

"Alexa!" shouted Zack, diving past Sydney and Janice and into the water.

The Nasty, Slithery Something yanked Alexa's leg out from under her, and she fell into the water with a splash. Since she was only standing in ankle-deep water, she landed on her rump with the water up to her belly button. But the Nasty, Slithery Something started to drag her out into deeper water, tugging her through the muck a few inches at a time.

"Help!" she screamed.

Zack belly flopped into the lake next to her, the shallowness of the water knocking the wind out of him as he landed. Even so, her big brother reached out and took hold of Alexa's arms as he fell, anchoring her in place.

The Nasty, Slithery Something seemed to understand its prize was no longer such an easy claim, and its spastic tugs grew stronger in response. Alexa struggled against the pull, shoving her free foot deep into the lake bottom for leverage. The Nasty, Slithery Something was stronger, however, and try as she might, Alexa was slowly but surely drawn toward deeper water.

"Guys! Help me!" called Zack, getting to his feet and straining to keep his little sister from being dragged to her death.

The elder Rothbaum girls were at his side before he'd finished his plea, and they quickly joined his efforts to save their sister. Between them, the three children were almost able to match the sheer power of the Nasty, Slithery Something.

Almost, but not quite.

"Help!" screamed Alexa in rising terror as her body ran taut like a rope in a game of tug-of-war. The top of the Nasty, Slithery Something broke the surface of the lake as it clung to her, and it was every bit as nasty and slithery out of the water as it was submerged. It looked like a giant slug, brown and gray and disgusting and covered with tiny little slits all along its skin.

"Hold on!" commanded Zack, straining with all his might.

She tried to do as she was told, but felt her grip slipping slowly out of his hands. With a final gasp, she realized her brother and sisters were going to lose the fight.

"Nobody breathe!" hollered their all-but-forgotten grandfather, stomping his way into the water, holding something in his closed fist.

Alexa didn't understand how not breathing could save her, but she put her faith in Grampy and quickly did as she was told. As did Zack and Janice.

"What do you mean, don't breathe?" asked Sydney, who

would very soon regret not holding her breath. "What are you—?"

With a final lunge, Grampy lurched past the three older kids and tossed whatever was in his fist toward the Nasty, Slithery Something.

A fine black powder floated down through the air onto the slimy skin of the Nasty, Slithery Something. Suddenly, dozens of the narrow slits on the creature opened up and sucked flakes of the powder into its system.

The creature sneezed.

The force of the powerful blast shot Alexa up and over her siblings, landing her on the shore of the lake. Without the Nasty, Slithery Something pulling against them, all three of Alexa's siblings toppled backward—Zack and Janice with a gasp and Sydney with a sneeze. Meanwhile, since every action needed an equal and opposite reaction, the Nasty, Slithery Something jetted uncontrollably backward across the lake in multiple, sneezy bursts.

"What was that?" asked a semi-dazed Janice.

"The powder?" asked Grampy as Sydney continued to sneeze in fits and starts. "Pepper. The creature? I don't have a name for it, but it doesn't belong here."

He quickly ushered everyone out of the water.

"You mean—*achoo!*—in this lake?" asked Sydney, her eyes watering.

"I mean in this memory," replied Grampy. He bent down to a knee next to Alexa. "All good?"

"That was nasty," she answered.

"Yes, they are," he agreed, hauling her to her feet. "We need to leave this memory. Right away. Follow me."

Without waiting for them to respond, he set off away from the lake in the direction of a tiny structure standing alone under a tree.

"What do you mean, it doesn't belong in this memory?" asked Zack, hurrying to catch up. "Where'd it come from?"

"I intend to find out," said Grampy, reaching the tiny structure.

"Is that what I think it is?" asked Janice, eyeing the little building dubiously.

"Could be," he answered. "What do you think it is?"

"An outhouse."

"Then you're right."

"Ew," said Janice.

"What's an outhouse?" asked Alexa.

"An outdoor potty," answered Sydney between sneezes.

"Ew," said Alexa.

"Luckily, whoever's memory this is never used it," said Grampy, opening the door wide to reveal a wall of black. "In you go."

The children hesitated.

"That thing will continue to grow," he explained. "Very soon it will pop out little baby things. Soon this whole memory will be swarming with them." He sighed and took a final look around the picturesque lake. "Shame. I liked it here."

As if in answer, a horrible, gravelly roar bellowed forth from the lake. The children quickly piled into the outhouse.

CHAPTER THIRTY-THREE

Zack Makes the Tough Call

THEY STEPPED OUT OF A STORAGE CLOSET AND INTO A CLASS-room.

Rows of desks faced a chalkboard, and a small, cramped table piled high with paper was tucked into a corner. A jiggly, matronly woman sat perched on a stool by the table, her flabbiness spilling over the top of the stool like muffins too big for the pan.

"Oooh!" she exclaimed upon seeing five strangers appear in her classroom. "Oooh! Have you come for me? I've always known someone would come for me."

"No, ma'am," said Zack, who was very practiced at being nice to teachers. "We haven't come for you."

"One of the children, then?" asked the woman with a quiver that took an extra second to travel all the way around her body. "I can well understand. A few of them are nice and plump."

Zack had no idea what she was talking about but was saved the bother of responding by his grandfather. "Just passing through," spat the old man, leading the children down the aisle to the door.

"Oooh," said the woman, a hint of disappointment in her voice. "Well, if you change your mind . . ." She patted her tummy and returned to her paperwork as they left the room.

Rows of full-sized lockers covered the hallway while pale industrial lighting gloomed down upon a far-too-shiny linoleum floor. Marcus carefully closed the classroom door before turning to his grandchildren and shaking his head.

"She gives me the willies," he said, more to himself than to any of them.

"What was that thing in the water?" asked Zack, ignoring his grandfather's musings and getting right to the point.

"And why'd—*achoo!*—why'd you throw pepper at it?" added Sydney.

"I said don't breathe." Marcus looked up and down the corridor and led them forward. "It's a mucus creature. Lots of nasal passages. Pepper irritates it."

"Where did it come from?" asked Janice, trying to keep up. "That's not real. Nobody 'remembered' it."

"No. It . . . evolved."

"In the MemorySphere?" asked Sydney with a sniffle, her eyes puffy and red.

"In a specific memory," he answered, frowning. "One of the first . . ." His voice trailed off. Zack saw a weariness in his grandfather he hadn't noticed before. He wondered what sort of life the man must have been leading trapped inside the MemorySphere all these years.

"However," snapped Marcus, suddenly back to his usual self, "I've never encountered it elsewhere."

"How'd it find us?" asked Janice.

"The memory man brought it," stated Alexa.

The others turned to look at the diminutive girl who, tired of all the walking, had flumped down onto the floor. As one, they waited for her to elaborate. She didn't.

Finally, Zack cleared his throat. "What memory man, Alexa?"

"The one that put the Nasty, Slithery Something in the lake. Duh."

Everyone just stared. "Huh," said Zack.

"Did you see the memory man?" asked Marcus.

"Sure," answered Alexa. "He waved to me. Then he put something in the lake. Then it swam over and attacked me. It was nasty."

"You mean someone brought that thing to the lake?" asked Janice with rising alarm.

"Not someone," corrected Marcus, growing red with concern. "The memory of someone! Walloping wallabies! I was right!"

"You know who it was?" asked Zack.

"Yes! Dimitri!" declared Marcus.

"No, Dimitri's innocent," said Janice. "Remember? He was tied to a chair."

"The real Dimitri, yes. But not his memory! Pliable penguins! The implications!"

Marcus at once set off on another back-and-forth pacing binge, mumbling and muttering to himself as his mind worked.

"I don't understand," confessed Janice.

"I think I understand," said Sydney. "I'm just not sure I believe it."

Zack tried to put it together in his mind. Was it possible? Could a memory of the quirky foreigner have been acting on its own? How?

"Why would Dimitri want to hurt us?" asked Alexa.

"Not Dimitri," reminded Sydney. "A memory of him."

"But he'd still be Dimitri, wouldn't he?" she asked.

"Not necessarily," said Marcus, returning from his mini jaunt. "He'd be of this world. The MemorySphere. And dangerous. If I'm right, he'd be very, very dangerous."

Zack was not thrilled with his grandfather's tone. "Why?" he asked.

"Because I think I know where he came from," answered a very guilty Marcus Tulving. "The same place that creature came from."

He swept a hollow gaze across his grandchildren, filling them all with dread.

"My wife's memory."

◆ ◆ ◆

"Your grandmother was a wonderful woman," remarked Marcus. He sat on one side of a table in the school cafeteria, with Zack and his sisters on the other. "Beautiful. Warm. Generous. Loving."

"Mom said you abandoned her," said Sydney, rubbing her eyes dry.

"Did she? Yes, I suppose she would. She didn't understand. Refused to understand."

"What happened?" asked Zack, trying to keep his grandfather on track.

"Agatha grew ill. Pneumonia. Nothing could be done. I lost her."

The children teared up over the loss of the grandmother they had never known.

"I was devastated. She was my life. But I had been so focused on my work. . . ." He sighed and wiped a tear from his eye. "It was Charlotte's idea, to use her mother's door. She hooked it up without telling me. While I was grieving. She visited . . . so many times." He stopped and put on his best "studious professor" face. "You understand what happens? When you enter and exit a memory over and over again?"

"We do," answered Zack with a shiver. The others nodded.

Marcus fidgeted in his seat and rubbed his hand across

the back of his neck. "Dimitri told me what she was doing. I went down there to stop her, but she was already inside. We followed. Dimitri and Gladys and I. It was a nightmare."

He stood and turned away, as if not looking at them would make the story easier to tell. "Agatha was . . . a monster. Those things were everywhere. And worse. She was worse. She was . . ." He turned back to face them. "I loved your grandmother. Have I said that?"

"Yes," answered Zack.

"It's true. I loved her. More than anything. But this . . . this was not Agatha. This was an abomination. Charlotte didn't see. She was blinded by love. But we saw. And we acted. Dragged Charlotte out of there. Shoved her through the door."

He stopped his narration, a puzzled look on his face.

"Twice."

The children perked up at this odd remark.

"Twice?" asked Alexa. "That's silly."

Marcus nodded. "I can't explain it. But we shoved her out the door. And then shoved her out the door again. Then I left. And then I left again. As soon as Dimitri was through, I slammed the door shut. We barely escaped with our sanity. Charlotte was furious. Ran off later that night. Never came back." He shuffled absently away, lost in his own thoughts.

Something about the story seemed off to Zack, but he couldn't quite put his finger on it.

Sydney, however, figured it out. "Dimitri only came out once," she said.

Marcus lowered himself onto a cafeteria bench, which for some reason had the consistency of Jell-O, bits of it squirting out from under his bottom. "I never really thought about it. But you're right. He only came out once."

"One Dimitri escaped," said Zack. "But the other . . ."

"Oh, dear Lord," murmured Janice in horror. "Trapped inside that nightmare."

"With nowhere to go," added Marcus quietly, a subtly comic squishy sound coming from his uncomfortable shifting about on the Jell-O bench. "I dropped my research for years. Opened no new doors. Added no new memories to the MemorySphere."

"And all that time . . . ," breathed Sydney.

"All that time," confirmed Marcus, "he would have been trapped among the few initial memories, the entire MemorySphere—his whole world—souring into a nightmarish prison."

A stunned silence echoed throughout the dumbfounded cafeteria. The children, who had experienced only fleeting moments of terror within the MemorySphere, went cold at the thought of spending years in a nightmare.

"He must hate you," observed Zack.

"Undoubtedly," agreed Marcus.

"But he's just a memory, isn't he?" asked Janice, determined to make some sense of it all.

"He's much more than that," assured their grandfather. "A sentient being? Born in here? Who knows what his limitations may be? Or if he even has any?"

"That's why he was able to switch out Mom's and Aunt Gladys's memories at the same time?" asked Sydney.

Marcus slowly nodded, putting it all together himself. "He can go anywhere. Once you have a memory of your own hooked into the MemorySphere, you're at his mercy."

"We'll never get Mom or Aunt Gladys back," realized Zack. "Anything we do, he can undo."

"What? No!" cried Sydney. "We have to get them back. We can't just abandon them!"

"We have to save Mommy!" urged Alexa. "And Aunt Gladys! They're our family!"

"There has to be a way to fix them," said Janice. "Maybe we can talk to this Memory Dimitri."

"And say what?" asked Zack. "'Sorry you were driven insane by our family years ago, but would you mind making everything all better for us?'"

Janice bit her lip and didn't answer. *Because there is no good answer,* thought Zack. *This Memory Dimitri obviously has it in for us.* Which left one alternative.

"We need to stop him," he said.

"How do we do that?" asked Sydney.

"We go to the source. Stop him from ever being created."

Marcus shot up in panic. "No! Very bad idea! You can't go into that memory!"

"We have to," insisted Zack.

"It's too dangerous! Those things! And Agatha! No. Out of the question."

"Is there any other way?" pressed Zack.

306

Marcus rose to his full height, suddenly seeming far larger and more intimidating than he had before. "That memory is not for you. It is evil. I went back in there when I first locked myself in here. I barely survived. Do you understand? I barely survived! And I'm an adult! What are you? Ten?"

"Eleven," mumbled Zack.

"I'm seven!" said Alexa proudly.

"Out of the question!" roared their grandfather. "The MemorySphere is . . . ! You shouldn't even be here! Any of you! Give me your doorknob—you're going home!"

He extended his hand expectantly.

"We can't go back—" began Sydney.

"You don't have a knob?" His eyes and nostrils flared with fury.

"I got it! I got it!" Alexa quickly pulled the knob out of her pocket and offered it to Marcus, shaking in fear the entire time.

He snatched it from her hands and marched to the door leading back into the school hallway. "You're all leaving!" he announced. "This instant!"

"They'll send us all away," complained Janice. "Split us up."

"I don't wanna move to Uruguay," complained Alexa.

Marcus reached the door and smacked the knob hard against the wood. The children all heard and felt that odd clicking sensation as the knob settled into place. "I'm . . . sorry," he said hesitantly. "But . . . there's no other way."

"We'll never see each other again," pleaded Janice.

"At least you'll be alive. And sane," finished Marcus, who then yanked the door open, showering the cafeteria with bright white light.

Zack shielded his eyes from the intense glare. "You're our grandfather," he said. "Our only hope."

But Marcus simply shook his head. "There's no hope for you in here."

Zack turned to survey his sisters. Janice was a wilted mess, Alexa was on the verge of tears, and Sydney was working herself up into a serious RAGE. A RAGE that would serve no purpose but to permanently scar their family. He knew what he had to do.

"Come on, guys."

He took Alexa's hand and gently led her to the beckoning whiteness.

"Zack, we can't just quit!" said Sydney, her face growing even redder than it already was.

"It's over, Sydney," he said. "Grampa's right. We're just kids. This isn't a playground."

He turned his back on everyone and, with Alexa's fingers curled tightly around his, walked out of the MemorySphere.

◆ CHAPTER THIRTY-FOUR ◆

Janice Plays the Hero

SEEING ZACK AND ALEXA SWALLOWED BY THE LIGHT SENT Janice's heart into anxious palpitations. Was he really giving up? Was he just going to let Miss Guacaladilla cart them off to the four corners of the earth?

The sound of teeth grinding against one another reminded Janice that Sydney was standing next to her. Her sister looked ready to explode, glaring daggers at—and, Janice was sure, through—the white doorway.

"I am sorry," repeated their grandfather.

"Sorry?" Sydney was revving up. "You're sorry?"

Janice stepped in, placing her hand on Sydney's arm. "Let's go, Sydney."

"No! We have to fight! We go into that memory and we stop him!"

Marcus refused to raise his head, becoming far more interested in the tops of his shoes than he had any right to be. Janice finally understood that the battle was lost.

"Come on," she said, tugging her little sister toward the door.

Sydney flared up, ready to resist, but Janice managed to stifle her with a glare of her own. Grudgingly, the furious girl allowed Janice to escort her out of the memory.

◆ ◆ ◆

Walking into the portal room, Janice felt as though a huge weight had been lifted from her shoulders. She put up a good show, but the truth was she still absolutely hated going into the MemorySphere. Aside from her brother and sisters, the only other person in the room was Dimitri, who was still tied to the chair. Aunt Gladys and Mom were nowhere to be found.

Sydney immediately shook herself free and ran to Zack. "You're just going to tuck your tail between your legs and give up?" she accused.

"Of course not, Sydney," he said, wearing what Janice felt was a self-satisfied smirk. "We're going into that memory."

For once, Sydney was speechless.

"How?" asked Janice. "Gramps won't show us where it is."

"No," agreed Zack. "So we need another way in." He turned to Alexa. "And I'm betting you can help us."

The littlest Rothbaum looked up, surprised. "Me?" she asked.

"Mom said she stole our doors so we could help her find Grammy's door," he explained. "She's been in your memories, hasn't she?"

Alexa's face turned red and she squeezed her lips closed, shaking her head.

"It's okay, Alexa," said Zack soothingly. "She told us she'd been visiting you."

"It's our secret," said Alexa.

"It's all right." Janice wasn't sure where Zack was going with this, but decided to follow his lead. "Mom would want you to tell us," she suggested.

Alexa squinched her face up, considering, then nodded. "Yes," she said. "Mommy asked me to find Grammy's door."

"And did you?" asked Sydney.

Alexa told them about her search and the locked door she'd found on the fifth floor.

"That's gotta be it," said Janice.

Zack nodded in agreement. "The problem is, if it's locked, we'll never find the key. Aunt Gladys won't remember where she put it."

"I open door," said the forgotten man from his chair.

Janice peered at him, a jumble of emotions. Here was the source of their problems. She knew, of course, that he hadn't done anything wrong. Not this version of him, anyway. But she was having difficulty separating the man from the memory. Her siblings were equally conflicted, and an uncomfortable silence descended upon them all.

As oblivious as he was, even Dimitri noticed eventually. "Children look at Dimitri funny," he said. "I have booger?"

The four children shifted uncomfortably in their shoes. "We should tell him," said Janice. Zack nodded.

Dimitri took the news as well as could have been expected. Janice couldn't tell if he was more upset to learn he'd been trapped in that nightmare all those years or that he was behind all the trouble plaguing everyone. Victim or villain?

Once Zack finished, Dimitri remained quiet a moment more, then he simply looked up at them, saying, "I open door."

A wave of relief washed over the children, followed by four weary smiles. "Thank you, Dimitri," said Janice, speaking for all of them.

"Is nothing," he replied. "First, I untied. Yes? Chair no longer comfy."

◆ ◆ ◆

They had to be careful not to run into Gonzo or Pixie as they made their way to the fifth floor. Dimitri explained that the two very large, very burly, very grim-faced, and very milk-covered men had forced their mother and aunt to lead them through the halls of the house in search of the children.

However, since neither Charlotte nor Aunt Gladys were presently all that familiar with the house, it wasn't exactly the most methodical search.

There was a close call up on the third floor when the children had heard their aunt's voice approaching and had to hurry and duck behind a pile of doors to avoid being seen, but they otherwise made it to the oddly locked fifth-floor door unnoticed.

"It's kind of weird to see a doorway with an actual door in it," offered Sydney.

This being his moment, Dimitri stepped up and tried the handle. "Is locked," he reported.

"That's what I said," reminded Alexa.

"Can you get it open?" asked Zack.

"One moment." Dimitri walked away from the children and closed his eyes.

"What's he doing?" asked Janice.

Zack shrugged. "Trying to remember where he saw the key?" he guessed.

That didn't sound right to Janice, but before she could say anything, Dimitri opened his eyes, let loose with a wild cry of "Ooooooooooookay!" and ran at the door like a madman. At the last second, he lowered his shoulder, and the force of the crash sent shock waves through the floor, causing the children to extend their arms to maintain their balance.

The door remained standing.

"That's your big plan?" asked Janice.

Dimitri backed away dizzily from the door and blinked his eyes a few times. "Is good plan. I go again."

"No, wait!" warned Janice.

Dimitri ignored her and charged the door again, this time knocking the door off its hinges and allowing access to the mysteriously locked fifth-floor room. It was small, dingy, and dark, and at first glance seemed entirely empty. A second glance, however, informed them that no, it was not empty. There was one thing in the room.

A door.

"We have to hurry," said Zack. "Those goons had to have heard that. They're probably on their way up here right now."

Everyone scrambled into the room and surrounded the door. It lay on the floor, as if unceremoniously dumped and left to rot, and seemed to gather the darkness of the small room to itself in an attempt to avoid being seen. Janice found herself shivering uncontrollably for no identifiable reason.

"That's it," confirmed Alexa. "Mommy told me to look for those scratches on the bottom. They're from Grammy's cats."

"It looks so normal," remarked Sydney.

"It is," said Zack. "Or was, at least. Come on, we need to hurry. Can you give me a hand with this Dimitri? Dimitri?"

The human battering ram remained outside the room, mouth open in horror, eyes locked on the simple wooden door revealed within.

"Dimitri?" repeated Zack.

"Is bad door," whispered Dimitri. "Is very bad door."

I guess that means it's the right one, thought Janice.

◆ ◆ ◆

The hike down to the portal room was even more nerve-racking than the trek up. Gonzo and Pixie had, indeed, heard Dimitri's door-banging and hurried over to investigate. Luckily, it was a big, confusing house and they were being led by two women who had no idea where they were going, so it took them a while to get there. The children heard their mother approach just as they reached the fourth floor and were able to duck behind a pile of doors (after first tossing their grandmother's door on top of the pile) to avoid being seen.

"Where do those stairs go?" asked the burly goon.

"Up, I think," answered Charlotte.

Either Pixie or Gonzo (it was hard for Janice to tell them apart) groaned and bounded up the steps, giving Janice and the others a chance to slip away. A great sense of unease beat down upon everyone as they made their way back to the central room. It was easy to tell where this uncomfortable feeling came from—their grandmother's door. Seeing Dimitri's discomfort regarding the door, Zack had volunteered to carry it down himself. Janice knew she should offer to help her brother, but the thought of touching that . . . that door . . .

She was extremely glad Zack had volunteered.

Inside the portal room, Zack and Sydney quickly hooked the door into the frame, while Alexa scurried about, giving orders they pretended to follow. Dimitri sat down in front of the bank of computers and began to make some adjustments—twiddling knobs, checking dials.

Janice became very aware that she was not helping. She chided herself on her laziness, but continued to remain aloof all the same. There was something about this door, something disturbing, something evil, that repulsed her. More than once, she considered quietly leaving the room before stopping herself.

No running away this time, Janice, she told herself. *You're really doing this.*

Sooner than she would have liked, the machine burst to life, Alexa fished another knob out of the drawer, and Zack donned a pair of rubber gloves and opened the door wide.

"I'm doing this," he said. "I'm not risking anyone else."

"Forget it, dunderhead," snapped Sydney. "You're not doing this alone."

"It's too dangerous," insisted Zack.

"Which is why you can't go in alone." Sydney crossed her arms defiantly.

"You're nine years old!" said Zack.

"And you're eleven. Get over it. I'm coming."

Janice knew they were both right. Zack couldn't go in there alone, but Sydney, tough as she was, would be better off outside, in reality. The answer was so obvious that Janice's mouth was open and her lips were moving before her brain even caught on.

"I'll go," she said.

Eyebrows were raised; surprised looks were shared. She didn't care. "I'm the oldest. If anyone should go with Zack— and no, you can't go in alone—it should be me." She tried to sound convincing but wasn't sure if it was working. "Alexa and Sydney will wait out here with Dimitri."

"No way. I'm going," insisted Sydney. "End of story. You guys need me. You'd be lost without me."

Janice managed to avoid rolling her eyes at her sister's bravado. Ridicule would not work with Sydney. In fact, it would backfire. So she tried a different tactic. "Look," she said. "Alexa can't go in there, right?"

"I wanna come!" piped up the little girl, only to be ignored by everyone.

"Yeah, okay," agreed Sydney somewhat reluctantly, as she pretty much knew where this was going.

"One of us needs to stay out here with her," continued Janice. "She can't be left alone."

"I not go in," reminded Dimitri, who was also swiftly ignored.

"I can too be left alone!" complained Alexa with a frown and a stamp of the foot. "I found the upstairs door all on my own! I'm handy!"

"You stay with her, then," suggested Sydney, once again blissfully ignoring everything Alexa was saying.

"I have to go with Zack. I'm sorry, Sydney. It really is for the best."

Janice waited for Sydney to verbally strike back but was relieved as her sister appeared to be giving in. Of course, the irony of the whole situation was that Janice absolutely, positively did not want to go back into the MemorySphere. But sometimes big sisters had to act like big sisters.

Unfortunately, her brave and selfless moment was interrupted by the voice of Aunt Gladys lilting in from the hallway.

"Well, look at that! That's a big door! We should look in there!"

"That's the room we started from," griped one of the very large, very burly, and very grim-faced men.

"Is it?" asked Aunt Gladys in wonder. "You're right, Mr. Gonzo! Maybe they doubled back!"

"They're coming in!" warned Sydney.

"Hide!" hissed Zack.

Janice looked around the room, empty save for piles of wooden doors. There was nowhere to hide. She groaned as the obvious dawned on her. *Bad idea,* she thought. *Only idea,* she thought right back.

"Into the memory! Everyone!" she cried.

Nobody had to be told twice. With a mad scramble, all four ran up onto the platform and vanished into what Janice just knew would be the ultimate nightmare.

◆ ◆ ◆

It was worse than a nightmare.

Janice could tell it had once been a bedroom, but if ever a memory had spoiled, this was it. The floorboards of the room were mushy and pulpy, and bursts of something really nasty-smelling shot up into the air from time to time like pus being squeezed out of a zit. The ceiling disappeared far above them. The windows, as near as she could tell, were bleeding. And a lot of the furniture seemed to be alive, which Janice found very upsetting. One chair in particular looked to be growing hair.

I was right, thought Janice. *Very bad idea.*

"I don't like this memory," said Alexa.

"Don't worry," said Zack, trying to sound calm. "It's only a memory. It can't hurt you."

"That circus was a memory, too," reminded Sydney. Zack shot her a glare but didn't respond.

Janice peered into the dark shadows at the far end of the room. She didn't see anything, but it was difficult to pierce the gloom. She knew they weren't alone, however. Their grandmother had to be in here somewhere.

A sudden, weak-sounding cry startled all four of them. Janice's heart skipped a beat as she imagined the most horrendous, evil terror jumping out at them from the dark, teeth bared, fire pouring out of its eyes. Then she caught sight of the source of the cry and actually grew even more afraid, if that was possible.

It was a cat.

Specifically, a small kitten. White with brown spots. Fluffy. Beyond cute. It was not covered in blood. It was not sprouting a mass of tentacles. It did not have a third eye. It looked perfectly normal.

Which really and truly terrified Janice.

"Kitty!" squealed Alexa, bending down to pet the creature.

"Alexa! No!" yelled Zack and Janice and Sydney at the same time. "Get away! It's evil!"

"It's not evil," said the little girl, reaching out and scratching the kitten behind its ears. "It's fluffy."

Janice was pretty sure fluffy could still be evil, but didn't know how to explain this to Alexa.

"Aunt Gladys said Grammy had cats," cautioned Zack. "It is a part of this memory."

"You said the memory couldn't hurt us," reminded Alexa, scooping up the suddenly happy kitten into her arms. It purred like a fine-tuned race car and quickly settled down in her embrace.

"Way to go," needled Sydney.

"Do I smell . . . faaaaaaamilyyyyyy?" creaked the most terrifying voice Janice had ever heard.

All four children were instantly paralyzed with fear. The unearthly, inhuman voice dug into their hearts with an icy grip, stealing the very breath from their lungs. Janice felt her mind go blank in response, her brain willfully shutting down rather than dealing with whatever horror lurked in the shadows.

As they stood and stared, transfixed, the owner of that wretched voice slowly crept into the light. The first thing the children could see were ten gigantic fingernails poking out from the darkness, each one finely whittled to a razor-sharp point. The fingernails seemed to hover, disembodied, for a moment, before the fingers themselves came into view.

Gnarled and grotesque, each individual finger was the size of a grown man's arm. Somewhere deep inside herself, Janice thanked her brain for shutting down, otherwise she was pretty sure she'd be screaming bloody murder right about now.

"Soooomeone come to viiiiisit meeeeee?" called the disturbing voice behind the enormous fingers.

And then Grandma's face invaded the light.

It was massive, even larger than they'd been led to believe from the size of her fingers. Dozens of bulbous warts sprouted and bubbled, much like the floor itself, across her face. Her hair streaked down in wet strands, and her lips were parted in a perpetual sneer. But for Janice the most horrific thing about her were the eyes.

All five of them.

Two in their normal places, a third halfway up her left cheek, a fourth just above her chin, and a fifth at the end of her nose.

I'm going to scream now, Janice informed herself. To which she responded, *Go right ahead.*

She inhaled a massive amount of air into her lungs in preparation for launching the scream to end all screams, but was interrupted by a blast of bright white light as the door through which they'd entered was suddenly flung wide open once again.

"Mom!" cried a much younger, far more lucid version of Charlotte Tulving bursting into the room. "I'm back! Like I promised! I'm going to help you. I'm going to save you!"

Even though Janice had intellectually known that they

were going to meet up with their mother from years ago inside this memory, actually seeing her was a shock. Luckily, Zack was on the ball enough to quickly grab his sisters and pull them into the shadows of the far wall.

"Saaaaave meeeeee?" asked the Grandma-Thing. One of her normal eyes rotated to glare at her daughter, as did the eye on her chin. The others rolled around in their sockets independently of one another.

"You're sick," explained Young Charlotte. "Suffering. But I can make it better." Totally unfazed by the abomination gyrating before her, she stepped forward, hands out like she was approaching a nervous puppy.

"Siiiiiiick," creaked Grandma. "Yessss. Soooo siiiiiick."

Even as the creature wailed and moaned, Janice noticed her oversized fingers flexing absently, grasping and clutching at the air.

"We need to get you out of this memory," continued Charlotte, speaking as naturally as if she were discussing the weather over a cup of tea. "It's gone bad. You're not yourself in here."

"Siiiiick," repeated Grandma. "Not myseeeeeeelf."

Janice watched one of those enormous hands quietly lower itself to the floor beside the bed—out of Charlotte's line of sight. What was going on?

"No. This isn't you," agreed Charlotte. "No matter what Dad says, this isn't you. This is not my mother."

"I smell faaaaamilyyyyyy," said Grandma, the eye on the end of her nose turning to face Janice and her siblings.

"That's right. I'm your daughter," said Charlotte, understandably misinterpreting her mother's meaning. "And you're my mother. We're family. Family does not give up on family." Having reached the bed, she smiled up at the horrific creature towering above her.

"Faaaaamilyyyy gooooooood," muttered Grandma, her voice low and menacing. The five fingers on the floor silently jerked forward, detaching themselves from the hand and crawling around the edges of the bed. With a start, Janice realized they were hunting her mother, who was oblivious to their existence.

"Zack, the fingers!" whispered Janice as loudly as she dared. "They're going for Mom!"

Her brother put a hand on her arm, holding her back. "Don't interfere," he hissed.

"She's gonna be torn apart!"

"This is a memory," he reminded her. "Just watch."

"Watch?"

"We're waiting for Dimitri," said Sydney, butting in on the conversation.

Janice couldn't understand why they were so calm. Didn't they see those . . . those things? Clawing their way forward? Preparing to seize Charlotte and rip her to shreds?

"Here's what we're going to do," continued Charlotte, unaware of the doom stalking her. She dug into her pocket and held up a doorknob. "You're coming with me. Into the real world."

"Reeeeeeeal worrrrrrrld."

"You'll revert to your old self, leaving this horrible place behind. Then we can insert you into a nice, new memory."

"New meeeeemoryyyyyy." The five fingers approached Charlotte from either side of the bed even as she kept her gaze lifted up toward her mother's face.

"Where you can exist in peace," finished Charlotte, beaming with joy.

She believes it, realized Janice. *She's convinced herself it can work.*

"In peeeeeeeeace," repeated Grandma, the eye on her cheek widening with expectation. In that moment, Janice saw the creature was toying with Charlotte. Playing with her like a cat plays with a mouse. It wasn't sick. It was evil.

And Charlotte had no idea.

"I love you, Mom," said the blissfully ignorant younger version of their mother, swelling with pride and closing her eyes to soak in the maternal love she imagined she was receiving.

The five finger creatures raised up to skewer Charlotte on their razor-sharp tips.

"No!" screamed Janice.

Her cry was drowned out by the sudden opening of the door yet again and the frantic calls of "Charlotte! No!" issuing forth from Marcus Tulving as he raced into the memory. He was quickly followed by Aunt Gladys and . . .

Dimitri!

Zack squeezed her arm. He saw him, too.

Grandma paused, annoyed by the interruption, and her

fingers quickly dropped down and away before Charlotte opened her eyes. "I smell faaaaaamilyyyyyyyy," she spat out nastily.

"Get back, Charlotte," ordered their grandfather. "Come away from her."

Charlotte whirled toward her father, her face reddening the same way Sydney's did when she set off on a RAGE. "Leave us alone!" she screamed.

"That's not your mother!" he insisted.

"You know nothing!" she replied.

"I love this part," whispered a calm voice from behind the children. "I honestly can't get enough of it."

Janice whipped her head around to find Dimitri leaning against the wall, smiling. Or rather, a memory of Dimitri.

The memory of Dimitri.

The children gawked in astonishment, mesmerized by his sudden appearance even as the drama of fourteen years prior unfolded behind them.

"Dimitri?" asked Alexa.

"Oh, I'm sorry if my words confuse you," he said, smirking. "Is this better?" He dramatically cleared his throat before continuing. "This favorite part. Love very much."

Hearing him mock his own style of broken English infuriated Janice. Zack was right, this wasn't Dimitri. Not anymore.

"Why are you doing this?" asked Zack. "What do you want?"

Instead of answering, Memory Dimitri slipped himself

between Zack and Janice and pointed at the gruesome face of Grandma. "Look at that," he said. "Terrifying, isn't it? Can you imagine spending years alone with her? The only escape into memories equally horrific? No respite from her appetite? Nothing but an eternity of misery and darkness with your grandfather's and grandmother's twisted memories? Can you imagine? No? Well, I can. Because I lived it!"

Janice and the others shrank back as if struck as he spun around and sneered at them.

"And it's about to happen all over again. Watch!"

He threw an arm back toward the action just as Marcus grabbed Charlotte and began pulling her away from Grandma.

"Let go! No, Dad! We can save Mom!"

"Someday, I hope you will understand," said Marcus sadly. "Gladys! The door!"

Aunt Gladys obediently pulled a doorknob out of her pocket and attached it to the bedroom door.

"Nooooooo!" wailed Grandma. "Doooooon't gooooooo!"

"Mom! Help!" Charlotte continued to struggle, threatening to break out of her father's grasp, until Dimitri stepped in to help.

"Must go now!" he chirped. "Is bad memory!"

"I was such a good soldier, wasn't I?" murmured Memory Dimitri.

Aunt Gladys yanked the door open and, at her father's commanding nod, stepped through to the other side.

"Mom!" yelled Charlotte in a last-ditch effort to break away from her father. "Mom, he's abandoning you!"

Janice felt Memory Dimitri lean in until his lips were inches from her and Zack's ears. "Wait for it," he whispered.

Grandma exploded.

Not physically, but psychically. A howl of primordial fury erupted from the darkness, sending out a shock wave of energy that knocked everyone off their feet. The blast of chaos released by the abomination tore through the fabric of the memory, stretching it beyond the boundary of under-standing. An instant later, the memory snapped back into place like a spent rubber band, but the damage was done. Everything and everyone in the room in that moment was duplicated, almost as if reality had just hiccuped. Janice felt as if she had been pulled out of her own skin, while at the same time she felt something deep inside her yank itself free.

From the boiling, bubbling floor, both Janices watched as two versions of her grandfather wrestled two versions of his struggling daughter into the doorway—one pair half a second behind the other. Finally, he shoved her through the door.

And then he did it again.

"Dimitri!" both grandfathers yelled after having inexpli-cably sent Charlotte home twice in succession. "Run!"

"Zack!" cried Sydney twice. "It's happening!"

The Zacks took a step forward, but two Memory Dimitris

blocked their path. "Just where do you think you're going?" they asked, one speaking a fraction of a second after the other.

Janice's mind, having more or less returned from its vacation, raced. They would get one shot at this, and the timing needed to be perfect. She looked out and saw the first Marcus Tulving step through the door. It was now or never. As each Zack tried to dodge around a Memory Dimitri, she launched herself forward and then followed herself a split second later.

"Go, Janice!" shouted both Alexas.

The Memory Dimitris twisted back around and spied both Janices making for the open doorway as the second Marcus left the memory. "Oh, no you don't," they said. But before they could stop her, the Zacks and the Sydneys all leaped upon the Memory Dimitris, bringing them to the ground.

"Now, Janice!" called both Zacks from the floor.

Janice reached the doorway just as the first Dimitri left the room. She reached the doorway again a moment later. With a cry of triumph, she shoved her arm against the door as it was trying to close, forcing it to stay open. She moved to shove her arm against the door a second time, but found it difficult to concentrate. The second Janice grew hazy, less distinct, as if reality within the memory was healing itself from the psychic explosion.

"What are you doing?" screamed the more solid of the two Memory Dimitris. "You'll ruin everything!"

The second Dimitri, himself looking less substantial, reached the door and paused momentarily, surprised to find Janice in his way. "Little girl?" he said. "I no underst—"

Janice pushed him through the door.

"Noooooo!" howled Memory Dimitri as the door closed, casting the room once more into near-total darkness.

A hush fell, broken only by the purring of the kitten in Alexa's arms.

Janice, utterly spent, slid down the door to the floor. "Tell me that did it," she said. In the back of her mind, she took note of the fact that she only said this once. Reality had been repaired.

"I think . . . ," began Zack. "I think we—"

"Curse you!" came the answer from Memory Dimitri, who had fallen into a heap on the floor. "Curse you horrible little children! You pushed the second me out of the memory! Now I won't be created! Now I don't exist! Why? Why would you do such a thing? What a world! What a world! To be vanquished by children!"

The Rothbaums looked at one another, uncertain. Something didn't seem quite right. For one thing, Memory Dimitri was being a bit overdramatic.

"Um . . . Zack?" said Janice, getting to her feet, worry gnawing at her gut.

"Only . . . ," continued Memory Dimitri. "If that's true . . ." He stood up, a look of false amazement plastered on his face. "Why am I still here?"

Zack grabbed Sydney and Alexa and backed away from

the memory man, who grinned maliciously at them. "Could it be . . . ? Could it be your brilliant plan wasn't so brilliant after all?"

Janice hurried to her siblings' side. Memory Dimitri leaned in, causing the children to lean away.

"Gotcha," he said.

The children screamed.

Memory Dimitri doubled over, laughing. "That was better than I even dreamed!" he said. "You should see the looks on your faces!"

"Wait," said Alexa. "It didn't work?"

"No, it didn't work, my sweet little lamb! I'm still here!" He spread his hands as if introducing himself to an audience. "And you know who else wants to say hi? Heeeeeeeere's Grandma!"

With a flamboyant wave of his hand, he gestured to the bed, where the horrifically enlarged, grinning head of their grandmother hovered, her eyes focused on the children— one on each with the fifth rolling absently to the sky.

"I smell faaaaamilyyyyyy," she groaned. All ten of her fingers inched out from the dark to approach, none attached to a hand. A flock of Nasty, Slithery Somethings emerged from under the bed as well.

"Now it is your turn to spend eternity in this nightmare, getting to know your wonderful grandmother," said Memory Dimitri. "I'm sure she has lots of neat stories!"

The room came alive. The bed dragged itself forward, bringing the full, reality-defying body of Grandma with it.

Janice was horrified to discover the thing's legs had melted into or merged with the frame of the bed. It was part of her. Meanwhile, her torso—tiny compared to her head and hands—was covered in red welts.

"Please!" cried Janice. "We never did anything to you!"

"You exist!" screamed Memory Dimitri, his voice climbing in pitch and fervor. "You are Tulvings! Marcus can hide in the MemorySphere if he wants. I'll take my revenge on everyone he loves! Eventually, he'll have to step outside to try to save his family. And then I'll control his memories! I will make him forget everything he ever knew—everyone he has ever known!"

Zack stepped up into Memory Dimitri's face. "You won't get away with this," he said.

"I already have," snapped Memory Dimitri. "Unless you're referring to the doorknob the little oaf has in her jacket pocket."

All eyes turned to Alexa, who backed up, clutching the purring kitty in her arms. "Go away," she said. "You're mean."

"From the mouths of babes . . . ," murmured Memory Dimitri before launching into motion. Before anyone could stop him, he grabbed Alexa and jerked her forward, as if to toss her to the encroaching fingers.

She was saved by a flurry of fur.

The cat, suddenly disturbed from its resting place, gave one defiant growl and flew at Memory Dimitri, teeth and claws bared. It hissed up a storm and landed on the cruel memory man's face, sending them both to the ground.

"Alexa! The knob!" yelled Zack.

Alexa took out the knob and threw it to Zack, who caught it and attached it to the door with a resounding click.

"Get this . . . stupid . . . furry . . . beast . . . off me!" demanded Memory Dimitri, throwing his arms in front of his face in an effort to ward off the memory of the kitty.

Zack pulled the door open, bringing the promise of freedom streaming into the room.

"Go!" he yelled.

Janice grabbed a slightly stunned Alexa and ran for the door, Sydney a step ahead. Behind her, she heard a high-pitched howl from the cat, a less-than-manly grunt from Memory Dimitri, and, from Grandma, a guttural cry of pure rage that felt like a thousand paper cuts on her eardrums.

Then she was through the door.

◆ CHAPTER THIRTY-FIVE ◆

Sydney Goes for Broke

IT WAS A SERIOUSLY SOMBER MOOD IN THE PORTAL ROOM.

The four Rothbaum children stood or sat silently at random spots, each needing a few feet of personal space but not willing to let any of their siblings out of sight. Dimitri stood awkwardly by the curtain in front of the vaultlike steel door, trying to be considerate yet also nervously keeping an eye out in case Gonzo or Pixie returned.

"It should have worked," said Zack for the fifteenth or sixteenth time.

"It didn't," replied Janice for the fifteenth or sixteenth time.

"I miss the kitty," whimpered Alexa. "It was fluffy."

"You've still got Ratty," said Sydney, pointing her thumb at the pet's cage resting against the wall.

"He's a rat," said Alexa, pouting.

Sydney sighed and looked down at their grandmother's door, which lay broken on the floor at the foot of the platform. Nobody had said anything, but once everyone had gotten out of that horrible memory, they had quickly asked Dimitri to snap it in half. All had breathed a sigh of relief when it was destroyed.

"I still remember being double," murmured Janice.

"That was weird," said Alexa. "I was petting two kitties."

"Something about when Grandma—" began Zack.

"That wasn't Grandma," insisted Sydney, feeling like she needed to stick up for the relative they'd never known.

"Agreed," said Zack. "When . . . that thing . . . screamed, it . . . it was too much for the memory to handle. Too much rage. Does that make sense?"

Sydney actually thought it did make a little sense. She remembered the force of that fury striking her body as if it were a physical thing. "So the memory, what? Split itself in half?"

"But only for a moment," clarified Janice. "Then everything kind of snapped back into place."

Sydney nodded to herself. It made sense, if any of this made any sense. By the time they got out of the memory, they were whole again. But Dimitri's two halves had been caught on either side of the doorway. Cut off from each other. One in the real world and one in the MemorySphere.

But if that was true, then why hadn't everything been

fixed when Janice shoved the second Dimitri through the door? They'd saved him, hadn't they?

Or had they?

"Is someone!" cried the real Dimitri, waving his gangly arms about in warning. "Is coming!"

Sydney quickly looked for someplace to hide, but there weren't many options. She saw Zack and Janice tense up but remain where they were. If Miss Guacaladilla walked in, there wasn't much any of them could do about it.

The heavy curtain was clumsily whacked aside, then whacked aside again after the initial whack failed to get it out of the way. "Oh, for . . . ! A curtain by the door! Of all the silly . . . !"

"Aunt Gladys!" cheered Alexa, running forward as the less-than-graceful woman finally managed to get past the curtain with Dimitri's help.

"Oh! You're back! You were gone, right? Now you're back. Am I fixed?"

All four children rolled their eyes.

"Do you remember us?" asked Zack rather hopelessly.

"Of course! You're those four children. Oh wait. That's not what you meant. Do I remember you? No. No, I don't. I'm not fixed, am I?"

"You're not fixed," confirmed Zack.

"Am I going to be?"

Alexa dropped her arms and walked away. Sydney watched defeat creep its way into the hearts and minds of her siblings and found herself equally pessimistic. What could they do? What could anyone do? Memory Dimitri had a hold on their mother and aunt. No matter what move the kids made, he would counter.

It was infuriating, but for once Sydney managed to hold back the impending RAGE. She simply didn't have the energy.

"I fix you," said Dimitri softly, gently bringing the terminally confused woman over to the swivelly chair by the computers. "You rest now. I fix you."

Sydney's heart broke to watch the two of them. There had obviously been some sort of connection between them, and now that connection had been forgotten along with the rest of Aunt Gladys's memories.

"So . . . ," began Janice, wary of breaking the fragile peace. "This is it? He wins? We're going to Uruguay?"

"Only one of us," said Zack.

No, thought Sydney. *No, no, no. This is wrong. This is all wrong.*

"There has to be something we can do!" she exclaimed.

"Should we eat cereal?" asked Aunt Gladys. "I like cereal."

"I get cereal," said Dimitri. He quickly scuttled out of the room.

"He's so much nicer than that other Dimitri," noted Alexa.

"Maybe his personality split," suggested Janice. "You know, like in that story? Jekyll and Hyde?"

A light went on inside Sydney's head. It was faint and flickering, but it was a light.

"We should probably figure out what we're going to say to Miss Guacaladilla when she returns," said Zack.

"The crying woman?" asked Aunt Gladys. "She's in the kitchen. With Princess."

The flickering light in Sydney's mind got brighter. There was something she was missing. Something obvious.

"Princess?" asked Alexa.

"That's not right. Penny? Pickles?"

"Pixie?" suggested Zack.

Aunt Gladys frowned in concentration for a moment. "That can't be right. That's a ridiculous name."

It was on the tip of Sydney's tongue. Something about Dimitri. And Memory Dimitri. And . . .

"So she's back," said Janice.

"And in the kitchen," agreed Zack.

"Dimitri's going to the kitchen," said Alexa.

"Stop him!" blurted Sydney suddenly. The light burst out in full force, illuminating her face with excitement. "Quick! Bring him back! Alexa, run!"

The littlest Rothbaum bolted out the door.

"What is it, Sydney?" asked a cautiously excited Zack.

She beamed with pride. "I know what we have to do."

◆ ◆ ◆

Their grandmother's bedroom was as dark as before.

The floorboards were just as mushy and pulpy, nasty-smelling gunk still shot up into the air, the windows were still bleeding, the furniture was still alive. The hairy chair remained incredibly disturbing.

But rather than enter the nightmarish world of the memory before the drama between the monster Grandma and her family unfolded, the children stepped right smack dab into the middle of it.

The hellish abomination that was the well-spoiled memory of their grandmother writhed and groaned and oozed pus and mucus from every pore.

"Get back, Charlotte," called Marcus to his elder daughter. "Come away from her."

Charlotte whirled around, furious. "Leave us alone!" she screamed.

"That's not your mother!" he insisted.

"You know nothing!" she replied.

"Back again?" crooned Memory Dimitri as the children quickly scrambled from the door to avoid being seen by the original participants of the memory. "You Tulvings are certainly gluttons for punishment."

He didn't notice, thought Sydney in triumph. Per the plan, the other children ignored him, but Sydney—relishing the challenge—took him head on. "We're going to save you, you know," she said.

He scoffed. "You're fools to return to the Memory-Sphere. You will not slip through my grasp a second time."

"Wanna bet?"

He started to give her a snarky response, but she put on

her best "I'm so much better than you" face, causing him to hesitate. "What are you up to?" he asked suspiciously.

"I want my life back," she answered.

"Get used to disappointments."

She smirked even more knowingly and returned her attention to the action.

"Let go!" demanded Charlotte as she was dragged unceremoniously by her father away from the monster. "No, Dad! We can save Mom!"

"Someday, I hope you will understand," said Marcus sadly. "Gladys! The door!"

Aunt Gladys obediently pulled a doorknob out of her pocket and attached it to the bedroom door.

"Nooooooo!" wailed Grandma. "Doooooon't gooooooo!"

"Mom! Help!" Charlotte continued to struggle, threatening to break out of her father's grasp, until Dimitri stepped in to help.

"Must go now!" he chirped. "Is bad memory!"

"He's so much nicer than you," commented Sydney to Memory Dimitri.

Aunt Gladys yanked the door open and, at her father's commanding nod, stepped through to the other side.

"Mom!" yelled Charlotte in a last-ditch effort to break away from her father. "Mom, he's abandoning you!"

Sydney closed her eyes. She didn't want to see this again.

Just as before, she heard the howl of primordial fury erupt and felt the shock wave of energy. This time, knowing it was coming allowed everyone to remain on their feet. The eerie sensation of being psychically ripped in half, however, remained disturbing.

"Shouldn't you be pointlessly trying to interfere right about now?" hissed the two Memory Dimitris.

The Sydneys calmly watched her grandfather fight her mother in duplicate in the doorway. The timing of this had to be just right.

"Well?" continued the Memory Dimitris, a touch of panic in their voices. "Aren't you kids going to do something? What are you waiting for?"

Both Sydneys remained silent, letting the memory men stew in their juices as Marcus pushed his daughter through first once, then a second time.

"Dimitri!" yelled Marcus. "Run!"

"You're all just going to stand there?" asked the Memory Dimitris incredulously.

Satisfied, the Sydneys turned around, smiling. "Nope," they said. "Go, guys!"

Two Janices dashed for the door. At the same time, the Zacks and Alexas turned around to face the Memory Dimitris, the Alexas holding furry kittens in their arms. The cats hissed.

The Memory Dimitris laughed. "Honestly? You don't need to block me from the door. I'm not going to try to stop you. We all know this doesn't work."

Janice reached the doorway just as the first Dimitri left the room. With a grunt of determination, she shoved her arm against the door as it was trying to close, forcing it to stay open. Her echo did the same.

"You should not have returned," remarked Memory Dimitri, though only once as the memory was returning to a state of equilibrium. "Now you will never escape your grandmother's memory."

"We're not in Grandma's memory of this moment," stated Sydney as calmly as possible.

Back at the door, the second Dimitri paused as he encountered Janice standing in his way. "Little girl?" he said. "I no underst—"

Sydney smiled and went for the jugular. "We're in yours."

Memory Dimitri's eyes widened as the implications struck him like a hammer to the forebrain. "What?"

Janice grabbed the other Dimitri and pushed him through the door.

Memory Dimitri's face turned the palest shade of yellow possible. "No!"

He launched himself forward, now only a single person, but Zack and Alexa held their ground, holding him at bay until Janice cleared the doorway and it was slammed shut from the other side.

"What have you done?" screamed Memory Dimitri. "You foul, miserable children! What have you done?"

Janice rejoined her siblings, and the four stood in a mixture of mute fascination and horror as Memory Dimitri began to peel away. Little holes in his skin appeared as if he were a sheet of paper held over a flame. But instead of bones and veins and whatever else ought to have been inside a human body, there was nothing.

"You made it out," said Zack.

"Which means you never existed," added Janice.

"It's called a paradox," explained Sydney.

"I never liked you," said Alexa, calmly stroking the now-purring kitten in her arms.

Memory Dimitri dropped to what was left of his knees and writhed about, not so much in pain as in misery and horror. As the holes of emptiness devoured his face, he turned his remaining eye toward the children and glared at them with utter malice.

And then he was gone.

CHAPTER THIRTY-SIX

Alexa Has Another Secret

"THEN ALEXA PULLED OUT THE DOORKNOB, AND WE GOT OUT OF there," finished Zack. "Grandma, or whatever that thing is, was losing it big-time."

"Her fingers were crawling toward us!" added Alexa, shuddering. "On their own!"

Their grandfather shook his head, smiling very sadly. "Yes, the memory of Agatha devolved into a nightmare. My one regret. She deserves better." Alexa nearly burst from the excitement of her secret. But not yet. She'd wait until Zack gave the signal.

Grampy sighed, then shook the melancholy away. "But enough! It's good to see you. All of you!"

The children were sitting in the front row of a pew in

a small church. Their grandfather sat on the steps to the altar in front of them, his two daughters on either side, with Dimitri sitting next to Aunt Gladys. Alexa grinned when she saw their fingers were intertwined.

"It's good to see you, Dad," said Mommy. "It really is."

He smiled at her, then looked over at Aunt Gladys, taking her in as well. Finally, he leaned forward to address the children. "I'm still fuzzy on how it worked, though. You made Dimitri walk back and forth through the door you purchased for Gladys?"

"It was brand-new, and she only went through it a couple of times," explained Zack. "Sydney marched Dimitri through it something like ten times—"

"Twenty-seven," interjected Dimitri.

"Right, whatever—"

"Is lot of times."

"Yes, okay—" continued Zack.

"Is very boring," added Dimitri.

"But it worked!" said Sydney, glowing with pride. "Going through it that many times made the door yours, so when we hooked it up, we entered your memory of that awful scene and not Grandma's. We went in, we shoved you out the second time, and suddenly you remembered coming out both times."

"Yes. Is freaky weird."

"Which meant no part of you remained behind, which made Memory Dimitri vanish! My idea! I rock!"

Everyone laughed. Alexa thought her sister was being a bit of a show-off, but figured that was okay. Just this once. Besides, Alexa still had her super-awesome secret.

"Dad," said Mommy, "this whole experience . . . it was . . ."

"Terrifying," finished Grampy. "I know."

"Too dangerous," admitted Mommy. "Things are wrong in the MemoryVerse."

"MemorySphere," corrected Grampy.

"See, that makes no sense." Alexa hid a smile as her mother and grandfather fell into the pointless argument. "It's not a sphere."

"It's not a verse," countered her grandfather.

"Hello? Short for *universe*?"

Grampy shrugged. "I discovered it. I get to name it."

"The point, Dad," interrupted Aunt Gladys. "There's a point. Memory hopping can't continue."

"Memory hopping?" asked Grampy.

"My own term," said Aunt Gladys.

"Not bad."

"You like that?" asked Mommy. "Over MemoryVerse?"

"We're shutting it all down," said Zack. Alexa was glad he interrupted because she'd been growing tired of the bickering. "Destroying the equipment. Getting rid of the doors. Everything."

"Yes," said their grandfather. "I understand."

"Do you?" asked Mommy. "No more doors. No more visits. The MemoryVerse might cease to exist."

"MemorySphere," corrected Grampy again, and Alexa thought she saw the hint of a smile on his face. "And it'll exist. It's its own reality. It can't be unmade."

"Will you come out with us?" asked Janice, even though they all knew the answer.

"No. Outside I would go hopelessly insane," he said.

"Are you sure?" asked Sydney. "We were able to fix Mom and Aunt Gladys. Why can't we fix you?"

Grampy sighed and sadly shook his head. "Their memories were altered by Memory Dimitri. Once you got rid of him, he never existed to alter their memories in the first place."

"But you altered your memories yourself," said Zack.

Grampy only nodded.

"Then . . . this is goodbye," said Mommy. She stood and opened her arms. Grampy rose to his feet as well and embraced his daughter.

"I want a hug, too!" squeaked Alexa, jumping up and barreling into her mother and grandfather. One by one, everyone else joined in, until the entire family was in one big group hug, even Dimitri.

"Is sad," he mumbled. "I cry now."

Everyone was crying, to the point where Alexa stopped crying because she didn't like being a follower. She looked up at Zack, eager to spill her secret, but he was busy hugging their grandfather.

"There is one more thing," said the children's mother once everyone had hugged it out. "We opened one last door."

Alexa felt the secret bubbling up from her tummy.

"Oh?" said their grandfather. "That explains it. I noticed another memory open. Just before this one. I assumed it was a mistake. I'll explore it later."

"It wasn't a mistake," said Zack.

Now Alexa felt they were dangerously close to spilling the beans, so she threw caution to the wind and jumped in. "We found Grammy!" she cried.

Her grandfather looked at her blankly. "You . . . what?"

"The old garden shed," explained their aunt. "She went in there. All the time. Not me. Not a gardener. And not you, either. Right?"

A sudden energy infused their grandfather as he shook his head. "Your mother was the green thumb, not me."

"That's what we figured," said Zack. "We hooked the door to the shed up to the machine, opened it for the briefest of seconds, and closed it again. So as not to spoil it."

"Then we broke the door," added their mother. "It can't be used again."

"Mommy's waiting for you," said Aunt Gladys. "If you go in there and stay, it won't spoil."

Grampy was speechless. A tear rolled down his cheek, followed by others. Alexa gave him a second hug.

"You're welcome, Grampy," she said. "I love you."

◆ EPILOGUE ◆

EDWARD ROTHBAUM OPENED HIS EYES WITH A SLIGHT GROAN.

He felt horrible. And weak. And sore. And thirsty. And horrible. And was that his wife standing next to the bed?

"Ch . . . Char . . . ?"

"It probably maybe isn't best for you to try to talk," said Nurse Hallabug. "Your body may need perhaps some more time to maybe heal up."

"Welcome back, Dad," said Zack.

Edward turned his head slightly to the side (moaning in pain from the effort) to see his four children standing together on the other side of his bed.

"Do you remember anything, Ed?" asked Charlotte, leaning down and taking his hand.

He took a breath to answer and felt a mild rush of pain in his chest, causing him to gasp. Which hurt even more.

"Oh! Sorry!" She quickly let go of it, as if holding it had somehow caused the pain.

"There's a very good chance that probably his lungs are maybe going to be perhaps a bit sore for a little while," cautioned Nurse Hallabug. "But don't quote me on that."

"Do you remember?" repeated the woman who, while technically still his wife, had been gone for over six years.

Did he remember? Remember what? How he had ended up in a bed? In a hospital? He closed his eyes and took stock of his situation. His entire body was sore, he felt utterly wiped out, and his lungs ached every time he tried to take a breath. What had happened?

"It is so miserably glorious to see your father alive and awake!" moaned a voice he did not recognize. "To think he survived that fire! Oh, it's too terrible to contemplate!"

Smoke. Burning. Yes, that fit. He'd been in a fire.

Ow.

He opened his eyes again to look at his children. Then he gingerly turned his neck to look at his wife. She looked different. Older (he supposed he looked older, too, under all the bandages), calmer. And also extremely guilty. He wondered what that was about.

"Char . . . ," he began.

"Shhhh." Charlotte softly pressed a finger to his lips. "There's a lot to talk about—and I've a lot to apologize for—but this isn't the time. Just rest. And know that . . . I'm sorry. I am so, so sorry."

There were tears in her eyes, which made Edward tear

up as well. He still couldn't believe it. His wife. Right here. Next to him. This was real. She was real.

"Do you think you'll ever be able to forgive me?" she asked.

"You have to forgive her, Daddy!" cried Alexa. "She saved Aunt Gladys! But then Aunt Gladys needed to be saved again and so did Mommy, and Grampy wasn't going to save her, so we saved her and now we're a family again!"

He had no idea what his youngest daughter had just said, but it sounded sincere. Particularly the bit about being a family again. That would be very nice. But could he forgive his wife for abandoning them like she did?

"You . . . left," he managed to whisper.

"I did," she sighed, then cocked her head to the side and raised an eyebrow. "In my defense, I did say I'd come back. So . . . I'm back." She smiled, looking like a little girl hoping to charm her way out of a scolding.

She was back. And all it took for her to return was for him to almost die.

"So can she, Dad?" asked Zack. "Can she stay?"

He slowly swiveled his head to look at his children again. The four of them looked so hopeful, almost bursting with expectation. They obviously wanted her back.

And so did he. It wouldn't be easy, but if they could make it work, it would be worth it.

He gave the briefest of nods before wincing in pain. Everyone cheered. He was pretty sure they were cheering his nod, not his pain.

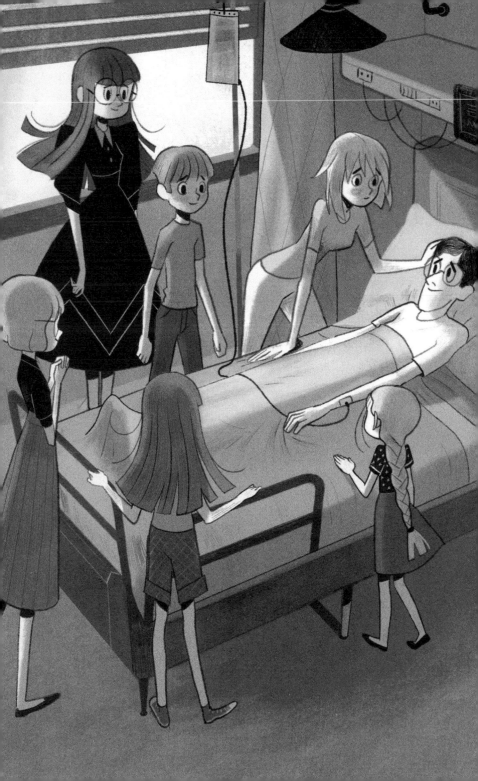

"How soon before he can come home?" asked Charlotte.

"He'll never go home!" moaned the unidentified voice. Man, whoever it was was a real downer.

"She means my house," said another woman, whose voice he didn't recognize but who looked a little bit like his wife. Didn't Charlotte have a sister? Was her name Gladys? He couldn't remember. "The family's temporary home. For now."

Wait. Temporary home? Why did they need a temporary home? What was wrong with the one they had?

"I really couldn't say," said Nurse Hallabug. "I would maybe suggest you think about asking the doctors, as that might perhaps be one possible way to maybe find out."

"Yeah!" Little Alexa clapped. "Daddy's coming home! We don't have to move to Uruguay!"

Uruguay?

"You don't remember, do you?" asked Charlotte again.

Remember what? Uruguay? No. Wait. Smoke. Temporary house. Sweet mother of pearl, his house must have burned down! And he must have been caught in the fire! He quickly swept his eyes back to his children, but they all seemed fine.

Did he remember his house burning down? Did he remember being caught in the middle of it?

No.

Thank God.

He couldn't imagine visiting that memory over and over again in his head.

It would be like living in a nightmare.

ACKNOWLEDGMENTS

Thank you to my editor, Emily Easton, for pushing me over the finish line, and to my agent, Eric Myers, for making it possible. Thank you also to my early readers Jerry, Judy, Bonnie, Jackie, Heather, and Antonia for poring over the initial draft as I doled it out in chunks—your comments were invaluable. Thank you to the Warner Library in Tarrytown, New York, for giving me the perfect place to write and edit. I know there are other people I need to thank, but for some strange reason I can't remember. . . .

ABOUT THE AUTHOR

David Neilsen is the author of *Dr. Fell and the Playground of Doom*. He is also a classically trained actor and story-teller, a journalist, and a theater and improvisation teacher. During the Halloween season, David can be found telling spooky tales to audiences of all ages or performing his one-man shows based on the horror author H. P. Lovecraft. David lives in New York's Hudson Valley with his family and cats. Visit him online at david-neilsen.com.